CURSED VINES

SUZANNE FERREIRA

Paperback ISBN: 978-1-7324367-0-1

Ebook ISBN: 978-1-7324367-1-8

Kindle ASIN: B07DLMJ43Q

Published in the United States of America

Book design by Suzanne Dixon

And, like the great damned souls,
     I shall always feel that thinking is worth more than
living.

FERNANDO PESSOA

ONE

HE CAN'T steady his hands to catch the hen, now determined to escape the altar it was tied to, but he carves the cleaver through its craning neck. A woman aged by the equator sun, wearing a white linen dress with embroidered accents, lights candles with wooden matches in a circle around him.

The glow trails the path of the thick crimson strings that slip from the bird along the crevices of the slab and into a clay bowl waiting on the tile floor below. Red specks smudge a large hand-chalked symbol marking the center of the room.

A drumbeat rises. A wooden clock hanging above the doorway strikes twelve. The old woman shuffles her bare feet around the symbol: a star, a pitchfork, and a crescent moon, circled in white. A few younger women join her dance, chanting Portuguese in unison as their twirling skirts tease the flames.

Male drummers in white drawstring pants emerge from the darkness, drums strapped across their shoulders. They thump their fingertips on the animal skin, eyes sealed and chins in the air.

The old man folds his sleeves, revealing a black tattoo of a snake eating its tail beneath his wrist, wrapped by a ring of lighter skin an inch wide. He slices the poultry carcass and arranges the pieces on a platter. Thunder rumbles through the vines outside, carrying a chilled gust of garlic and myrrh across the sanctuary. He sets the platter at the center of the symbol, crosses his legs beside it, and breathes a chant between his steepled fingers.

One of the dancers pours a clay bowl full of thick red liquid that coats the man's balding skull, forcing his eyelids closed and then splashing onto his robe. A bloodstained grin in his cheeks, he lifts his body with open fists in the air and shouts, "Long live the kingdom of faith! Long live Exu of the souls!"

TWO

"TALIA," she heard in a familiar whisper. "Time to get up, beautiful."

A thick hand brushed Talia's tangled auburn hair from her cheek, damp from the night's crying, and tucked it behind her ear. Talia jerked awake, kicking and punching.

"Sorry." Jared crouched to protect himself from Talia's swings, the edges of his tee rolled up from the night's restless sleep. His short blonde hair curled at the nape of his neck. "You've been calling out for your grandmother for the past five minutes. It's time to get up and get ready for … you know."

Although Natalia Braga, nicknamed Talia at birth, was fresh off the college graduation train, she had already outgrown her room and her family. Her degree in journalism balanced on the edge of her shabby desk, inked with names of boyfriends past. She itched to leave, to see the world, to report on all the glamorous and gory things she'd find. And then her mother got a call from New Falls General Hospital.

"It's a funeral," Talia said, her gut lurching. "She's dead and gone. You can say it."

"I wouldn't say it like that." Jared reached for a hug. "I know you're upset. I'm sorry."

The doorbell rang downstairs.

"Damn it. I promised your mother I would help with the deliveries," Jared said, petting the back of Talia's head. "How about you get ready while I'm gone? I can bring you something back. There are goodie baskets from all the local Portuguese bakeries on the dining room table. Fresh bread and pastries and cheese. You've got to be hungry. You barely ate last night."

"I'm not hungry," Talia said.

Her mobile phone buzzed on her desk, the screen blinking. She ignored it.

"How about something to drink?" Jared asked.

"I'm not thirsty."

"Okay." Jared exhaled into a frown that wrinkled his stubbly chin. "If you need anything, I'll be downstairs in the kitchen. Okay?"

Talia didn't answer.

"Okay?" Jared crossed his arms.

Jared's condescension got him into trouble with strangers on more than one occasion. New Englanders aren't keen on accepting help, let alone pity, and the mistaken assumption led to a few bar fights over the year they'd been dating. Talia warmed to this unusual characteristic by the time she accepted Jared's request for a third date, but she'd grown weary of it through the months they'd spent together since.

"Yeah, okay, fine," she said.

"Good. See you in a bit. Love you."

"Love you, too." Talia repeated it like an amen, a habitual afterthought. She meant it once. Maybe she still did. There was a time when she would giggle at Jared's puns and count down the minutes until she saw him next. She only felt numb now.

After the door clicked behind him, Talia dropped her head and forced a cry into her wet pillow, but she couldn't muster another tear. She must have drained her eyes dry the night before.

Talia's room in her parents' house in New Falls, Massachusetts was a time capsule of her tweens—from the band posters on the wall to the baby Jesus statue her mother insisted she display in her bedroom to keep her safe at night. Talia thought about protesting the baby Jesus many times since she first questioned her faith back in grade school, but she kept her angst for other more important rebellions.

The clothes Talia's mother ironed for her the night before hung on the knob of her closet door—black skirt, black shirt, black shoes on the floor. Even black underwear. It reminded her of the old Portuguese widows at church with woolen shawls draped over their heads, shoulders hunched, masking their worn faces even on the muggiest of New England summer days. Her grandmother, or Vovó, as she liked to call her, hadn't been like the rest. She defied her ancestors and colleagues by wearing brightly flowered satin shawls, even after her husband's death.

Talia closed her eyes and fixed the pendant necklace her mother gave her, wishing on its adjusted clasp that none of it had happened, that Vovó was downstairs waiting with flaky Portuguese pastries, wiggling her crooked nose one last time.

Vovó really did have a crooked nose. Its rounded tip leaned to the left. As a toddler, Talia pressed it into place and giggled uncontrollably when it popped back to its original state like a foam ball, Vovó snickering along. Talia couldn't swallow the thought of looking at that nose for the last time that day. She wondered if the mortician, in the pursuit of perfection, would set it straight again, permanently.

The late summer wake started on time at Saint Mary's cemetery, an extension of the church the thousands of Portuguese residents in New Falls attended. Talia's great aunts and uncles were buried there, along with her grandfather, near the plot Vovó was about to inhabit.

New Falls was one of the many small towns around New England with a large population of Portuguese people, each with their own churches, recreational centers, shops, and restaurants. New Falls, like some of the more populous ones, even held its own annual weekend-long festival, complete with a procession and parade.

Jared held Talia's hand as she stared out from her folding chair, expressionless, as strangers huddled around the varnished box. Vovó's casket sat by the fresh opening, prepped for its descent, and the old woman she once leaned on for guidance, outfitted in her best Sunday dress with her white curls set, rested peacefully inside.

"How are you doing?" asked Caryn, dressed in a vintage black Jackie Onassis dress with a slim collar and large buttons, her highlighted bob held by a gilded hair clip. Though it was a conservative dress, Caryn's bosom threatened to overflow when she dipped in for a friendly kiss on the cheek.

"I'm fine." Talia avoided the burden in Caryn's big brown eyes. She didn't appreciate being pitied.

"Here's some water. Can I get you anything else?" Caryn pressed the plastic bottle into Talia's hands, but Talia knocked it away with whitened knuckles.

"No thanks. I'm fine, really. It's about to start," Talia said.

Caryn nodded and sat on the opposite side of Jared, her heels digging into the field. They exchanged a frown.

Talia's mother sobbed beside her in the front row, comforted by her father's arm as Padre Vaz preached about the precious gift of life. To the priest's left lay the casket, to his right the most fragrant arrangement of white lilies Talia had the pleasure of smelling. It reminded her of the flower garden Vovó watered every morning for forty years. The scent trickled into the afternoon air along with the fragrance of shoveled dirt and freshly mown lawn.

Talia was able to hold off the tears then. Why did she only cry in her sleep? Why couldn't she cry when she was about to see her grandmother, her Vovó, her hero, for the last time? Maybe Jared was right. Maybe she was coldhearted.

Talia's hands shook and her stomach swirled. She knew Vovó's funeral would bring about a severe case of what she called her *paranoia*, but she had managed to suppress it until then. All she had to do was keep her mind from wandering.

And then someone spoke, their voice muffled as if through a train station speaker.

"Talia was seven years old when we moved out of Tina Batista's three family house into our new home." Talia's father stood on a footstool at the podium, his thick seasoned hair slicked back with water. He wore his best black suit with matching clip-on tie, because he hated the feeling of being asphyxiated, and a pair of shined shoes he brought out three times a year for Christmas mass, family weddings, and funerals. The Sacred Heart Jesus statue positioned to her father's right had been polished that morning and the sunlight flickered through the trees onto its nailed feet.

"Talia had a hard time understanding why we moved. A week in, she sneaked across town alone to visit her grandmother after waiting impatiently for me to finish speaking with our contractor. I was frightened, even angry, when I realized

Talia had disappeared, but I knew exactly where she was headed."

Talia had reached Vovó's house by the time her father found her that day. She spotted him outside the window as she sat at Vovó's kitchen table, munching on pastries dipped in whole milk. Talia could still feel the burning excitement as she rang the doorbell, and the devastation when her father drove her home.

That was the first time her father forced her to transcribe chapters of Portuguese history books. Her father didn't send her to her room, like her friends' parents. Instead, Talia's father obsessed over her knowledge of Portuguese history. This, combined with the dislike for his own messy handwriting, fueled his choice of punishment.

Despite having visited many of the historic sites mentioned in the books over several trips to Portugal her family took throughout her youth, the act of transcribing their history bored her. Not the calmest of children, Talia had memories of writing at the kitchen table for hours on end, wishing she could listen to her favorite song of the month for just one minute. It was no wonder Talia favored Vovó's kitchen over her own. Never did she sit there under penalty.

Though it was tortuous at the time, Talia had been complimented on her neat handwriting since then. Her ability to spout historical facts about anything or anywhere associated to Portugal led her cousins to dub her "Portugal's best tourist guide." But her father earned the title first. She was merely his apprentice.

Memories of her grandparents in good health flooded her mind. Their walks in the morning, lunch at noon, at which point Vovó would shout out the window, "Domingos, *almoço!*" until he replied. The best part was her grandfather's afternoon snores, when Talia and Vovó quietly watched daytime soaps operas until her grandfather would retreat to the basement to listen to Portuguese *futbol* on his dusty wideband radio, gulping one of the many glasses of wine his doctor advised him not to drink.

Vovó dressed him in a new green shirt every day to honor his favorite soccer team, *Sporting Clube de Portugal.* She knew from experience never to dress him in red, for he would refuse to wear it in any form. It was the color of the enemy, *Sport Lisboa e Benfica.*

É de pequenino que se torce o pepino, Vovó repeated, an old Portuguese proverb to remind Talia that bad habits learned young can last a lifetime.

———

HER FATHER STEPPED DOWN from the podium and Talia erupted into a sob. When she raised her head from her cupped hands, stomach unsettled, her cheap waterproof mascara staining her fingertips, the concerned black-cladded mass goggled at her. With the sense of urgency to retreat to a private location overwhelming her, Talia got up and marched toward the closest trail. She needed to be alone.

Jared and Caryn argued about who was to tail her. Caryn won and rushed to Talia's side.

"Hey," Caryn said when she caught up, breathless.

"Hey," Talia said, continuing at the same pace.

"Where are you going?"

"Not sure." Talia stomped on the grass field as if her shoes were molded with cement.

"I'm coming with you," Caryn said, removing her heels as she stumbled to Talia's speed.

"Fine." Talia swiped the swelling in her eyes with her bare wrist before the tears could hit her cheek.

"There are swing sets over the hill, if you want to go."

"Sure." Talia didn't have a preference. It could be anywhere, nowhere, just not *there*.

They wandered alone in silence, each claiming a swing when they arrived at the empty playground, swaying in unison as if they were back in the fifth grade. The cemetery now hid behind the hillside.

"I couldn't take it anymore," Talia said after some quiet swinging. The breeze crept up her skirt, the sun catching a glimpse of the Ouroboros tattoo on her inside ankle. She got the tattoo on a road trip to New Hampshire, with Caryn by her side, on the weekend after her eighteenth birthday. It was still bright and fresh, unlike the ones inked onto the old veteran in the next room that day.

"I don't blame you. I don't get funerals. They don't make anyone feel better," Caryn said.

"I've seen dead bodies before," Talia said, pushing her legs farther into the air to increase her speed. "But she was ... different."

"Yeah." Caryn caught up with a harder kick.

"I wish I didn't have to see her that way. I don't want anyone to see *me* that way."

"You could always get cremated. That's what I plan to do."

"It's times like these I wish I believed in God."

"Would it make you feel better?" Caryn slowed her pace.

"Maybe. I don't know. This makes me feel better." Talia closed her eyes to the wind. "Are you shrinking me?"

"Could be. Would you have a problem with that?"

Talia smiled. "She liked you."

"I liked her, too. She was a great lady."

"I feel like there was so much more she needed to tell me," Talia said. "I don't know. She always said she'd tell me more one day, when I was ready. I guess I wasn't ready soon enough."

"Everyone leaves things unsaid," Caryn said.

"She died so suddenly. I know she was old, but she was healthy. Just doesn't feel right."

"Well, you know I always believe your gut instinct. You've never been wrong about me. Remember that dream you had about Rob? *That* was a close call. I dumped him before he had the chance to cheat with that slut again. Ugh, that was months ago, why can't I get over it? You'd think with a degree in psychology, I could fix myself." Caryn said. "Anyway, don't you get to look through your grandmother's stuff next week? Maybe you'll find something that will give you some closure."

"I hope so," Talia said. "My mom said something about a jewelry box. My grandmother left me hers in her will. I wonder if it's the same one I saw her open. The one with the picture and the amulet."

"The one with the little boy you think is your uncle?" Caryn asked.

"That's the one. Maybe she'll tell me in death what she meant to tell me in life."

Caryn sighed. "Me-a-vue, you know."

"Me-a-vue also."

Although Talia wouldn't admit it, a silly word among friends as a secret way to say, *I love you,* genuinely made her feel better. Neither of them was even sure of its exact creation date, but they'd been repeating it since grade school. Caryn always sensed when she needed the boost, ever since that first day of second grade, when Talia sulked in the cafeteria alone with her milk until Caryn decided to set her tray beside her.

"I'm not going back there, I don't care what my parents say," Talia said.

"I know. I get it."

"I got another story." Talia confessed to the latest article she had planned for the local newspaper, *The New Falls Sun.*

She had been submitting unsolicited articles there since she conducted an undercover investigation into her estranged cousin's murder at the seasoned age of eighteen, and found a lead. Talia considered it a self-promotion from her position at the *New Falls High School Tribune.* Her parents cried tears of pride and fear when Talia broke the story. The police weren't as supportive, earning her both enemies and allies in the two years since. *The New Falls Sun,* or rather its managing editor, Jill Barrett, had a more complicated relationship with Talia.

"It's a double murder, pre-teen twin sisters. They say it's occult-related. I haven't told Jill yet, but I have some theories."

"Yikes. Is this what you want? You just lost your grandmother," Caryn said.

"I got a message from my contact in Portugal. The one I met online. The police keep saying the case is getting cold, but my gal had an interesting lead. She said an amulet might be to blame. I know it sounds weird, but I keep thinking about my grandmother's amulet. Maybe it has something in common with this amulet my contact claims is the murder weapon."

"Definitely a possibility." Caryn kicked her bare feet into the air.

"Let's go to Portugal."

"Excuse me?" Caryn slowed her swing.

Talia followed. "It's the summer after college. Our first as real adults. We have to do something crazy. Let's go to Portugal together. You, me, Jared. Blow off some steam. Maybe it will give me some closure. I need to get out of this town."

"Love this idea. Go on." Caryn caressed her invisible beard.

"And … my informant heard rumors the suspect may have

fled to Portugal." Talia just couldn't keep a juicy secret from her best friend.

"Ah, here we go. You want to go investigate this thing, huh? I admit, it does sound fun."

"Maybe this is a sign," Talia said. "We can sightsee *and* investigate a crime."

"Win, win. I'm in. Now, what about Jared?"

THREE

TALIA SAT at Vovó's green Formica kitchen table, which tried its best to look marble, save for the glued edges. Her small legs dangled off the chair, scissoring faster and faster as if peddling her bicycle down a steep hill, until Vovó finally brought over her favorite Portuguese dessert—*malasadas,* a Luso version of carnival fried dough. Vovó only slaved over *malasadas* for special occasions like Christmas, Easter, or in this case, Talia's tenth birthday.

"Don't get so excited," Vovó huffed, her soft arms jiggling with the pastry platter. "I know you love these *pasteis,* but you need to eat them slowly, even on your birthday. And don't forget your milk."

Talia could hardly contain her enthusiasm as she bit into the soon-to-be crumbly mess on the table below her. Instead, she got a mouthful of fish paste and salt water. She spat the half-chewed pastry onto Vovó's kitchen floor and chugged her milk, raising her head in anticipation of Vovó's horrified reaction, only to find herself in Vovó's backyard at the age of sixteen.

The whole family gathered for a weekend afternoon of

picking grapes from her grandfather's vines hanging on a steel pergola, just as every harvest season in Talia's memory. Familiar faces approached her in a procession line, commented on her pale white expression, and kissed her on each cheek. Vovó was last.

As she walked toward her, the sunlight reflected on a large broach Vovó kept pinned at her heart to clasp the shawl over her head in place. She smiled at Talia and lifted her weak head in to kiss her on the cheek, but instead she breathed in her ear, "*Que horas são?*" The smell of Vovó's floral perfume stung Talia's eyes.

The old woman didn't wait for the time. Instead, she stepped into the woods behind the house, the sun eclipsing her profile. Talia screamed for her as she strode into the horizon. She looked to her wrist to find drawn onto it with felt marker a watch bearing the military time 00:09.

———

TALIA JOLTED awake in the dark with a deep moan, having again kicked half her sheets to the foot of her bed. She swung her head to the side to check the time on the alarm clock sitting on her nightstand. It read 12:09 AM.

Talia gnawed at her stubby fingers. She was accustomed to strange occurrences, like seeing a random little boy in her dreams and then finding that same boy riding a bike for the first time near her house the very next day. This one with her recently deceased grandmother irked her more than usual. A piece of her walked away with Vovó that night, lost for good in the woods behind her childhood home.

The next morning, still groggy from an anxious sleep, Talia met her mother at Vovó's townhouse on Maple Street and collapsed onto the mustard yellow couch that had decorated her living room for as long as she could remember. It was as if the old woman had never left for the nursing home after her husband passed.

Talia's mother couldn't bring herself to sell the property her family owned since they immigrated in the 1970's. It sat vacant for months, gathering dust in the crevices no one could reach. The scent of cough drops and lemon ammonia lingered. Not a single trinket or frame out of place, yet the drawer in which she once saw Vovó hide her jewelry box, left to Talia as part of her inheritance, was empty. Or so her mother claimed.

"I know it's in here somewhere." Talia sprung up to search her grandparents' bedroom for the first of many times that morning.

"I know how upset you are about your grandmother, but it's not here." Her mother dabbed her blotched cheeks. Talia's erratic behavior since the funeral had started to reflect in her mother's disposition.

Talia pressed harder. "It's here. She said she left it for me. It has to be here."

"I've searched for days, it's not here. You have the gold watch she gave you. That should be enough."

Vovó told her tales about the watch and its many generations within the family tree. Her ancestors bought it as an investment. Vovó's side of the family came from a time when Portuguese gold was regarded as the highest of riches. This reverence originated in the spoils of Brazil in the 1700's, when Portugal colonized the country and excavated it for gold and silver. The greatest riches were discovered in the current Brazilian state of Minas Gerais, named after the mines that permeated that area of the country, now mostly closed after being burrowed dry.

This gold watch belonged to my grandmother and then to my mother—

your great-grandmother, Vovó said. *Your mother and I decided it should be yours now.*

Talia stretched her right arm and waited as Vovó fastened the heavy gold watch loosely around her thin thirteen-year-old wrist. The numbers on the face were Roman numerals etched in gold to match. As Vovó fiddled with the clasp, Talia could see an inscription underneath the face: *Destrave seu ser interna,* or in English, *Unlock your inner being.*

Vovó advised her to keep the gold watch in a safe place until she was old enough to wear it. She placed it in a maroon velvet pouch, pulled its braided rope handles, and handed it to Talia.

"It's not about the jewelry, Mom. It's the principle. She wanted me to have that jewelry box for a reason. I have to find it." Talia tore through the living room closet, snowballing the clutter of clothes and knitting yarn she had left behind minutes earlier.

"You're cleaning this up later."

"I don't understand why she didn't keep it safe somewhere if she wanted me to have it—if it was important enough to leave it to me in her will."

"What do you think you'll find in this thing anyway?" Talia's mother asked, hands on her round hips.

"Answers," Talia said.

"To what questions? I've answered everything there is to know."

Talia rolled her eyes. "For one, that little boy in the picture."

Her mother flushed to a beet red. "I don't know who you're talking about."

At age ten, Talia caught Vovó's reflection hunched over a drawer in her commode, rummaging through a wooden jewelry box underneath her neatly folded clothing. Inside was another of Vovó's many brooches hidden by a torn sepia photo of her grandparents with two children. One resembled her mother as a toddler; the other, an older boy around Talia's age at the time who resembled her grandfather. The little boy gazed into the mountains, as if awaiting something extraordinary, her grandfather's firm grip on his left shoulder. Before then, Talia assumed she was the only daughter of an only daughter, and after a long interrogation, Vovó shrugged him off as a deceased cousin.

"You know who I'm talking about," Talia said.

"I don't know. A local boy, a friend of the family, a cousin maybe." Her mother shifted her eyes away from Talia and nibbled on her already ragged fingernails. "He probably moved back to Portugal. He could be dead for all I know."

"Big help," Talia said. "How about what Vovó might have had in that jewelry box?"

"I told you. I don't know. Your grandmother never talked to me about anything. Not the way she talked to you." Her speech cracked.

Talia's mobile phone buzzed in the pocket of her jeans. It was a message from her informant: *Follow your instincts.*

So she had to look one last time. Her mother chased a fixated Talia back into Vovó's drawers. She shifted Vovó's delicates around without luck, except this time the clothes caught a corner of the drawer liner, peeling it up to reveal a marking in faded blue ink. Talia tugged at the corner, skinning the liner from its drawer. Once she saw what looked like a handwritten address, she ripped it off and folded it.

"I'll find out in Portugal," Talia said.

She already suggested to Jill her plan to follow her lead to Portugal to investigate the murder of the twin girls. Jill didn't quite accept her offer to use some of her European vacation to investigate the case, but as usual, she cautioned but never discouraged. After all, Talia served her well in the past. Jill will thank her when she lands the story of her career.

Being bi-cultural and bilingual with a passion for news helped Talia secure a few stories in the Portuguese communities around eastern Massachusetts, though it wasn't often that they involved a double murder. Talia was unfazed by the gory assignment. She had chased after crime stories like those for the school newspaper, only to be denied by the dean, who found the subject matter "inappropriate for college students." That didn't stop her from trying.

Around the anniversary of her grandfather's death a couple years prior, Talia found herself in the midst of a similar crime scene in New Falls. In between interviews, Talia took a window seat in a noisy café on the main Portuguese strip in town, as she often did. While sipping on a Portuguese-style latte and reviewing her notes, she heard a faint scream.

Talia fought the urge to jump up, but no one else in the café seemed to react. All were too involved in their conversations or devices to notice the muffled cries from the alleyway. When Talia heard a car peeling away, she ran towards the sound, mildly aware of the murmurs and gawks of the customers as she crashed out the belled glass door.

Ten feet into the alleyway Talia slid to a stop on the asphalt, salted from the last winter storm a few days prior. A pool of blood spread across the ground near the rusty dumpster, staining the napkins and wrappers that escaped along the sides. Talia traced the puddle to a lit red candle peeking from behind the corner wheel. Confused, Talia tiptoed a few feet closer and noticed the base of the candle was, in reality, a limp hand.

Without blinking, she fumbled through her bag for a phone and dialed 9-1-1. Pressing the mobile phone so tightly to her ear that she perspired, Talia inched towards the hand as the operator told her to stop walking. Lying to the operator, she continued down the path, unable to contain her curiosity. The dusk and clouds fell in between the buildings, passing with them a chill that put a lump in her throat.

Talia slackened her pace, and leaned in for a closer look. A lifeless body sat up against the dumpster, blood trickling from his hollow eyes, his peppered mane snarled with clumps. That older man was Talia's first murder investigation. His discovery boosted her budding career, and brought her back in touch with an old boyfriend, who had just graduated from the police academy for the New Falls Police Department.

During the investigation, Talia was brought in for questioning herself, a fact she kept from Jill for fear she'd lose her story. Ben O'Connor, the old boyfriend in the force, saw her in the waiting room and helped her maneuver through the legal process, no strings attached. He would become her contact from that point forward. It would turn out that the body Talia found belonged to an estranged cousin, a fourth cousin if she remembered correctly, whom she barely knew through the family grapevine. Armando Palmeiro was a drifter whose side of the family didn't stay in touch with Talia's, and it surprised no one when he would disappear for months at a time.

Excluding his parents, Armando had no family, no wife or kids. She heard of him through family gossip or the occasional Portuguese whisper at church, and it was never positive. Stories of alcoholism and domestic violence, the nature of which were harsh enough to incite a hush whenever Talia walked past gossipers as a child.

Her mother groaned. "You are not going to Portugal. You can find out everything you need here."

Talia held a sticky drawer liner up to her mother's face. She nodded at the scribble that resembled that of her Vovó, a proud woman who hid her illiteracy from most.

"What is that?" Her mother was a bad liar.

"An address in Portugal. Know it?" Talia asked.

"*Não sei ninguem em Lisboa.*" Talia's mother released the squint from her eyes as if she were being filmed. Her mother always concerned herself more with the appearance of things than the actual reality, more fearful of the gossipers at Sunday mass than the truth behind their whispers.

Luckily, Talia knew Portuguese well, and studied it throughout her academic career, as her family spoke a mixture of Portuguese and English on a regular basis. Her parents paid for classes two nights a week at the local Portuguese Club during middle school. The Club had always been the go-to for wedding receptions and parties for the local Portuguese communities in the United States, as well as the annual weekend-long summer festival where drinking wine, eating grilled meat, and traditional dancing were encouraged. Throughout her life, Talia had visited Portugal many times with her parents to visit family. Though she'd never tried before, she knew she could navigate the country alone.

"If you don't know anyone in Lisbon, then I guess I'll figure it out myself. Is Tia Maria still in Alfama?" Talia asked.

"Your great-aunt? She doesn't know who she is. She's not even living in her apartment. She's in a retirement home a few blocks down. They call it a *Lar*. Why?"

"I have a contact. A fellow journalist, I think. She's been helping me with some of my articles. I got a story about a double murder in town."

"You're going to investigate a murder?" Talia's mother asked, her face now a lighter shade of olive.

"I'm a journalist, not a cop, Mom. It's about those twin girls in the news. You heard of them, right?"

"Yes. Your grandmother used to know a couple that lived near that bakery we get our sweet bread for Easter. I took you to their house once when you were little, remember? They had that big sunroom. The girls that were murdered were her granddaughters. Your grandmother once told me they were distant cousins."

"Everyone's a distant cousin." It was a long-standing joke in her family. Every visit to Lisbon, Talia would meet a new forgotten cousin who, for some reason, was never in town the many other times she'd visited. "I think I remember that sunroom. And meeting them. So you're saying they are, I mean were, my cousins?"

"Yes. And I think you did meet them once. I can't believe they're gone. I have to call your aunt. What does this have to do with Portugal?"

"Well, they thought it was a run of the mill murder at first, and then they realized it might have been some sort of ritual sacrifice—witchcraft or something," Talia said.

"*Bruxas! Ai Jesus!*" Her mother gasped. "They think that's how your grandfather's best friend died."

"He died? When?" It was not like Talia to forget such a big detail. Then again, in order to keep her mom sane, Talia often left out the gritty minutiae of her day-to-day. If she knew that Talia had interviewed cellmates in prison or suspected criminals in their homes, she was quite confident her mother would cease to sleep at night.

"Last year. I thought I told you. They say it was a heart attack, but there are rumors."

"Rumors?" Talia asked.

"They say he was cursed."

Though she would rather call herself an Atheist, Talia knew the label didn't suit her. Though she didn't quite believe in God, growing up in such a deeply pagan culture, it was hard to shake the belief in curses and witchcraft, like carrying garlic around known witches, or visiting a witch doctor when the medical doctor can't find what ails you.

Her grandfather's best friend was allegedly cursed by the substitute nurse who visited him that day. She was a known witch in the Portuguese community. Nobody's sure why she did it, but some claimed the old man had a wandering hand.

"Why do you need to go to Portugal if the murders happened here?" her mother asked.

"The police traced the murders back to someone in Portugal. They aren't sure who yet, and the Portuguese government isn't quick at giving a hand. Bureaucracy, you know how it is there."

Her mother nodded. She too waited in line while the cashier at a local market in Portugal continued a ten-minute-long conversation with the customer in front of her in line, and sat for hours in the pleather chairs of a European bank lobby.

"I'm excited, to tell you the truth. It's only a week and I have to pay for it myself, but I have some money saved."

"What you're looking for doesn't exist."

"That jewelry box does exist. I've seen it," Talia said.

"You were young. Even if you saw it, it's probably long gone by now."

"Mom, this is so obviously a clue. How can you not see it? You're more superstitious than I am," Talia said. "This timing can't be coincidental."

"I think you want it to be a clue," her mother said, "but it's not, *querida*. I promise you, there is no one waiting for you in Portugal."

FOUR

THE NEW FALLS alleyway reeked of restaurant dishwater from the night before, which still dribbled into the storm drains running along its center. Talia avoided dampening her flats in the sludge by hopscotching around the puddles, much like she imagined the twin girls did moments before their death. Step on a crack, break your mother's back.

Yellow police tape crisscrossed in front of the crevice between the buildings, marking the alley where the double murder must have taken place. She wasn't supposed to visit a fresh crime scene, but Talia convinced a sweet old Portuguese neighbor to give her a heads up when the police stopped patrolling the area, and by surprise, Talia got a call that morning.

Being a petite gal didn't always work in Talia's favor, but on rare occasions, like being able to avoid a low-hanging branch without having to duck, it came in handy. Talia snuck underneath the yellow tape and tiptoed down the alley. A shiver in her gut caught her by surprise. The echoes of her footsteps pounded louder. A bead of sweat stung her eye, the stuffy air confining her between the tall building walls. It had been a muggy late summer, generators and air conditioners nearby whirred in a competition for the loudest note.

Knowing the little girls were her cousins didn't help Talia separate her emotions from the crime. Her usual focused demeanor while reporting waned at the thought of a mother losing two young children. Talia wasn't close with the twins, she only met them once, but just knowing they were family irked her.

Her cousin Armando's murder also took place in an alleyway. Besides the location, nothing about the two murders matched. Armando's autopsy suggested he bled to death, while the girls had not bled at all. Talia helped locate Armando's murderer and the police convicted him. Last she heard, the suspect was serving time for murdering Armando, who allegedly slept with the suspect's wife. Like most people in prison, he maintained his innocence, appealing in the courts several times to no avail.

Talia's left ear burned as if she had again spent too much time at the beach without reapplying suntan lotion. She placed her icy fingers on her earlobe to cool it, but it only worked for a moment. Somebody was talking about her and it wasn't good.

Burning ears are a sign of gossip in Portuguese folklore, but the side of the ear determines its intent. Though she assured herself it was all irrelevant, the age-old Portuguese superstition had been retold in her family time and again. She knew a lot of Portuguese folklore had religious connotations. In Christianity, the left side is considered the path to hell, while the right path took you to heaven.

Had Talia's right ear burned, she would have pictured her mother gushing to her friends about her promising future as a reporter, but it was her left ear that burned instead. Its timing took Talia by surprise, as if the alleyway itself was creating the sensation.

If they're talking about me, they're leaving someone else alone, one of her mother's popular nuggets of advice. Talia's mother was better at giving advice than taking it.

Her cell phone rang, and Talia shrieked. It was her editor, Jill. She had a tendency to call Talia at the most inopportune moments, like in the middle of an interrogation of a skittish suspect, or while Talia hugged the toilet before a big interview. It was one of Talia's most common paranoia rituals, and she learned to accept it.

"It's been a week. Just making sure you're not getting yourself in trouble," Jill's voice echoed.

Talia hated when Jill put her on speakerphone. "I'm not. Who's there with you?"

"It's just me this time. Multitasking." This actually meant that Jill didn't feel like holding the phone up to her ear. It was a Friday, the day she dressed up for her weekly date night, and she hated to remove her earrings for phone calls.

"I interviewed their mom this morning. She said there's word on the street that it was a man with a hood." Talia's voice shivered.

"Like a hoodie?"

"No, more like a trench coat with a hood. The guy was pretty far away and the police haven't gotten much from his eye witness account, but I just have a feeling about it."

"Trust your gut, Talia. I have faith in you. You leave tomorrow, right? Be careful. I don't want you getting injured, especially when this is supposed to be under the radar. If this gets back to my boss… I'm taking a chance with you," Jill said. "You're my link to the Portuguese community. I can't lose you."

It was an unemotional way of saying she cared, but Talia understood. It was about as warm as Jill got, and Talia knew where she stood. Talia was as much her protégé as Jill was her mentor, ever since they met five years prior during Talia's Career Day field trip to the local newspaper her junior year of high school. There's a certain amount of detachment a crime reporter develops over time. A cold body lying in a pool of blood starts to feel more like a scene from a movie than real life. They understood each other.

"I promise to be careful." Talia failed to mention her location before she said her goodbyes. She didn't want Jill to worry.

A dusty velour blanket concealing a pile of junk rustled in a recess of one of the brick buildings. Talia squealed, certain it wasn't a breeze. Her pace quickened, but the tall structures hovered over her, squeezing out the few rays of light that snuck through the narrow walkways. Her throat constricted with the sudden thinning of air, as if she climbed a few thousand feet of elevation in just one block. Fearful of what might be behind her, Talia fought through her racing heart and arrived at the scene of the crime just as her parked car at the end of the alley eclipsed the setting sun.

The alcove just beyond her looked torn apart from a search by law enforcement weeks before. Parts of the walls and dumpster had been dusted for prints, boxes of trash were emptied onto the pavement in the corner, and sticky beer bottles and soda cans had spilled out of a torn plastic bag leaning against the back wall.

It didn't take long for the stench of soured milk and wet asphalt to invade Talia's nostrils. She let out a moan of disgust, and consciously started breathing from her mouth. Talia hung in her step as if a steady gust of wind held her in place.

"Get it together, Talia." She raised her chest, marched towards the crevice, and stopped at the corner. Digging into her bag without ungluing her eyes from her careful step, she pulled out a travel-sized flashlight, and aimed it towards the pile of rubbish.

Lying underneath the pile of used paper plates and utensils, an unscathed blue mesh bag of herbs tied at the top with a rope, tipped on its side. Though pocket-sized, its bright hue appeared to glow, a mirage in a gray desert. With all this trash, it should have been destroyed, unless it was thrown away after the fact.

Talia read about mixes of herbs and spices that can induce a person into a coma or paralyzed state. It was considered a common practice in the black arts, often as a part of rituals or sacrifices. Concoctions such as this one were almost certainly used by her own family in the past, to ward off bad luck or bring wealth into their home. A bowl of colorful herbs always sat on the counter of Vovó's bathroom. Talia could tell by its potency of mint and rosemary how recently it had been refreshed. She hadn't thought much of it until then, chalking it up to a natural, old-fashioned way to eliminate bathroom odors.

It seemed unlikely that the murders were part of a ritual. Talia knew those rigid affairs must take place on specific days and hours, planned ahead of time by a group of likeminded people, not in dark alleyways in daylight by a lone gunman. These murders could not have been planned. There was no way of knowing the girls would be there, unless he lured them there.

Talia placed the flashlight on the ground with the beam facing the trash. Reaching again into her backpack, she removed a pair of disposable gloves, slipped them over her hands, and pulled out a resealable bag. Talia snatched the potpourri on the ground with her protected hands, and threw it in the sandwich bag as if it were on fire.

She sniffed at the opening and scrunched her nose. Black licorice, her least favorite smell. The detectives probably found the potpourri bag and threw it back. No one would think it was a clue to a murder. Cops don't understand pagan rituals, and they'd think she was crazy for suggesting a bag of potpourri could be a murder weapon. Ben would have definitely thought she was crazy.

Dried poppy flowers dotted the mix of cedar wood and licorice with sparks of orange, and shriveled white berries tumbled in between. Talia wrapped the bag of potpourri and shoved it in her purse. She pulled out her mobile phone and tapped the herb names onto the screen, followed by the words "witchcraft" or "spell." As she suspected, they weren't innocent ingredients. Licorice is used in black magic to control people's movements, and poppy confuses and dominates enemies. Talia wasn't certain a small bag of herbs was enough to kill two innocent children, but she couldn't say it was impossible. For now, it was the only lead she had.

———

WHEN TALIA GOT BACK to her house later that afternoon, she answered a frantic call from Ben. "What's wrong?" Talia asked.

"Your antics are gonna get me in trouble." His breath heavy, his Boston accent thickening with anger. He dropped R's as if they were on fire. Ben's voice had matured since their brief stint back in her freshman year of high school—his senior year—but his capacity for patience had not. "Someone called into the station saying they saw some chick snooping around a crime scene this morning. I'm guessing that was you?"

"That's a big assumption, isn't it?" Her heart beat faster.

"Am I right? You're putting me in a jam here, Talia. I said I would help you, but you're gonna get me fired."

Ben was an abrasive fellow, to say the least, but he was loyal, which was a rare trait she admired. He was a good guy, underneath the curmudgeon. Talia couldn't remember why they broke up, but she knew well why they hadn't gotten back together.

"No, I won't. You've always been such a tight ass. No one's going to get in trouble." She couldn't be sure of that, of course, but she said it anyway.

"Fine. Was it worth it? Did you find anything?" Ben asked. A man shouted obscenities above the din of chiming phones in the background.

"Maybe."

"What did you find, Talia?" Ben asked.

"Nothing you guys would find interesting. A bag of potpourri."

"A bag of what?"

"Potpourri. You know, a smelly herb concoction your grand-mother probably kept in her living room?"

"You think it has something to do with the murders?" His voice quieted with the background.

"Possibly. You know the rumors that the murders were occult-related? Well, this could be evidence of it."

"You know that's just in the media right? No one here believes that crap. Look, I don't know all the details. All I do know is, off the record, the coroner doesn't think it was a poison-ing. As of now, it's inconclusive, but I overheard some guys say the twins were stunned to death. Like they froze in fear. Obvi-ously, we don't want the press to know that yet. So keep your mouth shut and don't do anything stupid."

"Aw, sweet Ben, you know that's hard for me, but I'll give it the old college try. Thanks for everything. Gotta run. I've got a plane to catch." Talia didn't wait for a goodbye.

FIVE

"I CAN'T BELIEVE we're here. I've never even been out of New England." Caryn beamed as she emerged from the double horseshoe entrance of the Rossio Railway Station in Lisbon, and Jared and Talia stood by her side, bags in tow.

The station's cast-iron architecture was layered with a Romantic façade, three levels of round, gated windows, and a Roman numeral clock crowning its top behind them. That neighborhood in the Baixa district of Lisbon had been nicknamed Rossio since the Middle Ages. Rossio translates to "large public square," and although there are many squares throughout the city, none of them bear this title.

Rossio Square is officially named *Praça Dom Pedro IV*, after the former king of Portugal, who was also Brazil's first emperor, led the colony through a successful revolution for independence in the nineteenth century. His 23-meter-tall column monument stood at the heart of the plaza, commanding them from above as they walked beneath it.

Caryn took a seat at one of the outdoor restaurants that lined the pedestrian-only cobblestoned *Rua Augusta*, one of the four streets that intersected with the square. "So exciting!"

"Pretty sweet," Jared said.

"I told you guys Portugal was amazing." Talia smiled.

The waiter greeted the trio in Portuguese and handed them each a menu and a glass of water, with no ice.

"Okay, um, I can't read this." Caryn giggled, flipping the menu to all its sides.

"I'll give you suggestions," Talia said. "Just remember the shrimp have heads and most food is fried."

"Ew, shrimp with heads." Caryn frowned.

"You'll be fine. I'll have steak, any kind," Jared said, widening his chest.

"I think you'll love the *Bitoque*. Fried tenderized steak with a fried egg on top served with French fries and rice on the side. A Portuguese classic," Talia said. "My man loves his meat, don't you baby?"

Jared winked at Talia as he caressed her thigh.

"French fries *and* rice?" Caryn asked.

"Yep. We love our starch," Talia chuckled. "I think you should stick with the *Bacalhau a Bras*, Caryn. I know you love cod. It's a fish stew with eggs, onions, and potatoes. It's delicious. I am ordering *Dobrada*. I've missed it so much."

Dobrada, a tripe and white bean stew served mostly in the winter, is a strange love for Talia, who doesn't usually gravitate toward the exotic parts of an animal, especially after being a vegetarian for a short stint in high school. Talia's mother had a tendency to lie about the ingredients in her meals, knowing Talia was picky, and that the thought of pig ears, squid tentacles, and blood sausage revolted a finicky child of any nationality. Every so often, when her mother boiled one of the rabbits stored in the freezer in case of Armageddon, she tried to convince Talia it was chicken. It only worked a handful of times before Talia recognized the gamey stench of stewed bunny and refused to eat it. And she hadn't since.

"To hell with it. We're on vacation," Caryn said. "Waiter, I'll have the *bacalhau*."

When the waiter brought their dinners ten minutes later, Caryn mentioned their perfect excuse to visit Portugal. Talia was surprised it took her that long.

"So, what's next? You know, for the murder investigation." Caryn's voice softened.

"I forgot to tell you, I read through all the case work the day before we left and decided to go speak with the sisters' family. I got their address from my mom. The cops asked me not to bother them, but I just had to."

"Talia has always been known for her tact," Jared said.

Talia pursed her lips and ignored him. "After my mother told me they may be distant cousins, I had to find out for myself. I'd definitely been there before, just like my mom said. The lady even remembered me, which sure did help get me answers. Get this, she said the two girls had been seen with a man no one in town knew. Her uncle's cousin saw the whole thing."

Caryn stopped mid-chew. "You think they're hiding something?"

"Not sure. It could be that I just didn't get all the files, but who knows? His account was pretty out there. Well, out there for the average person, not for me." Talia grinned.

"So was it really occult related?" Caryn asked.

"Oh boy," Jared said, rolling his eyes. "Not this again."

Jared often scoffed at Talia's family traditions and cultural beliefs. She found a way to overlook it most times. Other times, she held back the urge to smack him. It was the main reason why she didn't introduce him to her extended family until the funeral.

"Apparently, one minute the two girls were approached by the guy, the next they fell down in unison," Talia said.

Caryn gasped.

"Crazy, huh? Ben said the guy never even touched them, just spoke to them. He wasn't sure if they even got to answer, it happened so suddenly. And they never got back up. He said they froze in fear."

"That's crazy." Caryn shook her head.

"I didn't know you were still talking to Ben," Jared said.

"He helps me with my articles sometimes. Anyway, their mother said the witness seemed pretty spooked. He couldn't even identify the suspect because he was wearing a hood. I guess he was far enough away for the police to question his vision, far enough to not be the first person on the scene."

"So he could have been seeing things," Jared said.

"Or not seeing things," Caryn said, a curve in her eyebrow.

"Exactly. So, I snuck back to the crime scene to see if they missed any clues."

"You did what?" Jared tossed Talia a concerned glare.

"I had to. Strangely, I found something the police didn't," Talia said, leaning into the table. "A small satchel of herbs. But they weren't just any herbs."

"Magic herbs?" Caryn asked.

"They weren't necessarily magic, but they all did have some sort of magical purpose. All of the ingredients in it have been used in spells for centuries. And not the happy, attract-a-lover kind. The evil kind."

Jared shook his head.

"The girls didn't even bleed. Autopsy results say their hearts stopped, but they aren't sure how yet. They still had smiles on their faces."

"I'm sorry, ladies, but I'm sure there's a logical explanation for how those little girls died. Maybe he blew anthrax in their face or something," Jared said.

"Don't mean to play the pre-med card here, but Anthrax wouldn't kill you that suddenly," Caryn said, adjusting her invisible glasses.

"Their mother certainly believed the guy's story," Talia said. "Maybe she'd believe anything at this point, but she took me aside later and whispered in my ear that I may be her only hope to find the killer. That because I was Portuguese, I understood."

Talia noticed the conversation didn't sit well with Caryn, who played with the food on her plate and then crossed her fork and knife on top.

"You shouldn't cross them," Talia said, knowing full well what argument would ensue.

"I can assure you it doesn't invite the devil onto your plate," Jared answered, on cue.

"It's actually from your plate through your mouth," Talia said. "I know it's silly, but don't we do the same by saying, 'bless you,' when someone sneezes? It comes from the same belief that a person's soul is vulnerable. Open to evil."

The custom of saying, *God bless you,* for a sneeze began as far back as the first century, with the rise of the plague during the papacy of Pope Gregory the Great. The power of this prayer seemed to work: the plague of 590 AD was brief compared to other plagues of its time. Some Christians now believe that a soul is thrown out of a person's body when they sneeze, and the power of prayer helps guide them back. According to Portuguese folk stories, sneezing opens a gateway in which the devil can sneak into your body and possess you. Blessing the sneezer protects them from this evil invasion.

"You doubt my knowledge of the Curse of the Crossed

Silverware?" Caryn playfully rearranged her knife and fork to lie parallel on her plate. "There, no evil. See?"

"Thanks, Caryn." Talia rose from her seat. "The ladies' room calls. I'll be right back."

She skirted her way through the bistro into a tiny room at the back harboring a yellowed toilet with a rusted pull-cord suspended from the low ceiling, a shared sink sat outside. On her way back, Talia overheard a news story on RTP1, Portugal's first federally-owned television station, chiming from the small flat screen hanging above the pastry case. She leaned on the counter to watch, careful not to smudge the glass with her skin. The man behind the counter stared at Talia for a moment and then served another customer.

"A recent surge in occult-related violence in the Porto area has local law enforcement scrambling for clues," the dark-haired woman anchor reported in Portuguese. "Remains of what is believed to be discarded animal sacrifices are showing up on some properties down the coastline, accompanied by strange symbols believed to be Brazilian Voodoo."

A tall man spiced with sandalwood and tobacco snuck up from behind Talia and asked with a thick, unusual Portuguese accent, "Does voodoo interest you?"

Talia jumped.

"I did not mean to scare you," the man said. "You looked very interested. *Eu sou Nuno Morães*."

He reminded Talia of her father in all but height—dark olive skin, green eyes, and unruly chocolate locks. A long nose complemented his tall, lean physique.

"I'm Natalia Braga, but people call me Talia," she said as she stretched out her hand for a shake. "Voodoo is intriguing, I suppose. Do you know anything about these murders?"

"Do I look like I do?" he asked with a roguish grin. "All I

know is what they have told me." Nuno pointed his thumb back at the screen.

"This is the first time I've seen it on TV. Has it been all over the news?"

"Only since yesterday," he said.

"I wasn't in town yesterday," Talia said. "So do they think the guy is up north now?"

"*Asho que sim*," Nuno said. "*Desculpa*, do you know Portuguese? It means, *I think so*."

"I do. A little," Talia lied. "You don't sound Portuguese."

"That is because I am from Brazil," Nuno said. "You are very observant."

"That's what they pay me for. I've always been a bit more curious than the average person. Just call me Alice in Wonderland."

"Alice?" Nuno asked.

"You know, she's very curious."

"*Oh, sim.* I know," Nuno laughed.

"Hi there," Jared chimed in.

"Oh, hey, Jared. Nuno, this is Jared, my boyfriend. We got to talking about the occult murders. They aired a story on TV."

"Nice to meet you, Nuno," Jared said, shaking his hand. "I was wondering where you ran off to."

"Sorry, got caught up in the story, you know how it is," Talia said.

"Your girlfriend says she knows some Portuguese. Do you?" Nuno asked.

"No, I don't. Talia, are you ready to head back?" Jared straightened his shoulders as if in a contest for the tallest man in the room.

"Um, yeah, sure," Talia said. "*Boa noite*, Nuno."

"*Até já*, Alice," Nuno called out with a wink.

"I would prefer if you didn't usher me out of conversations," Talia whispered as Jared pushed her through the restaurant.

"He's a stranger in a strange land," Jared said. "Right, Alice?"

"You were once a stranger," Talia said.

"That's what I'm worried about," Jared said, his grip on her upper arm tightening.

"Jealousy is not sexy." Talia eyeballed Jared for a reaction.

"Can we just move on with our night?" Jared asked.

"Yes, let's," Caryn said as they arrived at the table in an attempt to avoid bearing witness to another squabble. "Let's bust this joint."

SIX

ON THE TRAIN up the coast to Lisbon's beaches, Jared, Caryn, and Talia stopped to nibble on a *Pastel de Nata*, a mouthwatering, flaky custard pastry tart that no Portuguese festivity goes without, at its birthplace in the *Antiga Confeitaria de Belém*.

The ornate pastry shop overlooking the marina always brimmed with locals and tourists, its blue-vested staff weaving around the glass counters at its center and the cases of untouched liquor that lined the walls. On weekends, customers leaked out into the street in front of its blue awnings, treading the cobblestoned lettering that has marked its name since its grand opening in 1837.

Further along the train line at the seaside cliffs, fittingly named *Boca do Inferno*, or the Hell Mouth, Jared feigned falling off the cliff side, frightening both girls for a quick laugh.

Talia's father warned her of the legend behind its gory name. No one who ever fell in was rescued, their bodies never recovered. It is presumed that the tall surf pummeled them into a chasm between the jagged rocks of the cliff, and then dragged their battered bodies deep into the Atlantic Ocean.

Boca do Inferno is also known for its ties to the occult. Aleister Crowley, a well-known English occultist and self-proclaimed Satanist, faked his suicide there in 1930 with the help of the Portuguese modernist poet, and fellow occultist, Fernando Pessoa.

The two occultists first made contact when Pessoa, who once aspired to be an astrologer, wrote a letter to Crowley citing errors in the horoscopes published in Crowley's infamous *Confessions*. After more letters were exchanged, the two made plans to meet in September 1930 in Lisbon, Pessoa's home his entire adult life.

Crowley arrived in Lisbon with his lover in tow, but the two had a falling out which resulted in her departure from the country shortly afterward. A dejected Crowley convinced Pessoa to assist him with a fake suicide note left on the side of the cliffs of *Boca do Inferno*, while he instead escaped Portugal through western Spain.

Pessoa spread rumors about the meaning behind the symbols sketched throughout Crowley's note and then claimed to have seen his ghost the very next day. Due to Pessoa's reclusive nature, the newspapers believed his deceits and published many sensational stories about Crowley's self-inflicted demise.

Weeks later, after basking in the media frenzy, Crowley shocked Europe by appearing at an art exhibit of his own paintings in Berlin.

"Be careful, Jared!" Talia yelled, having heard reports of tourists leaning off the cliffs to pose for their final photo.

A pretty girl in a bikini top, her olive skin oiled, her dark hair styled into beach blown curls, jogged over to Jared to help save his life and he milked it like a teenage boy. Talia cringed.

"You know he doesn't mean it," Caryn said, but she didn't know the whole truth.

A few days before Vovó's death, Jared was making a sandwich in Talia's kitchen when his cell phone buzzed on the coffee table in front of her in the living room. Talia didn't want to look, since she wasn't the type to snoop on her boyfriend's phone, but it glared at her, dared her to read it. The text from a girl they once met from his dad's firm read, "How about tonight?"

On the cliff, a wave of irritation rubbed across Talia's shin. When she bent to scratch, she saw a black cat snuggling with her right foot. Considered a place much like the ends of the earth, *Boca do Inferno* had become a haven for abandoned felines, who meandered around the touristy masses and rickety fences, mewing for scraps and attention.

"Oh no, bad luck." Caryn pointed at the mangy cat, whose dark skin masked the missing blotches of fur on his spine and hind legs.

"Actually, in Portuguese folklore it's good luck to own a black cat," Talia said. "It's supposed to absorb all the evil directed at its owner. So when it dies, it saves the owner's life."

"Oh look, good luck," Jared joked as he approached the girls.

"Told you." Talia smiled.

"Superstitions are an interesting part of the human psyche," Caryn said. "They're a form of obsessive compulsive disorder. I'm guilty of it myself, but superstitions are a ritual performed— or not performed—for luck, which is a myth. There's no such thing as luck."

"That reminds me of the saying, *se Deus quiser*," Talia said. "It translates to the English phrase, *God willing*. My older family members always say it when we say our goodbyes, as if trying not to tempt fate by implying we'll see each other again. So morbid."

"It makes a strange sort of sense when you think about it," Caryn said.

The three walked up and down the hills that traced the cliff side, the din of waves crashing beneath them.

"Do you think superstitions work?" Talia asked. "Suppose you believe something will happen, will it be more likely to happen?"

"You mean just because you believe it will?" Caryn asked.

Talia nodded.

"There are studies theorizing that positive and negative energies do impact the world around them."

"The power of positivity, like *The Secret*," Jared said.

Talia slapped Jared's forearm with a smile.

"Actually, a lot like that," Caryn said, wearing a severe face that Talia pictured her in during future therapy sessions. "There have been studies done on plants and snowflakes where the energy emitted from human emotion has been shown to affect a plant's health or a snowflake's symmetrical shape."

"Sometimes I forget how smart you are," Jared said.

"Um, thanks?" Caryn gave Jared a sarcastic smirk.

"Don't listen to that chauvinist. This is why I keep you around," Talia said with a wink. "It's good to have a doctor in the house."

"Anytime you need help with the crazies, you know where to find me." Caryn said.

"Lately, it seems the crazies are all around us." There was another itch on Talia's ankle. The little black cat could not be shaken. He followed Talia around the park and back to the train tracks, purring on her toes at every pause.

"That cat really likes you," Caryn said.

"I've noticed," Talia said. "When I was younger, I always

found a cat friend here. None as friendly as this one, but still odd."

"Animals like you. My parents' cat loves you," Jared said.

"I think only cats like me," Talia said, not recalling a time when a dog enjoyed her company. "Maybe because I saved one once."

"You saved a cat?" Caryn asked.

"When I visited once as a tween I heard a meowing kitten agonizing in pain. My dad tried to stop me, but I was already on its tracks. I followed his cries into an enormous stack of restaurant chairs three rows deep. He was trapped between some legs," Talia said, gesturing her arms. "My dad helped me move the chairs a little and the cat wobbled out all broken. I convinced the restaurant owner to feed him scraps until we left. Who knows how long he lasted. Probably not very long, but longer than he would've without me."

"My angel of kittens," Jared teased as he pulled Talia in for a side hug.

"I don't know how you can hear any living thing sobbing like that and not want to help it. I have a heart," Talia said.

"And a good one it is." Caryn wrapped her arm around Talia's neck. "You have passed the psychopath test."

"Good to know." Talia laughed.

"Side note, there are a lot of hot boys here," Caryn whispered as she watched a flock of shirtless boys grabbing plates of grilled seafood from the stand. "Don't hate me if I want to take one home with me."

———

"SAY *QUEIJO!*" Caryn shouted from behind Jared's treasured Holga camera, showered in the morning sun.

With their feet buried in the soft sand bordering Portugal's western coast at Talia's favorite beach, Cascais, Talia and Jared locked lips, the warm breeze fanning sand and hair into their content faces. The crisp, white Atlantic waves crashed against the teeming shore behind them in a rhythmic beat.

For a moment, Talia forgot the mounting arguments with Jared throughout the last year—over Vovó's death, the demanding nature of her soon-to-be career, and stupid things, like Talia taking too long to get ready. All their cares washed away with the waves. For good, she hoped.

Talia favored Cascais over the other two major beaches off the coast of Lisbon—Estoril and Carcavelos. There's something quaint and untouched about the enduring fishing village with its origins in the twelfth century.

Despite the growing tourism that spilt in from the largest casino in Europe found in Estoril and the many expatriates living in Algarve, Portugal's southern coast—the area Talia likes to call the Portuguese Riviera—Cascais held on to its old world charm.

Talia's father would tour her through the castles that stripe the coastline and tell stories of King John II, who in 1488 built a small fortress near the sea to repel Spanish troops (to no avail); he'd tell her about the earthquake of 1755 that destroyed half the village, long before there was a yacht harbor and over a dozen golf courses in the outskirts.

An older couple sauntered in front of Talia and Jared, and then scurried away with an apologetic wave when they caught sight of Caryn setting up a shot with the camera. Caryn smiled at the bronzed couple in bathing suits two sizes too small as they fell out of view, and then pressed the shutter button.

"Nice one, guys!" Caryn shouted again as she plodded through the sand in their direction.

The ocean breeze cooled Talia's pinked shoulders as she

wrapped her arms around Caryn and Jared. "I want to thank you guys for coming with me to Portugal and, you know, supporting me in all this."

"How could I say no to the Mediterranean?" Caryn winked.

"You're my Mediterranean," Jared flashed a perfect smile at Talia, his blue eyes reflecting the early afternoon sun.

Talia smiled, her cheeks toasted, and Jared pulled her into a kiss.

"Okay, you guys. That's enough. I can handle it for pictures, but no more," Caryn said, crossing her arms. "Ooh, guys, gotta go! I'll be back, promise."

Caryn shoved the camera into Jared's hands and dashed for the café, almost tripping over the raised plinth of the statue of King Carlos I positioned at the heart of the mosaic boardwalk.

"Short attention span that girl has," he said, wrapping the camera strap around his wrist. "My brother would be so jealous if he was here."

"That's why he isn't. He's still pining over her, I'm guessing?"

Jared's younger brother, Steve, had been carrying a torch for Caryn since they met. Steve crashed into Caryn at a frat party, the same party where Talia first met Jared. In fact, Steve's infatuation with Caryn was what brought Jared and Talia together that night. Steve wouldn't leave her alone, which was a sure way to send Caryn running.

"He says he's not, but I can see it in his eyes when I mention her. He still lights up, the fool. I try to help him, but he never listens," Jared said. Steve was also not swayed by Jared's attempts to control him. "He has a girlfriend now, though, so that's something."

"You can't help who you love," Talia teased, pushing her wet bikini top against his bare chest with a playful grin that encompassed her entire face, scrunching her eyes.

"I guess not." Jared smiled, touching his nose and then his lips to Talia's forehead.

In an optical illusion from the corner of her eye, Talia stared through the statue Caryn walked behind in an attempt to guard her, but Caryn wasn't in sight.

The statue of King Carlos was not the only statue in town depicting the king, who was assassinated in 1908 along with his eldest son by two revolutionaries. His youngest son, Prince Manuel, who took a shot to the arm, was crowned the last reigning King of Portugal seven days later.

Baptized as *Carlos Fernando Luís Maria Víctor Miguel Rafael Gabriel Gonzaga Xavier Francisco de Assis Luis Simão*, King Carlos was given the sort of long-winded Portuguese appellation that inspired Talia's mother to leave her without a middle name of her own.

Who doesn't have a middle name? A rhetorical question she had been asked dozens of times in her life by strangers and friends alike. In Portuguese culture, children take their mother's maiden name as one of their middle names. Many of her family members hoarded three or four of them, passed down from generations. Not Talia. When she complained to her mother about her curt forename, her mother threatened Talia with her maiden name, which Talia didn't fancy. Who needs a middle name anyway?

Jared and Talia escaped the sun on a bench nearby and awaited Caryn's return. When Caryn reemerged, an older man stood at her side, possibly in his mid-forties, dressed in casual business attire and sockless penny loafers, his hair slicked back, face smooth-shaven.

"Guys, this is *Pierre*. He's from *Paris*." Caryn elongated her French pronunciation of his name and hometown to emphasize his appeal.

Talia and Jared stared at each other, desperate to veil their creeping laughter.

"*Bonjour*, I'm Talia," she said as she stretched her arm out to Pierre.

"*Bonjour*, Talia," Pierre said, his fingers slithering out from her firm grip in what Talia often described as a dead fish handshake, a sign of a lack of confidence.

"Hi Pierre, I'm Jared."

Pierre grabbed Jared's hand with force. "*Bonjour*, Jared." His unmistakable machismo overwhelmed Talia with an impulsive wrath, but she tamed it before causing a scene—a skill most girls learn by their teens.

"So what brings you to Portugal, Pierre? Business or pleasure?" Talia asked.

"He's here on vacation. Isn't that right, Pierre?" Caryn interrupted.

"*Oui*." Pierre attempted a half-smile, the dancing fluorescent overhangs reflecting off a snarled bottom tooth.

"*Oui*! So cute." Caryn's brown eyes glossed over as if he were her first kiss in junior high, Patrick Fitzgerald.

It was Talia's last clear memory of Caryn's mother while still healthy. She died of cancer a year later when Caryn was only thirteen. Caryn and her mother lived alone in a low-income apartment community close to the state park the stoners in high school used to frequent for quick trips to Mars.

Caryn made sure her mother didn't get the notice for a half day that Wednesday, so she could invite Patrick over for her first kiss. She had chosen him, she said, because he smelled good and picked her flowers from the school gardens. Talia wasn't a big fan of Patrick, but she played along, keeping an eye out for Caryn's mother, who would often come home for a late lunch unannounced.

Caryn was a different girl then, nervous and afraid of change. The death of her mother made her impulsive and impatient, even though it took her two hours to muster the nerve to kiss Patrick that afternoon. Talia gained some respect for Patrick that day. He was a patient soul.

It was inevitable Caryn's mother would walk in when Caryn sat mid-kiss on the living room floor. Caryn's mother screamed some obscenities Talia heard for the first time that day. When Patrick realized what had happened, he ripped free and ran for the door, while Caryn sobbed into her cupped hands. Patrick didn't kiss her again.

"Do you guys want to join us for a drink at the bar?" Caryn asked.

"Sure," Jared said before Talia could muster a syllable.

The two girls located a freestanding spot near the abused foosball table while the two boys ordered drinks at the bar. Talia had almost forgotten about the younger drinking age.

"Four Super Bocks please," Talia overheard Jared ask the bartender. He then turned to Pierre and said, "Best beer in the country. But I'm guessing you're more of a wine person."

Pierre smiled and carried two beers back for Caryn and himself. Talia caught Jared winking at the bartender with a low cut sweater, and then followed Pierre.

"*Merci beaucoup*," Caryn hiccupped.

Pierre leered at Talia, setting her ill at ease.

"So, what do you do for a living, Pierre?" Jared cut through the steely silence.

"My family owns a few hotels in the south of France," Pierre said.

"That must be *Nice*." Jared chuckled at his own play on words —always the guy who breaks character on a sketch comedy show. Talia rolled her eyes and Pierre faked a snicker.

Caryn startled herself with an unexpected snort and everyone stared in awe. "What? It was funny."

"Thank you, Caryn," Jared said, the pride returning to his face.

"*Et vous*, Jared?" Pierre asked. "Why are you here?"

"Jared and I are here to help Talia catch a serial killer," Caryn blurted.

Talia tossed Caryn a concerned brow, to which Caryn responded with wide, apologetic eyes and a mimed apology. Though Talia didn't have anything to hide, there was no need for a random stranger to know her business, and certainly not one of Caryn's strange guys.

"That and celebrate our graduation. We start real life when we get back, so this is our last hurrah." Caryn tried to save herself, but it was too late.

"I'm also a crime reporter," Talia said. "I'm here for personal reasons, but also to investigate a murder back in the U.S."

"Her grandmother died a month ago," Caryn blurted, buzzed from the alcohol she had already been drinking before Talia and Jared arrived. Caryn was what people called a "cheap date" and so Talia always stayed close when Caryn had a few sips too many.

"My sympathies to you," Pierre said. "*Cuídado*. There are many places to hide in this country."

"Talia's a pretty darn good sleuth," Caryn said. "She thinks there's a clue at her great-aunt's house in Alhambra."

"Alfama. Alhambra is not even Portuguese, Caryn. It's Spanish." Talia could not restrain a fleeting giggle, but then gathered her composure. She found it endearing when Americans tried to speak Portuguese. "I hope to find out more during our visit."

"*Bonne chance*," Pierre said.

Pierre sized her up one last time and winked. Talia shuddered behind a phony smile. He spoke a combination of French and Portuguese, not unlike those taught through the Portuguese education system.

For the promise of a job in retail or tourism, most schools in Portugal teach children from a young age three different languages: Portuguese, French, and English. This hybrid European language is not to be confused with the rampant *Portuglish*—an Americanized melding of Portuguese and English often spoken by Portuguese immigrants residing in New England, where Talia was raised. Her parents were fluent in it.

Pierre muttered something to Caryn, she nodded, and he marched to the back of the bar.

Talia took to Caryn's side for a better view of Pierre's whereabouts. "Where did he go?"

"To the *toilette*." Caryn raised her chin with satisfaction.

Talia stood watch as Pierre walked into a hallway marked with a metal sign reading *W.C.*, and reemerged a minute later on his cell phone. He was excited and animated, resembling a schoolboy in the midst of recanting a new story to his best friend for the first time.

Talia tried to read his lips like she did sophomore year of high school, when Caryn whispered in French class and Talia had to figure out whether she meant Pete or Peyton that day. Caryn had a weakness for guys whose first names started with the letter P.

Portuguese was a bit harder to read, but Talia was sure it wasn't French that Pierre spoke to his old friend. The occasional Portuguese word rose above the din of the bar, like *segura* and *moças*, safe and girls. Was he talking about them?

Talia caught Pierre's eye. His big ears twitched as he u-turned down the hallway. A minute later, he approached Caryn, put his right hand on the small of her back, and whispered in her ear, cupping his left hand over his mouth for privacy. Talia noticed a band of lighter skin on his ring finger. Was he a divorcée or an adulterer?

Caryn nodded her head and smiled. "We're going to the bar down the boardwalk a ways. Meet you guys later?"

Talia couldn't shake his piercing gaze. "Wait, you're taking off?"

"*Oui*, they could join us," Pierre said. "How do you call it? Double date?"

"They need some time alone to do the mushy stuff without us." Caryn pouted. "And then we can get mushy without them."

With a mouthed, "Me-a-vue," Caryn started towards the entrance, hanging off Pierre's arm.

Talia whispered, "Me-a-vue also," and watched them weave through the tables out the glass doors, propped open by a menu sign listing drink specials in ornate lettering.

"I don't know about this." Talia did her best to squint out the setting sun as she looked up at Jared, who stood over a foot taller than her, especially in flip flops.

"She's a big girl, Talia. She can take care of herself," Jared said, rubbing her exposed back in the same spot for too long.

"We're in a foreign country." Talia pressed her fingers against her forehead. "Don't you think we should be a bit more careful?"

"It's not foreign to you. You've been to Portugal a gazillion times. Weren't you just telling us earlier about how King Carlos set up the first oceanographic lab in the country in the late 1800's? You're a certified nerd," Jared said, "and a worry wart. I understand why Caryn took off. She feels like the third wheel. You can't blame her. Plus, she's allowed to go out and have a good time. We're in Europe, you know. It's exciting to us at least."

"I suppose you're right." Talia smiled. "I *am* a nerd."

Jared smacked Talia's behind with an echoing crack, making

the locals flinch more than its owner, and they chased each other back to their towels before heading to the hostel to prep for dinner in town.

———

THERE ARE a lot of places to hide in this country. Talia chewed through her thoughts and the food on her dinner plate with quiet concentration, no matter how much Jared tried to ease her anxiety.

"Are you sure you're okay?" Jared interrupted the silence. "You're starting to worry me."

"I'm fine, really." Talia munched on her food as if it were day-old bread.

Pierre's eerie gape still haunted her. Her stomach revolted at the thought of his crooked smile, the memory of which augmented its severity to a bucktoothed grin. She couldn't shake from her mind Caryn's urgency to leave with a whisper from a man she barely knew in a country in which she had hardly spent forty-eight hours.

Jared was right. This wasn't unusual for Caryn, but it didn't make it any less troublesome. One day, Caryn wouldn't be able to get herself out of one of her dramas, and Talia couldn't fathom the thought of doing nothing to prevent it.

Later after dinner, Caryn never showed. Talia masked her anxiety with casual conversation, and Jared played along with her act. Two hours after Caryn had promised to return, Talia got a text message from her number that read:

> *Having too much fun.*
> *Don't worry. Be back soon.*
> *Love, Caryn*

She exhaled and snuggled next to Jared, who was lying on his side of the bed, reading, or rather staring at the pictures in a Portuguese soccer magazine.

"What's up? Was that Caryn? Is she okay?" Jared asked.

"I guess. She's spending the night with the creepy Frenchman," Talia said.

"You go girl," Jared said with a snap of his fingers.

Talia slapped him on the shoulder, and he burst into laughter. "This isn't funny, Jared. The Catholic guilt is creeping up on me again. What if something happens to her? That guy looked slimy."

"All Euro dudes look slimy," Jared said.

"Nice." Talia scolded him with terse lips and brows. "And then her signature … she never tells me she loves me. You know that. We always say, 'Me-a-vue.'"

"Again I say, Caryn is very capable of taking care of herself. How about you stop playing mommy with her and start playing sexy French maid with me? Uh huh huh!" Jared joked in a stereotypical French accent, pinching at Talia's thighs and waist.

"Stop it. I'm genuinely worried about her," Talia said. She tried to remain stern, but a childish wiggle took control when Jared snuck his fingers into a sensitive spot under her arms. She stifled a giggle as he dug his fingers in for a deeper tickle. "I just hope she's okay."

Jared stopped to kiss Talia's bare shoulder. "She just told you she was."

"I guess." Talia slumped her shoulders.

"Come on, Toots. I think I know a way of taking your mind off things," Jared said, reaching around to kiss Talia's pursed lips. "Good news is, we have the place to ourselves tonight. You show me yours …"

SEVEN

"NO, PLEASE, STOP," Talia heard Caryn's voice cry from a hospital corridor stretching far into the darkness. Fluorescent lights flickered in and out of view the hundreds of half-open doors to the left and right. She sprinted around abandoned gurneys and intravenous poles to glance into every opening. The rooms were deserted, and the more she ran, the further Caryn's cries, until Talia's heart pounded every other sound out of her ears.

"Caryn? Caryn?" Talia shouted, but she was nowhere in sight.

Reaching the end of the hallway, she located an open door leading to a dim stairwell. She clambered down a few flights and ran out the door as if to freedom, only to find herself in a dark basement, the walls and cabinets painted forest green, the color flickering with the lights above.

It was her grandfather's basement.

Talia spotted the familiar wall sink with a rusty white medicine cabinet at the far end of the wine cellar and navigated towards it as if it were the North Star. As she turned the faucet knobs, a pale face appeared in the smudged mirror, whose cracked pieces dangled off its metal frame.

The consistency of the water not quite right, Talia cocked her head to find purple fluid gushing out of the eroded faucet. The trailing stench of unfiltered wine eased her mind, and she exhaled as if she had been holding her breath underwater for too long. Wine she could handle.

Peering into the mirror again, she witnessed an unrecognizable reflection of herself with vacant eyes and a bloated pallid face, framed with a plum stain and matted hair to match. Her violent screech loosened the shards of mirror, which shattered on the cement floor.

———

TALIA SCREAMED HERSELF AWAKE, but Jared didn't budge. He was already accustomed to her daily nightmares. She wished she could shrug off her visions as easily—they were exhausting.

It was the morning after Caryn left with Pierre and she still hadn't returned to their hostel room in the Baixa neighborhood of Lisbon. Talia brushed her damp hair, staring down the full-length mirror on the back of the bathroom door as if its reflection had been her worst regret. It was a better replacement for gnawing her fingernails down to such a brittle mess they could pull a sweater.

Why her grandfather's basement? She hadn't been there in years. And Caryn was in the hospital, but she wasn't. None of it helped her anxiety.

"I'm sure she's fine, Talia," Jared said, his voice coarse from sleep.

"I didn't say anything," Talia said.

"I can tell you're worried. Honestly, babe, your hair is not the issue."

Talia paused mid-brush and eyed Jared's reflection stretching his back behind her. "You're right. It's only 9:00 AM. I'm sure she's not up yet."

"Exactly. Especially after a night like last night. She was toasted before she even left and the sun wasn't even down yet."

Talia shook her head. "I should *not* have let her go."

"You say it like you had a choice. The girl would have gone anyway. There was nothing you could've done to stop her," Jared said. "Why are you so worried? It's not like it's the first time she's run off with a guy."

Talia brushed her hair again in a deliberately relaxed pace. "I know. I had another one of my bad dreams. You know how they get to me."

"What?" Jared called from the bathroom.

Talia looked over to the empty bed where Jared had recently been resting and grumbled. Of course he wasn't listening. "Nothing. Are you almost ready to go to the bookstore?"

Jared strolled out of the bathroom, wiping his face with the white hostel towel that he confessed he'd pack with him when they left. He tamed his hair with a mixture of water and musky hair cream.

The smell of sawdust and eucalyptus instilled in Talia images of brawny men hiking the Andes. Although trying to hide them, his defined arms peeked through the short sleeves of his blue tee, Talia's favorite because it matched his eyes.

Jared licked the toothpaste off the corners of his mouth and replied, "I'm not just ready. I'm ready, Freddy."

———

THE SUN ESCAPED through the clouds hanging over the Chiado district of Lisbon as the crisp morning breeze nipped at her neck. Hunger pangs diverted Talia and Jared to a café nearby for a quick bite to eat before they began their research at *Livraria Bertrand*.

Café A Brasileira, the oldest café in the country, is a tourist staple in the aristocratic old quarter of Lisbon, which has been inhabited since the Roman Empire. Over the last few centuries, the Chiado has become the cultural and commercial heart of the city, home to the Royal Theater, awe-inspiring architectural museums and cathedrals, and the oldest bookstore in the world, *Livraria Bertrand*.

Outside the café's arched stone façade, atop an elevated mosaic stage, a bronzed Fernando Pessoa sat with crossed legs beside an empty chair, awaiting an audience of one. One of the most notable literary figures of the twentieth century, Pessoa was also fluent in English and French, leaving behind a prolific bibliography of prose and poetry in all three languages, most of which were published posthumously.

Loved by artists and intellectuals alike, the *Café A Brasileira* was frequented by Pessoa, who either sipped on absinthe or the Portuguese version of a shot of espresso called the *Bica*—which was born in that very café in 1905—while he constructed his newest verse in one of his many alter egos.

One pseudonym was not enough for the many works of the poet, who wrote in the point-of-view of over seventy-five personalities. These personalities served as a way for Pessoa to voice unpopular themes such as occultism, astrology, and mysticism. Pessoa openly admitted that he suffered from prophetic visions and the ability to view a person's magnetic aura. He believed, as did many surrealists at the time, that his personalities inhabited him during their respective writings, sending him into a trance, guiding his arm and transforming his face in the mirror to their likeness.

The fact that Pessoa had suffered some of the same out of body experiences Talia had faced since Vovó's passing didn't give her the comfort she'd hoped for. The gaze of his likeness pierced through her gut, and she turned away, the vision of her bloated discolored reflection dancing in his metal eyes. Did she see her own death? Is that how she's going to die, drowned in a vat of wine?

Talia struck the thought from her mind, flashing a forced smile to Jared as he ordered them *Bicas* with butter and cheese sandwiches from the busy glass counter. The black and white checkered floors pair with the chiseled gold walls stretching with gilded mirrors to create the illusion of width in a narrow space. The coffered peach ceilings were pleated with gold to match the brass chandeliers that hung low above the glass cases teeming with freshly baked sweets and breads.

The caffeine steam that floated above her mini teacup awoke Talia from her daydream.

"Are you okay?" Jared took the first bite of his sandwich.

"Not really," Talia said. "I had another weird nightmare last night. I don't know what to make of it."

"It's probably an anxiety dream," Jared mumbled through a mouthful of bread and cheese. "You've been under a lot of stress lately."

"You sound like Caryn." Talia grimaced.

"Well, then I'm right, since she's the expert on this stuff," Jared said and then took another bite.

"Possibly. What would you say if I said I may have seen my own death?"

Jared stopped mid-bite, almost choking on the crumbs.

"Never mind." Talia patted Jared's back. She didn't expect a different response.

"I would think maybe you were overreacting," Jared said, still wheezing. "You can't dream your own death, babe. What you saw probably symbolized something entirely different."

Talia nodded. Psychologists have suggested that most objects and people in dreams symbolize something else—anxiety about taking a test at school reflects a conflict in life you're not prepared to face, being paralyzed means you feel powerless about some aspect of your home or work life, death foretells inevitable change or reinvention.

"You've been having these dreams for a while. Have any of them come true yet?"

"I guess not," Talia said. Contrary to popular belief, Talia accepted that Jared was right at least part of the time.

"See, you have nothing to worry about," Jared said, risking a sip of his *Bica*. "I promise you they're just stress dreams. They'll pass."

Talia daydreamed about the warmth and solace of a good night's rest and the peaceful day when these nightmares would end. It was not yet that day. If she witnessed her death in her subconscious, she must have done so because there was still a chance to alter it. Were Talia to believe Jared and his hypothesis, there was a chance she could miss the opportunity to save herself. Talia hadn't made sense of why she'd visit her grandfather's old wine cellar, but Caryn could be in a hospital, hurt and alone, while Talia wasted time dissecting her dreams for clues.

"Maybe we should check the hospitals for Caryn," Talia said.

"Let me guess, Caryn was also in this nightmare?"

She nodded, gnawing on her sandwich with caution. Talia knew from experience Jared's reaction, how he'd strike her down when she worried, whether or not there was good reason.

"There are dozens of hospitals in this city. How do you think we'll find her?"

"Just because it's hard doesn't mean we shouldn't try," Talia said, reciting advice she once read in a self-help book.

"Caryn has been gone *one* night. I think you may be overreacting. She wouldn't even be considered a missing person yet."

"It's been almost twenty-four hours," Talia said, checking the clock on the wall. "I've got this nagging feeling is all. But you're right, it's just stress."

Without the energy to fight, Talia placated Jared with the illusion that she had let go of the nightmare, at least for now, and swallowed the last of her coffee.

———

A FEW BLOCKS down from the *Café A Brasileira*, blue frescoes tiled the corner of the *Livraria Bertrand* and trimmed its original brass-lettered sign. Talia surveyed the bookstore, the oldest in the world, having been in business since 1732, and then at this corner location in the Chiado neighborhood of Lisbon after the first location was destroyed in the earthquake of 1755.

As Jared jetted to the history section, Talia located an empty seat and tapped into the free Wi-Fi through her phone to check her email. It was better than paying for international roaming.

She pretended not to notice Jared talking up an attractive store clerk, her thick hair up in a bun, her high heels lengthening long olive legs, her skirt hugging her round hips. The woman helped him find a book on the shelf, and threw him a wink as he walked back.

"So what did this suspect of yours look like?" Jared plopped down a large book the size of an unabridged dictionary with a thump and then settled himself on a chair nearby. The volume bore some resemblance to the history books Talia was forced to transcribe as a child as punishment. The binding read: *História de Crime na Europa: 1975-2000.*

Talia curled her eyebrow.

"Call me old fashioned. I like a long read," Jared said.

"How are you planning to *read* that one?" Talia played along.

"I've learned a little Portuguese since we've been together, thank you very much." Jared bowed his head.

"No one has an I.D. on the guy who killed the twins, I told you," Talia said. "The witness said he was wearing a hood that covered most of his face. He was kneeling down so he couldn't even gauge how tall the guy was."

"That's not very helpful." Jared slumped his shoulders. "Did you ever get back in touch with your chick out here?"

"No, unfortunately. She disappeared a few days before we left. She never sent an email," Talia said with her head buried in her phone. "No, wait. I think something just came in."

"What's the chick's name?"

"Actually, I don't know. Her screen name is Padilha999," Talia said.

"Maybe Padilha is her last name," Jared said.

"I don't think so. She's a self-proclaimed witch and Maria Padilha was a revered Portuguese queen from the days of the Inquisition. She was convicted of witchcraft, beheaded by her lover, King Pedro de Castella, and declared queen posthumously, but she's considered a saint to followers of Brazilian Macumba."

"Your contact is a witch?"

"Maybe? I think she practices Umbanda. It's allegedly the light side of magic." Something flashed on Talia's phone. "Finally!"

Despite being a tiny but lofty bookstore, the echo was that of a majestic symphony hall, empty but for one lone French horn blaring on stage.

"Sorry. *Desculpa.*" She glanced around the room at the many angry faces.

"Okay, what did you find, crazy?" Jared teased with a smile.

Talia sat down to settle her nerves. "She thinks she's got a lead. She sent a picture but the Internet connection here is absurd, took forever to load. Look." Talia shoved the mobile screen into Jared's face.

"It's a picture of a piece jewelry," he said.

"Yes. I think this is the amulet the murderer might have used on the girls."

"I thought he used the satchel of evil herbs?" Jared snickered.

"See, thing is, I wasn't very convinced at first that the herbs were enough to kill my little cousins. They are supposed to enhance experiences and increase probability, but they're not enough to put two girls to sleep forever. This amulet could be the answer. Amulets like this are known to possess great powers, if used correctly."

Golden brass vines sprinkled with sapphire wrapped around a jade cameo. It reminded Talia of the brooch Vovó presented her a picture of as a child.

It's a very special brooch with very special powers, the old woman said as she raised her head to view Talia's reaction, her snowy hair a halo in a ray of Sunday afternoon sun filtering through the curtained window behind her. The dark living room enhanced the dusty sunbeam, which traced the furniture, illuminating that which was most important—gold-framed photos of grandchildren and lost loved ones, fading porcelain knickknacks, and the all-in-one record player skipping occasionally on a traditional Portuguese Fado.

The male and female singers bantered in the classic Fado tune.

The woman's voice lilted at every chorus, while the man tapped on his accordion keys, squeezing and stretching the bellows to elongate the woman's pain. Talia understood about half of the lyrics, they sang too quickly to translate. She heard enough to know it wasn't a song of joy, but rather one full of the heartache of a hardworking sailor shipping off into the unforgiving seas to feed his family.

This amulet gives its owner ultimate protection from all evil—even from the curse of a witch, Vovó said. *Rainha Maria Padilha, the most sacred of all queens, blessed it. Some of the most evil people have been known to own it —including Salazar.*

The old woman whispered the former Portuguese dictator's name by force of habit, afraid she may invoke his spirit to haunt her, or worse, the ones she loved. Her family recounted many stories before then of the fearful era of António de Oliveira Salazar's oppressive New State for forty-two years until its fall in 1974. Talia's grandfather refused to censor his thoughts, and often spoke against Salazar in public places, even after countless tales of the suspicious disappearances of those who openly protested the longstanding authoritarian regime.

The oval broach was the size of a knob on Vovó's vintage stove. The ivory cameo encrusted into the jade gemstone was in the shape of a woman's profile wearing a crown, encircled by three multi-colored gemstones in an ornate gold frame. The gold was heavy, darker than any gold Talia had seen in person. The darker the metal, the purer the gold.

Though hard to believe these days, Portugal was once a world superpower, dominating global sea trade from over fifty-three territories around the world. The Portuguese Gold Coast, known today as Ghana, sailed limitless amounts of gold and ivory into Europe, along with, unfortunately, the most sought after commodity at the time: African slaves.

The coast was discovered by one of Prince Henry's trained navigators, whose teams built two forts around the area in the fifteenth and sixteenth centuries. Millions of pounds of gold nuggets passed through these forts in their prime, and to this day, Portugal's gold reserves are among the highest in the world. As of 2015, a total of 382 tons of gold sat in the Bank of Portugal in Lisbon.

"He killed two girls instantly with an amulet?" Jared asked.

"I asked my contact if there was anything the suspect could've used to shock the girls to death, and legend has it that this is the amulet used in some of the most notorious and unsolved occult crimes of this century. Thing is, my grandmother thought it was used for protection, not harm. At least that's what she implied."

"So you've seen this amulet before?" Jared tapped his fingers against the table.

"Yeah, I think so. I think my grandmother showed me a picture of it when I was a kid," Talia said. "I wasn't sure why then. Frankly, I still don't know why. She did a lot of things I can't seem to understand."

"I suppose a witch would be a more credible source for this insane hypothesis of yours than your grandmother," Jared's leg bobbed in his creaky chair like a hyperactive schoolboy.

"Can you give me a logical explanation for how these girls could have died? Because if you can, I'm listening."

Jared grumbled.

"I didn't think so. I'm just trailing all leads here. That's my job. If their mother thinks it could be occult related, I have to give it a shot, no matter how crazy."

"I'm just being devil's advocate." Jared leaned in and whispered, "You've been researching this stuff a little obsessively since your grandmother died. I just think you shouldn't jump into anything too quickly. You're still digesting the loss."

"Working helps keep my mind off things, like say, Caryn." Talia knew Jared meant well, but she also knew he rarely believed a word she said.

"How about this for getting your mind off things? The translation says a man named Carlos Batista was born in Portugal in 1959 but moved with his family to the United States, where he spent his teenage years. That was your uncle's name, right?" Jared read from his enormous book, changing the subject. "Once he was old enough, and Salazar ended his rule, Carlos moved back, where he lived as a gypsy on the streets, swindling money off people by pretending to be handicapped."

"My parents told me stories about people who did that," Talia said. "Old wives' tales about bucking the system. One urban legend has it that a man dressed as a gypsy every day for five years, considering it his job to beg for money. Meanwhile, he stashed a hundred fifty thousand Euros between his mattresses."

Talia paused. She tried to imagine what her uncle would look like on the streets and in the subways while she vacationed in Portugal as a child. Vagabonds with oversized rags for clothing lying on the pavement, their soiled faces wincing in pain, pleading for a bite to eat for themselves or their dejected, sunken-eyed children rocking beside them. Talia wondered if she had ever passed by her uncle without knowing his real identity. Would her mother recognize him, or worse, ignore him?

"Okay, this is weird," Jared said. "It says in the *Journal de Noticias* that a man who looked like Carlos Batista is known to have ties to a cult from Brazil. No proof though. That's all it says. What is Macumba exactly?"

Talia pursed her lips into a frown.

"Oh, no. I know that face," Jared said. "You make that face when I leave food wrappers in your car."

"I don't even know that they're there, Jared, until they smell," Talia said as Jared laughed under his breath. "Anyway, Macumba is an umbrella term for a group of syncretic religions that combine Christianity with African Voodoo. It became popular in Brazil and the mainland after Portugal invaded Africa and took slaves there. Spain and France performed massive witch-hunts and punished those that practiced Macumba, or any of its sects."

"Sounds pleasant. Let me guess, Portugal followed their lead?"

"Actually, Portugal was different. Their Inquisition was a quarter the size of the others. Instead of shunning the occult, the Portuguese incorporated it into their Catholic beliefs, often as herbal remedies or folk superstition. My family performed a lot of pagan rituals, like making three wishes while eating twelve raisins just as the clock strikes midnight on New Year's Eve. I doubt they even realized what they were doing, but they believed in it."

"Sounds crazy, Talia."

"It does, I know. But crazy thing is, sometimes it works."

"Only if you believe," he scoffed in a familiar way, but Talia ignored it.

"I think it's ingrained in me by now," Talia said. "When my dad brought me weird herbal concoctions in the middle of the night to cure my cough or nausea, I believed they worked. And they did. It's hard not to believe when you feel it happen. Anyway, my contact said this amulet has been missing for years, but it was last seen up north. She didn't say where, but I have to go look for it. It could be the key to this case."

"We're not going anywhere. We're going to stay here and enjoy ourselves."

Talia squirmed in her seat. She hated when Jared told her what to do, expecting she'd bend to his will at his almighty command. Just an inkling of his control brought out the fighter in Talia. Like mother like daughter. She pounded the feeling down over and over throughout their relationship, but she could no longer contain it.

"I knew you didn't take this trip seriously. 'Let Talia get it out of her system, and then we can go back to basking in the sun and having sex all day.' Is that what you wanted?" Her heart beat faster. "I think I'm onto something here, Jared. What if that Carlos Batista guy was really my uncle, and he killed my cousins? I know it sounds far-fetched, and I'd still have to figure out the motive, but I can't rule it out."

"How implausible is that?" Jared asked. "We don't even know if your uncle exists. And if this is the same guy, he couldn't have made it through customs as a wanted criminal."

"Nothing's impossible, Jared," Talia said.

"I never said impossible. I said *implausible*," Jared raised his voice and it echoed.

"You were just saying he could be a criminal under the radar, and that he has ties to Macumba *and* now he has ties to the victims. He's their family for Christ's sake. It makes a strange sort of sense. People with his kind of money get away with a lot worse."

"It would be extremely coincidental. I don't buy it." Jared folded his arms and turned.

"Yes, it's all *circumstantial* for now, but I plan to change that."

"We should relax first. It would do you some good before you got yourself all worked up over this again," Jared said. "You haven't been the same since your grandmother passed. I know how close you were to her, but you have to move on. This obsession is controlling you."

Talia stood up and marched through the front door, causing it to almost knock into Jared on its return as he chased her out. She took a few long paces down a side street and stopped. "I can't stop thinking about it. I can't sleep. I have nightmares every night warning me of what's to come. I can't take another day of waiting. I have to do this now."

"You travel halfway across the world over a nightmare, and you wonder why I'm worried," Jared said.

"It was a vivid vision." Talia continued her pace. "Plus, I'm not here just for that. I'm investigating a story."

Jared sneered. "We both know the assignment is just an excuse."

"Carl Jung believed that our dreams are the key to unlocking our subconscious, and they can sometimes provide insight into our path ahead," Talia said. "Our conscious and subconscious minds work together to get us through this life, like yin and yang. You need them both to make you whole."

He opened his mouth but a hush followed. His silence implicit, Talia knew whatever she said afterward didn't matter, that he had already shut her out. She felt a sudden urge to state her mind, to do what she'd been longing to do since they made plans to travel together.

"My grandmother has been haunting me in my dreams for weeks now, Jared. She's trying to tell me something. I can feel it. Just like my great-grandmother and the ghosts of bees she haunted me with at night when I was a kid, this has meaning. I just wish I knew what my grandmother was trying to say. I know you don't believe in this stuff. I don't know why I bother telling you."

"Your deceased grandmother is not talking to you in your dreams. It's all in your mind." Jared shook his head. "I thought you'd forget all this once we got here. I wanted to get you off this madness, but you won't let it go."

"I can't!" Talia yelled. A few pedestrians nearby paused to eavesdrop, so she quieted. "I feel it in my bones. Even if it isn't my grandmother communicating with me, just my subconscious mind, I have to listen. I wish you could support me on this."

"I'm worried about you." Jared reached for Talia's arm, but she pulled away.

"I can take care of myself. This is my family. I need to know what's going on. I mean, I may have a long lost uncle. Don't I owe it to myself, to my family, to find him?"

"Why do you have to be the one to do it? Maybe your family disowned him for a reason, Talia. Maybe you should listen to them."

"You sound like my mother. Two girls were murdered, Jared. No one else is willing to find their killer. Am I just supposed to let him get away with it?"

"It's more than that and you know it. You believe all these unrelated events somehow connect. You just want them to connect, so that you have a reason to find your uncle. A lot of people in Portugal practice black magic without even realizing it. You said it yourself. What makes you think this one infamous guy, who could by some crazy coincidence be your uncle, is the only murderer in town? There have to be at least a dozen more logical suspects than him."

"Like you said, this is too much of coincidence not to be true."

"That's not quite what I said," he said. "If you believe in synchronicity so much, maybe the world didn't want you to find that box, or you'd have it."

"Maybe you're just not meant to come with me to find it," Talia asserted, folding her arms. "Honestly, Jared, I'm sick of you trying to control me. This is my life and my trip. Maybe it's my fault for not making it clearer when I asked you to come with me. This investigation is why I'm here, and why I have to follow my gut. With or without you."

Jared frowned. "I can't support you on this, I'm sorry."

"I can't even remember a time when you supported me, so it doesn't surprise me. Goodbye, Jared. If you see Caryn, please tell her to call me."

"Wait," Jared shouted as she continued walking.

Talia turned to face him. "I saw a text from your dad's intern. I didn't mean to, but I did."

He ran his hand through his hair, sculpting it into a short blond Mohawk. His jaw hung open and he shook his head. "What text? Babe, I don't know what you're talking about."

"You know exactly what I'm talking about. I was trying to forget, but you keep—I've just had enough." Talia slammed her arms to her side and walked away.

"So you're just going to leave me?"

"I need to do this alone, Jared. If you really love me, you'll leave me be." Talia headed towards the bus station, resisting the temptation to look back.

Their hostel room sat empty with no sign of Caryn's return in the meanwhile. Talia dropped her backpack from her achy shoulders onto a pile of clothes, and plopped down on the squeaky bed. A gleam reflected off something in her bag's unfastened pocket. In a panic, Talia unzipped the canvas compartment all the way open to discover Vovó's gold watch rattling outside its velvet home. She lifted it out, blew on it, and inspected the face for any scratches.

With sadness in her distorted reflection, Talia flipped the watch over. She read the inscription again, aloud and in her best Portuguese, "*Destrave seu ser interna.*"

"Unlock your inner being," Talia mocked. "This should be written on a fortune cookie, not engraved into a thousand dollar gold watch. I need a real clue to where my grandmother would stash a wooden jewelry box."

She relaxed for a moment, zoning into a pair of Jared's navy boxer shorts, which sported dozens of identical Red Sox logos. Maybe she was as cold Jared said, but at least she wasn't a cheat. She wondered if he'd chase after her. Did she even want him to?

Talia shook it out of her arms. "I need to get out of here."

She packed chaotically, first by folding her clothes and then by rolling them up and throwing them into her bag. Realizing she had tossed one of Caryn's shirts in with her own, she dug it out, accidentally dragging her cell phone out with it. It teetered on the shirt and cracked when it crashed onto the thin gray carpet that concealed the concrete floor underneath. She picked it up and stuffed it in her jacket in between curses. She should have put it in her pocket, but she was afraid she'd get pickpocketed.

Talia zipped her backpack and inspected the room one last time before leaving. Her favorite of Jared's sweatshirts hung over the steel desk chair near the window and she tied it around one of the straps of her bag.

EIGHT

A BUSY SIGNAL emerged from Talia's phone. Caryn wasn't answering. Talia had been fiddling with her phone's cracked screen for the entire cab ride through *Alcântra* to the eastern end of Lisbon, which has been deserted since its development for the Expo fair in 1998. Much like the World Cup and the Olympics, many of the contemporary buildings in the *Parque de Nações* neighborhood were designed specifically for the event, which spanned the course of four months, and then abandoned due to lack of maintenance funds.

The futuristic site converted some of its buildings to a few keepers—the Oceanarium, Europe's largest aquarium at the time of its construction, a regional shopping mall, and Lisbon's second casino. This neighborhood of Lisbon was home to over twenty-five thousand residents and eighteen million visiting tourists a year, yet hundreds of apartments and commercial spaces outside the central zone have been left vacant for years.

It didn't look like an area of town Vovó would know well, having moved to the United States long before it was built and visiting few times since. Talia always forgot the area existed. It was not part of the landscape when she was a child, and it didn't offer much when she visited other than a nice walk along the marina and an ultramodern aquarium.

Talia didn't care much for the idea of fusion food in Portugal. She instead longed for the everyman comforts of her ancestors, who often feasted on the basics while living off the land. And also, pastries.

Talia dialed Caryn's number a few more times, but the calls always ended with a busy signal. It could be due to Talia's maimed phone, or Caryn's line could be in use. If Caryn was on the phone, then she must be alive. Unless someone else was using it.

No matter how hard she tried, the voice in her head always battled her attempts to soothe herself. It always offered a contrary view that was never far-fetched enough for Talia to write off as one of her paranoias. Instead, these thoughts infiltrated her brain and clouded her judgment. She tried to brush off the voice as she paid the driver and walked up to the house that matched the address penned onto the liner of Vovó's dresser drawer, pinching the torn paper between her index finger and thumb like a winning lottery ticket.

Set against a background of clean-lined buildings, this old-world structure stuck out, as if it belonged to a stubborn old woman who refused to let the city buy her out of her lifelong home. Only a floor tall, it cowered to its towering steel neighbors. The stone building reminded Talia of the hand-built structures Vovó's generation called home. Talia wondered who Vovó would know around that area. Who was important enough to permanently mark a part of her bedroom furniture, but dangerous enough to keep it hidden in a spot no one could find?

The stone steps to the porch were so loose, Talia held onto

the side of the hovel to climb the stairs, concerned they couldn't support much weight without jiggling out of place. Blue paint chipped off the weathered door slab and a black hole replaced the doorbell button.

Before striking the door with her knuckles, Talia peeked into the window shaded by a sheer tribal tapestry draped on the inside. A fog of incense and candle smoke wafted through the half-opened pane, infusing Talia with serenity. The front door swung open and drew Talia closer.

"*Qual é a problema, menina?*" asked a leathery man wearing loose, white linen scrubs embroidered in blue, similar to a doily her mother would crochet.

Her problem was that Vovó knew him in some way. When were they? It was as if she traveled back in time. The yellow door braced the man's frail body. The living room behind him appeared more like a yoga studio than a place to live, no doors but the one to the bathroom. Half of the beds in the far left corner were occupied, and a young couple sat on a rug on the floor to the right, their hands clasped, eyelids shut, murmuring chants in unison.

"*Bom dia, sou —*" Talia began.

"Natalia?" the old man asked. "Is that you?"

Talia stepped back. "I'm sorry, have we met?"

"Your grandmother and I were friends. She was a good soul. I was expecting you. *Por favor*, come in."

Talia wasn't comforted by his claim to know Vovó, but she felt compelled to follow him into his compound. It could have been their similar stature that put her at ease, but Talia remained concerned for her safety. The young couple was unfazed by Talia's presence as she tiptoed by them, and a family sobbed over a young boy who laid in a comatose state in the far corner.

"*Não te preocupes*. Don't worry. He has been possessed by a demon, I am sad to say. We are working on him every hour. No luck yet."

"Shouldn't he go to the hospital?" Talia asked.

"The doctors tell his family nothing is wrong, but as you can see, there is something to be worried about," he said. "*Ele está sob um feitiço.*"

Talia wondered if the the boy was under a spell or on some strange drug. "What do you do here, exactly? What is this place?"

"It is a place of worship and healing," the man said. "I am *Pai Santo Paolo de Osain.* Welcome to my home."

"So you're a priest. And this is your … church?"

"*Sim*, you can say that," the man said. "We live here, all of us who need healing. Your grandmother needed healing. We all do at least once in our lives."

"My grandmother lived here?" Talia asked.

"No, no." Pai Paolo shook his head and closed his eyes. "She visited for a few years. She was troubled over her family's safety. She wanted to create a spell that could protect her family—her entire bloodline."

"When was this, do you remember?"

"It was so long ago." He rubbed his wrinkled forehead. "I do not remember much anymore."

"Do you remember if she ever brought a young boy with her?"

"Your mother was the only child I met."

"Did she speak of others?" Talia insisted.

"Is this why you've visited me today?"

"No. My grandmother had your address written in her dresser drawer back in the States."

"You came all the way from America to find *me*? I am honored," he said, patting his shirt against his chest.

Talia was still not willing to admit her true intentions in

Portugal. "How did you know my grandmother died? Or even that I was her granddaughter?"

"*O periquito me disse.*" Pai Paolo wiggled his little finger near his ear.

Vovó often recited the proverb Pai Paolo just spoke, which translated to "the parakeet told me." It was an inside joke within her family, or so she thought, which alluded to a mystical source of knowledge, a magical bird that fed the truth directly into their ears. More transparently, it was an excuse not to divulge their sources. First rule of journalism: protect your sources. No wonder, it was in her blood.

"She wrote me a few months before her passing to tell me you would be visiting me upon her death," he said while rearranging multi-colored jars full of herbs in tall wooden cabinets. "She knew you would come looking for me."

"I still don't know why I'm here."

"I think you do." He tapped his temple.

"Do you think she knew she was going to die?" Talia asked.

"Your grandmother had a good instinct. She knew a lot of things she should not know."

Talia glazed over the dark figurines on the blue altar at the back wall that reminded Talia of African art she observed at museums. The puffs of incense evoked an air of divinity around them as she contemplated other possible secrets Vovó may have kept from her. How much time did Vovó spend with this guy?

"You said she thought my family was in danger. Do you have any idea why she'd think that?" Talia asked.

"She did not speak much of her family," Pai Paolo said. "But with the work we were doing, I knew."

"I'm not even sure what your work is."

"I like to think it is to fight demons."

"So she was paranoid," Talia concluded. Vovó was the most

pragmatic person she knew, high principles backing every deci-sion. This was a side she never showed Talia.

"I believed her," he said. "Just because I could not see the danger does not mean it does not exist."

"So you think someone was after her—after my family?"

"It looks that way, *sim*," Pai Paolo said, averting Talia's gaze.

She lingered, forcing herself to process this information without emotion. "I believe the vendetta against our family continues today." Talia paused with a grimace. "Members of my family have been murdered, and there's no clear reason how or why. Two young girls, my cousins."

"In an alleyway, *sim*. I can see it." He bowed his head, his eyelids sealed.

"Is that all you see?" Talia asked, adjusting her seat.

Pai Paolo's eyeballs stirred inside his lids as if sifting through books in a library. She could feel his warmth.

"I am afraid so. I am sorry. I do not choose what details I see. He does," he said, pointing upwards. "I would say your family had a curse put upon it. Do you believe your grandmother had an enemy so spiteful he or she would want to cause your family to suffer for generations?"

"It'd be the most rational explanation, as weird as it sounds," Talia said.

"Life is not rational."

Talia remained silent in bewilderment. She appreciated his honesty, but she never understood how a culture so rooted in Christianity could be so Pagan in practice. In any other situation, Pai Paolo's accounts would be improbable, even downright lunatic. Yet Talia trusted this man she'd known for less than an hour on what she could only describe as a strong hunch.

"She would be very proud of you," he said. "You are on the right path."

"It would be nice to know what that path is. I feel lost right now. Maybe everyone's right, I am crazy." There was something about the candles on the altar, the quiet calm of the chants sung by the young couple in the background, or the soft aura that surrounded the old man that led Talia to confess to a priest in a makeshift temple.

"If you're crazy, then so am I," the man said.

It wasn't a helpful thought.

The old man chortled. "You think I am crazier than you?"

"Possibly." Talia smiled to cut the tension. Did he just read her thoughts?

"I admire your honesty, Natalia. I know I may seem strange, but your grandmother was very special to me. Please trust that I would do you no harm," Pai Paolo said. "In fact, I think I have what you are looking for."

He picked dried leaves from several unmarked mason jars shelved in the cabinets behind him and blended them together in a short tin canister. From behind, it looked as if he slicked his hair back that morning, but half of it had bounced back to its natural bushy state.

The peppered curly bush on his head reminded Talia of her father's when he put off a haircut for too long. That laziness caused her father so much grief when traveling—he was consistently chosen for random bag searches—that her mother forced him into the habit of trimming his hair and mustache before flying overseas.

"Ginger root for protection. Cinnamon for luck. Mint to break spells and jinxes. Anise to defend against the evil eye and boost your awareness," Pai Paolo said as he dropped each herb into the jar. "And a few rose petals for luck in love."

"I don't need luck in love." The last thing Talia needed to think about was love, or Jared.

"Everyone needs luck in love, *querida*," Pai Paolo said, addressing Talia with a term of endearment that comforted her like family. "Oh and I almost forgot. Jasmine, to help you sleep."

"How–"

"I know a lot of things I should not know, Natalia," he said. "Your visions mean something. You need to listen to them carefully. They are the gateway to your soul."

"This gives me a thought." Talia rummaged through her backpack and pulled out a sealed sandwich bag containing the satchel of herbs she removed from the scene of the crime in New Falls. "I found this near where my cousins were murdered. Do you know if the herbs may have had any mystical pull on them? I'm not completely sure of the terminology, sorry. Maybe you can even tell me who used them."

"I am not that good, Natalia. If I could find criminals that easily, I would have chosen a different profession." Pai Paolo unsealed the bag Talia handed him, wedged his nose into it, and then resealed the bag as if its contents were toxic. He paused for a moment, meditating while repeating a short chant underneath his breath.

"Do you know what's in that bag of herbs? I thought I smelled some black licorice. Terrible."

"It is definitely terrible." Pai Paolo shuddered. "There is licorice, you are correct. There is also calamus root, ague weed, patchouli, and wormwood. These are not good herbs, Natalia. What you have here is a special blend of evil."

"Evil?" Talia held her breath. Good thing it got through customs.

"This may not have been enough to kill the little girls, but it could have hurt them," he said. "This is not a good omen, *querida*. I am worried for you. If the man you seek is the man who created this, you are seeking the devil himself."

"That's my job, I guess. To find this man and help put him in jail," Talia said. "I can't turn back now."

"Careful, Natalia. This is not a game," Pai Paolo warned.

Talia sat in a trance on a folding chair near the medicine cabinets, paralyzed as the man stared into her eyes, examining her soul. Feeling empowered once he looked away, Talia rose up from her chair and prepared her belongings to leave.

"*Espera.* I want to add another herb to your mix," Pai Paolo said, sliding the tin can across the laminated table. He took a tall, thin canister labeled *Palhas de Basoura* from the shelf. "This should help keep you safe."

Pai Paolo sealed the tin can and handed it to Talia, who brushed the man's hand. Before she moved away, the old man grabbed her wrist, his eyes rolling up into his head, his grip tightening.

"What are you doing?" Her stomach clenched.

"*Cuidado,* Talia," the man groaned in a voice Talia no longer recognized. The color drained from his cheeks as the bruise on her arm spread. "*Não sabes quem é familia, e quem é inimigo. Destrave seu ser interna.*"

Talia gasped. *Destrave seu ser interna.* That was inscribed into Vovó's watch.

"Vovó?" Talia called without forethought.

Pai Paolo's grasp loosened and he buckled like a puppet on strings. One of the little boy's aunts rushed across the room to tend to his frail body sprawled on the floor, but Talia stood firmly in place, leaning on the tin canister as if it were a cane.

Careful, Talia. You can't tell who's your enemy and who's your family. It sounded like a warning.

"*Não vais me ajudar?*" The boy's aunt pleaded for help as she tried to lift the unconscious old man, but an electric shock coursed through Talia's spine. The shock tethered her to the canister. She couldn't let go to break the live current.

"I–I can't," Talia said.

The current stopped. She released the canister from her hand as she dropped to the tile floor. The room swirled into blackness.

———

"*DESCULPA, QUERIDA* NATALIA," Pai Paolo called from above as he waved a satchel under her nose.

Talia unsealed her eyes one at a time, disembodied heads hanging above her. "Don't be sorry. I spoke to my grandmother."

"I heard," Pai Paolo said, smiling at the women as if they were all in on the same joke, one Talia didn't understand.

"Are *you* okay?" she asked as she jerked up from the bed. The room appeared different from this angle, bigger. The women, now certain that Talia had recovered, returned to their nephew's vigil.

"I am okay." Pai Paolo cleared his throat.

"Oh, good." Talia moaned as she propped herself to a seated position, wobbly and off-balance. Her left elbow throbbed, it being the first body part to make contact with the floor. "How did you do … what you did?"

Pai Paolo laughed. "I wish I could say I had something to do with it. Your grandmother took control of me. She did not ask permission."

"Can she do that when she's—you know?"

"This is not normal, of course, but it is not new. Your grandmother was, how do you say, a natural. She chose a different life, but she had a command over people that is not typical of any man on the street. *Era muito forte.* I saw her strength, but she did not agree with my assessment."

"Maybe she didn't want this life," Talia said. "No offense."

"This is not a life many would seek, I will admit, Natalia," Pai Paolo said, resting his hand on Talia's forearm. "But it left her unprepared in the end."

"What do you mean?" Talia hunched over as if it would improve her hearing.

"Your grandmother did not tell me much when she was younger. I tried to look into her soul, but she built a wall around herself. *Antes*, earlier, when she came to me, I saw so much I should not know. Things I should not tell you … about your uncle."

NINE

THE MONOGRAMMED HANDKERCHIEF does nothing to muffle Caryn's cries. Tugging her chafed wrists forward above her, the jagged stone wall cracks with her weight, loosening the metal pulls that hold the rope tied around her arms.

Unable to focus on the ritual at hand, alone in a dark room lit only by flickering candle sconces, the old man who holds her captive erupts into a rage and lunges at Caryn from across the tiny dungeon.

"Help me!" Caryn screams as she knocks her head against stone wall and into unconsciousness.

The old man sighs with a slighted smile and resumes his chant in Portuguese as he slices a wood-handled knife across Caryn's left palm. "I offer you this blood as a sign of my undying devotion. As a act of faith to you, my great Exu, that I will keep my promise if you keep yours."

Caryn's blood pools at the creases of her palms as the old man clenches her fist. A few drops escape onto the dirt floor near the candles at her feet before they land in the hand-fired clay bowl the old man aimed underneath her. Every drop evaporates into smoke as it touches the ridges of the clay, leaving behind a burnt orange pigment.

Before the old man has the chance to repeat the ritual on her remaining hand, Caryn awakens and clenches her jaw around his forearm with the force of a pit bull, leaving a bloody wound to match the size of the Ouroboros tattoo a few centimeters lower on his wrist.

The old man screams in agony, and the bowl crashes onto the ground, cracking it into a handful of pieces on the packed dirt. As he tends to his wounds, Caryn rips her arms forward, fracturing the wall further, its dusty pieces settling on her disheveled hair and sweaty shoulders. The commotion knocks over a few statuettes of Fátima and other deities.

The old man lunges at her again, knife in hand. "You will live tied to that wall, or you will die escaping. Which do you choose?"

The blade slivers a fold in her neck, and a tear wipes Caryn's cheek clean as she bows her head in agreement.

The old man chuckles. With a snap of his wrist, he slices Caryn's right palm and swipes the largest shard of pottery to catch the first drops. They continue to dissolve into tiny plumes of smoke as they make contact with the clay, despite its condition.

"I offer you this blood as a sign of my undying devotion," the old man repeats. "As an act of faith to you, my great Exu, that I will keep my promise if you keep yours."

TEN

A BOUQUET of brewing coffee and baked sugar bloomed in the air above the cobblestone streets that blistered Talia's heels that morning. She escaped into the shade of one of the umbrellas at the *Casa Suíça* in Rossio for a snack before visiting her great aunt's house in Alfama. One last stop before Porto.

Reaching around the tin canister in her canvas bag for her journal, Talia took in the air and her surroundings. It took less than half of the late eighteenth century to rebuild that entire area of town after the earthquake of 1755, now named the Baixa. Over seventy thousand people died and over seventy percent of the city was leveled from the devastating tremor and tsunami. Now it was paved with waves of mosaics bookended by the majestic Rossio Station and the Palace of Independence, the only surviving monuments from the quake.

A visit to Portugal was not complete without indulging in an authentic Portuguese pastry from *Casa Suíça*. Talia considered it a rite of passage. After she swallowed the first bites of her *Bola de Berlin*, a sugar coated ball with custard filling, she felt equipped to begin her journey, alone. She hesitated in abandoning Pai Paolo earlier that afternoon, fearing for his safety, especially after what he divulged about her uncle. Pai Paolo let slip that her uncle was last known to live up north. He said he felt Vovó sending Carlos a letter to an address in Porto. The rest of the address was fuzzy, except the number 1209. Too many of Vovó's memories had flooded his mind that morning to make sense of the rest.

An elated Talia itched to hear more, even though what had been alleged so far was horrifying. If the man Jared researched was indeed her uncle, he was rumored to have taken dozens of innocent lives as sacrifices—lives that some offered freely as gifts for his congregation. He controlled his followers like a puppeteer, forcing them to do his evil deeds.

You don't know who's your family and who's your enemy. There's nothing like the combination of evil and the power to put that into action.

The revelation about her uncle didn't bring her any closer to finding him. None of Vovó's memories contained a clue as to where her son may have been hiding for twenty years, nor what new name he may have been passing himself off with now. Talia assumed her uncle must have changed his name over the years to successfully hide from his notorious life, and if he were a smart criminal, he wouldn't be anywhere near where he was last seen.

Porto is a sprawling old wine town, its southern side bordered by the Douro River where vines of Port grapes grow like weeds. On the other side of the river is a town nicknamed the Gaia, its full name *Vila Nova de Gaia.* Both cities, and some surrounding neighborhoods, make up the district of Porto.

It was a large expanse to cover in a short time frame, and Talia had no clue where to start. It was doubtful her uncle lived anywhere near Porto, his last known address and the address

Vovó wrote in Pai Paolo's vision. Wild goose chase or not, it was her only lead, and wanted men rarely sat still for long.

Talia wiped her sugar-powdered fingers on a waxed napkin she tore from the dispenser at the center of the table. It was just as ineffective at cleaning off her hands as she remembered. She checked her inner jacket pocket for her shattered phone. It was a little after three o'clock. Catching the autumn sun before it escaped, she took a moment to jot down some notes while she felt the inspiration.

Her mother was certain her great-aunt, Tia Maria, wouldn't remember she had a sister, let alone acknowledge her recent death. No one visited for over three years. Talia felt compelled to go, not just to learn more about Vovó, but also to pay her respects to an ailing aunt before it was too late. If she'd learned anything from Vovó's passing, it's that life can end abruptly.

Talia stretched her legs under the table and snuggled into her black jacket while meditating on the bronze angel perched over one of the two fountains in the square. Her father claimed the statue was imported from France along with the rest that lined the courtyard.

A blonde tourist couple canoodled on the stone bench surrounding the fountain, their sunglasses reflecting the falling daylight on the water. They distributed two coins between them, kissed, and then tossed them both into the Baroque fountain in unison.

She batted away the urge to cry. Jared should've been there, teasing the waiters about their silly black bow ties, Caryn flirting with them to score free food.

"*Do prato à boca perde-se a sopa,*" a young man with a familiar accent interrupted as he slid into the empty chair next to hers. "Is this seat taken?"

She gasped, smiled in agreement at his Portuguese proverb,

and washed down a mouthful of pastry with a gulp of her luke-warm *Galão*, the Portuguese version of a latte, served in a tall milk glass with a metal handle. "Sure. I mean, *sim*, this seat isn't taken. Didn't think I'd see you again."

"It is … a small world. Is that what they say?" Nuno asked.

"Yes, that's what they say." A smile crept into the corner of Talia's mouth.

"How are you, Talia? Or shall I say Alice?"

Talia offered Nuno her cheeks to kiss, respecting Portuguese tradition. His deep gaze and intoxicating scent of lavender and cloves piqued her curiosity. The sly accent alone was ample distraction from her jumbled thoughts of Jared, Caryn, and Vovó.

"Your friends are gone? A pretty girl should not travel alone," Nuno said.

"They're around," Talia said. "We had different ideas about what we wanted from this trip. I wanted to get a head start on my research."

"Ah *sim*, I remember, the story about voodoo."

"Yes, and the article's a good excuse to tie up some loose ends and find some old relatives," Talia said. "I am in the motherland, after all."

"*Claro*," Nuno said. "Which relative?"

"No one in particular. Just finding my roots, as they say back home."

She shifted her hips, prompting Nuno to change the subject with boasts of his childhood in Brazil. Talia knew his storytelling aimed to intrigue her, and yet it still did. She snorted at his Portuguese anecdotes and traditional tall tales, covering her face with embarrassment.

"*Meu Português não é muito bom*." Talia apologized for her caveman Portuguese.

"It is good enough," Nuno said, edging closer.

"You know, I actually have somewhere to be right now. But it's nothing that can't wait until tomorrow," Talia said.

Though it was a good dodge, it was true. She did plan on visiting her Tia Maria that afternoon, but Talia had a hunch Nuno could help her somehow. His admitted knowledge of Macumba could fill in the gaps, especially since he was raised in its birthplace.

Nuno's tone grew somber when he spoke of his deceased father's remains, enclosed in a brass urn on the mantel of the family fireplace, cold for years, how they sat in disappointment at the way his mother raised him. He hinted about the young misadventures this allowed him, from late nights wandering the bar with his mother, to underground gambling, to hustling on those frequent afternoons when she was too drunk to notice his absence.

Feliz ao jogo, não feliz aos amores, his mother said as all the subsequent father figures snuck out the back door. He waved his hands when he spoke of her, highlighting each tense moment and poignant revelation with a heavy smack on the table, disturbing the silverware.

It looked as if his persistent high energy had hidden from those around him the disappointment lurking inside him. He peered into Talia's eyes, as if searching for a clue that he had fooled her, too. She managed to convince him with a forged void in her eyes.

"At ten years old, my mother fell ill. The doctors insisted it was her drinking, but she knew it was something more. Like you said, voodoo. Late one night, she brought me to a small *terreiro* in the middle of the urban jungles of Bahia and told me to wait outside while she visited the witch doctor. When he let my mother in, he stared at me with his one shifty eye. I was worried about my mother, so I peeped through the gap in the sheets covering the front door and watched him perform his ritual."

Candles and incense burned along the curve of the tent as everyone sang. Nuno's witch doctor chanted while waving his trembling hands over his mother as she lay on a cot at the center of the room.

Nuno relived it all in detail. "The doctor never touched her, not even to help her in or kiss her hello. She walked out of the tent in a daze, and was cured."

The scene he set reminded Talia of the altar at Pai Paolo's house—he also lit candles while clothed in linen robes. "Is that what made you believe in Macumba?"

"I believe what I saw that night. The next day, my mother told me she never felt better. She even stopped drinking for a long time."

"My mother used to make me carry garlic in my pocket as a kid to ward off the evil witches in her hometown, especially the Evil Eye."

Nuno chuckled. "Sounds like my mom. She told me never to eat anything a stranger gave me because it could be cursed—the curse of envy."

"Mine too! Our moms are crazy," Talia laughed.

Nuno half-heartedly joined her.

"I mean, you know what I mean," she said as she knocked over her empty coffee glass in a nervous jerk reaction. "Sorry, *desculpa*. I'm a little clumsy today. Or in general."

"It is okay." Nuno placed the unscathed glass upright in its metal holder.

"Looks like you believe in it yourself." Nuno pointed at Talia's neckline.

Talia looked down at the jade pendant hanging from her necklace. It must have slipped from beneath her shirt when she leaned over. "The Figa? I thought all Portuguese people wore these."

The Figa is a common Portuguese symbol of a clasped fist with the thumb in between the index and middle fingers, originally taken from African culture during Portugal's invasion of Africa's eastern coast in the early sixteenth century. Their meld of voodoo and Catholicism created a ritualistic and superstitious belief in Jesus and, especially, in the Mother Mary.

Received as a gift, the Figa is thought to bring good luck, prosperity, and protection to the wearer. Talia's mother had given it to her as a child, after she had it blessed by their priest.

"The people who believe in it wear it. Do you believe in it?" Nuno asked.

Talia tilted her head and squinted. "I don't know. Never really thought about it."

"Then why do you wear it?"

"Because my mom gave it to me," Talia said. "She believes in it. I suppose a part of me must still hold onto a little superstition."

"May I have a look?" Nuno asked, and without waiting for an answer, he lifted the jade charm from Talia's collarbone.

Talia flinched at first, but then allowed him to tug at her neck for a closer view.

"This one is very unique," he said. "The jade and silver make it very powerful at keeping away evil. Your mother must have known this."

Talia smoothed down the goose bumps creeping up her arm. "Maybe. She never seemed that knowledgeable about these things."

"She may have known more than you think."

"I suppose all parents know more than their kids think they do."

Nuno stretched his arm around her chair. "So where is your *namorado?*"

"My boyfriend? Now, that's a long story."

"I have time."

"I don't want to get into it. Let's just say I don't have a boyfriend anymore."

"Oh," Nuno said, shirking a smile.

"He doesn't understand why I'm here, and I guess I don't feel like he supports my decisions unless he agrees with them. I don't know. I don't want to talk about him." Talia felt too embarrassed to mention Jared's wandering eye. She was ashamed she let him get away with it, as if she was somehow to blame for his indiscretions.

"Why *are* you here?" Nuno asked.

"Bringing out all the hard questions this afternoon, aren't we, Nuno? *I'm* supposed to be the reporter."

"*Desculpa,*" Nuno apologized.

"No, it's okay. It's a good question. I'm not exactly sure why I'm here. To investigate a murder, I guess. Jared seems to think it's more than that."

"Do you think it is more than that?"

"Why do I feel like you are shrinking me?" Talia asked. "Maybe I do need therapy. Since Caryn's not here to do it."

"Is that your friend? Where is she?" Nuno asked. "Is she with your boyfriend?"

"No, nothing like that. She took off with a French guy. Pretty typical. Not so typical is never calling. That's another issue altogether."

The invigorating scent of his natural cologne eased Talia's instinct to defy his advances. Channeling advice from Caryn to enjoy the moment, she accepted Nuno's invitation for a drink at his hotel bar down the street off *Rua Augusta.*

By the time the two stepped onto the boulevard, Nuno got the first of his odd calls that night. His eyes widened when he saw the number flash on the screen of his vibrating mobile phone and wagged his finger at Talia to wait as he plodded down the street to answer.

Talia listened as he scolded the person on the other line, his arms flailing. He pulled a soft box of cigarettes from the front pocket of his well-ironed pants and lit one with his free hand. She pretended to stare at the stars as she paced the uneven sidewalk, avoiding the bars that already teemed with young Europeans hunting for a vacation companion.

"*Ó pá!* Stop calling. I told you, I am busy," was all Talia could comprehend over the din of tourists chatting in multiple languages from the outdoor seating, muddled with American music playing in the brand name stores sprinkled in between.

Someone had been stalking him. Possibly an ex-girlfriend.

It would not have surprised Talia if Nuno kept a few lovers. He seemed well versed in the art of meeting women. However, his tone was a bit cold for this particular call to be from a current girlfriend. Talia speculated that it must have been a former connection who was finding it hard to say goodbye. Whoever it was, it was definitely not a close friend. At least not anymore.

Nuno reappeared from behind one of the trees that lined the square and Talia watched a couple of girls taking drags off their cigarettes, fingers in the air, their boisterous laughter echoing down the alleyways.

"*Pronto, vamos,*" Nuno waved Talia over.

The bar roared and Talia let go to enjoy the moment, as Caryn and Jared always insisted. In spite of the noise, Talia found herself enthralled by Nuno and his stories. Especially after a couple *Caipirinhas*—a deceivingly delicious drink with muddled lime and Brazilian *cachaça*, a strong, clear liquor made of distilled sugar cane.

"I couldn't wait to leave Brazil and travel the world. *Afim, aqui fiquei*," Nuno waved his hands and placed them at his side.

"And here you are," Talia affirmed with a raised glass. "It may have been *um pouquinho* early for drinks." Talia teased Nuno with a slur, stretching her right index finger and thumb an inch apart, near her face, winking to further accentuate her point.

When she lowered her hand, Nuno smiled at her, his eyes glossy, and went in for a kiss. She stopped him before he got the chance, placing her fingers on his lips as she looked in his eyes. She let him continue, and he left her lips fruity and tart. Her stomach fluttered for the first time in months.

"I shouldn't," she said, but she couldn't stop. She slid her fingers behind his ears and led him back to her lips.

The girl at the beach, the woman at the library, the intern. Laughing, pointing, taunting. Their faces smeared Jared's memory, and cheered her on with Nuno. But they faded away with Nuno's warmth, and she embraced the peace it brought her, even if just for that moment.

Nuno escorted Talia back to his hotel room. Focused on balancing one hand under the back of her sweater, he used the other to unlock the rustic door of the room with an old fashioned skeleton key. He hooked onto the belt holes on Talia's jeans as he fiddled with the light switch. She smiled at the children playing down the hall when the door creaked open and Nuno drew her inside his room.

Talia tugged on Nuno's loosely buttoned shirt tucked in his trousers and unbuckled his belt as they tripped across the room onto the bed. He slipped his long fingers down the front of her jeans and unbuttoned them one-handedly with a flip of his index finger and thumb. Biting her bottom lip, Talia stripped off her black sweater.

She pressed his shoulders further into the mountain of red pillows with her open palms, rubbing her inner thighs against his loosened pants, and nibbled on his earlobe. Nuno's faint moans traced Talia's neckline, leaving behind raised goose bumps in their path. Talia draped her slender arms around his neck and brought his head in for another kiss, enveloping him in her long auburn hair.

———

IT WAS SCARCELY past the usual late European dinnertime when they fell to bed in exhaustion. The down pillows exhaled an air of lavender that flooded Talia with a sense of calm satisfaction. She could hear the rustling footsteps of passers-by below the open second-story balcony door as Nuno wrapped her into his ciliated chest. She traced his sternum with the tip of her finger, as he played with her hair.

"*És mesmo linda*, Talia," he said.

Talia lifted her head in a hazy smile and kissed Nuno's swollen lips. "I bet you say that to all the girls, and I bet they melt with that sexy accent of yours."

He smirked and kissed her deeper.

"My grandmother told me to stay away from boys like you. She knows your type."

"And what type is that?" He played along with a smirk.

"Oh, you know." She tapped his chin with the short tip of her index finger, and then swayed her head to the side with a pout. "She used to say I had plenty of time to find the right man. I realized later that she got pregnant later in life to snag my grandfather. And now no one even knows where that son is. They say he's up north somewhere. Who knows? It's amazing how many secrets you can take with you to the grave."

The air in the room stagnated.

"That didn't work for my mother." Nuno ended the silence. "My father still left us."

"I thought you said he passed away?" Talia perked up.

"He did, a few years later. My parents never got divorced, so when he died, my mother and I had to arrange things."

"That's awful. How did he die?"

"Overdose. Pills and alcohol. They say it was an accident. He left us one Sunday afternoon. I did not see him again until I identified his body three years later."

"I'm so sorry." Talia caressed his stubbly chin with the back of her fingers. "Your mother did a good job of raising you alone."

"I do not think she would agree. *Agora,* we will never know." Nuno paused. "You remind me of her. *Um pouco.*"

"Is that good, getting compared to your lover's mother? Even a little?" Talia smiled.

"It is love that is essential. Sex is just an accident." Nuno surprised Talia with an excerpt from Fernando Pessoa's poetry.

Nuno laughed off his frown with a long blink, and then pinned Talia down to bite her neck, which was already chafed pink by his three o'clock shadow. As she fell back, she caught an upside down glimpse of a sealed cardboard box tucked behind the maroon plush chaise near the bathroom.

Nuno's wandering lips on her outstretched neck won her attention back, but it was interrupted seconds later by another ring of his mobile phone—this time it was a Portuguese polyphonic Fado that reminded her of young boys and girls dressed up in traditional embroidered peasant attire dancing in a circle to an accordion ballad. It startled them both.

"Not this time, *gatinha*. I am all yours." He winked, kissed her forehead, and slid out of bed. *"Mais vinho?"* he asked, wielding a bottle of port wine.

"Então, mais um pinguinho de tinto." Talia asked for another glass, mimicking the men at the bar of her hometown's Portuguese Club.

"Wine is good for men when it's the women who drink it," Nuno recited another Portuguese proverb.

"Hey now, that's not nice," Talia joked. "Us women are fun sober, too."

She grinned as he moved his boxer-briefed hips to the dance music wafting along with the cigarette smoke from the club a few doors down. She snuck another look behind the couch when Nuno turned away to open a new bottle. There it sat, a strange manila box. No labels, no addresses, nothing. It was too neatly sealed to peek in, but Talia was anxious to pick it up and feel its weight. Maybe she could deduce what was inside.

Why would he bring a box to a hotel? A box without a single identifying mark.

As a child, Talia always found the Christmas presents her mother squirreled away in the months preceding the holidays. The search was only the first step. What Talia enjoyed most was the meticulous unwrapping of the gifts, discovering the contents within and then refurbishing them to their original cloaked state. None would be the wiser until the last and crucial step—the surprise act come Christmas Day. Talia's brutal honesty gave her away to her scolding mother, who never appreciated that the opportunity to sleuth remained Talia's favorite gift.

She slipped into the white terrycloth robe hanging off her bedpost and tiptoed to the manila package.

"Where are you going?" Nuno asked, a jitter in his throat.

"Casa de banho. Is that okay?" Talia winked and veered from

the strange box toward the bathroom as if never intending to head that direction in the first place.

"Of course! Your *vinho* will be waiting."

He watched Talia inch into the oversized lavatory. She lost her view of the box, but once she locked the door behind her, she heard Nuno tap a number into his cell phone.

"*Sim senhor.* I have the box. *Não se preocupe.* Everything is ready for tomorrow. *Sim. Ciao,*" he said.

Talia wiped her raccoon eyes with a bundle of rough toilet paper she dampened under the faucet. She took one last frustrated look in the Victorian gold-framed mirror that hung just low enough to reflect everything above the tip of her nose, including her bushy brows, but only while standing on her toes.

Staring into her own hazel bloodshot eyes, she felt a longing for Jared she hadn't felt since she met Nuno, sloshing with the pang of guilt that unsettled her belly full of alcohol. Jared took care of her, maybe more than she liked, but at that moment she wished him there to give her advice. Just this once, she might heed it. Of course, that would be after he tackled Nuno for all the things he had just done to her.

How was she going to explain this to Jared? The text he received from his father's intern could have been innocent. She didn't catch Jared in the act. But Talia had just crossed a line she could never uncross.

A sudden wave of nausea rushed through Talia's gut and up her throat. She rushed to the toilet, barely making the shot into the bowl, pink droplets splashing onto the rim. Her hands trembled as she watched her wavy reflection in the toilet water. What had she done?

Nuno paced outside the bathroom, his step louder as he passed the door, back and forth. Talia scrambled along the uneven slate tiles to wipe the toilet and flush before he noticed.

"*Tudo bem?*" Nuno asked through the door.

"*Sim.* All's good," Talia called back. She rinsed out her mouth with water, let out a breath, and wiggled her arms to shake off the fear before she opened the door. Startled by Nuno's presence on the other side, she gulped and stepped back.

"*Desculpa.* You took so long, I got worried. Your *vinho*," he said, thrusting a full glass of red wine into her clammy hands.

Nuno's arm weighed down Talia's shoulder as he led her back to bed. Half a glass of red wine later, her heart settled. Half a bottle later, she forgot all her paranoia.

"There is nothing more metaphysical than chocolate. Religion does not teach us much more than a candy shop," Nuno recited an excerpt from Pessoa's *Tabácaria*, in Portuguese, much to Talia's delight, while offering her a chocolate from the mini bar.

Talia could name a few people who believed chocolate was divine, but her family would've cringed at the comparison of faith to confection.

"Nice choice in poetry," Talia said. "Couldn't have said it better myself."

"You know Pessoa?" Nuno asked.

"What self-respecting Portagee doesn't?" Talia couldn't resist laughing at Nuno's dirty jokes, acted out by his large gestures and ascending accent.

Most Portuguese jokes revolved around a play on words, or a pun, and Talia enjoyed all the ones Nuno told. He chortled at his own tales, as though he hadn't heard them spoken before, and it was just dorky enough for Talia to join him. His long-winded stories and local clichés reminded Talia of her father, who could talk for hours about nothing. It was endearing, comforting.

"You may have heard this one before, but I will tell it again," Nuno began. "There was a woman who had a daughter who was very ill. All the doctors told her that she was fine, but every night she became sicker. So one day, her mother brought her to a witch doctor. He told her to feed her a new meal every night for a week, but to not allow her daughter to finish everything on her plate. The woman was to take the small, uneaten portion of each night's meal and save it. On the last night, she was to feed it all to a wild animal."

This urban legend had been told in Talia's family hundreds of times. The woman did what she was told, and on the last night, she fed her daughter's scraps to a stray dog in the alley behind her house. The next morning, after her daughter woke up healthy, the woman returned to the dumpster to find the dog had finished his plate and died a short while later.

"Poor pup, but lucky girl," Talia slurred, and then blurted, "I think I may be psychic."

Nuno censored his laugh.

"No, really. I have prophetic dreams. They creep me out and lately, it's been getting worse. I'm having nightmares about my grandmother. It's been about a month since she died, and in my dreams she's trying to tell me something, but I can never figure it out."

"Have you had these dreams before?" he asked.

"My whole life I've had terrible nightmares predicting the future," Talia said, trying not to stare at the manila box on the other side of the room. "Some have already come true. I'm afraid of the rest. But the priest I met this morning, that was a trip."

"You met a priest?" Nuno asked.

"I guess that's what he is," Talia said. "He felt more like a witch doctor, to tell you the truth. But he told me a lot of things I'm not sure I should know."

"Maybe you're not as prophetic as you think, if you did not already know what he would say." Nuno winked.

Talia laughed. "Fair enough."

"So what did he tell you?" Nuno asked.

"Just some family secrets. But then, there was a weird encounter with my grandmother."

"Your grandmother who just died?"

"Yeah, I told you it was weird." Talia picked at her nails. "Anyway, I don't even know what to think about it, or whether I even believe it's real. It's all a little fuzzy now."

"What was his name?"

Talia paused. "Pai Paolo."

Nuno cocked his head. "*Tu–* you met Pai Paolo?"

"Yes. Why, do you know him?"

"Not exactly," Nuno said. "I have heard of him. He is well-known around *Lisboa.*"

"He wasn't so popular this morning. There were only a few of us at his house."

"You entered his home?" Nuno's voice crescendoed.

"I guess it was his home. It looked more like an abandoned church on the inside. Should I be worried? Because you're certainly acting like I should be."

"His house is not safe, Talia," Nuno said, clutching her knee. "He is known to practice voodoo."

"It didn't look like voodoo. It looked like a hippie commune." She chuckled.

"Promise me you will not visit him again."

"I don't think he's as bad as you say, but I doubt I'll visit him again. So sure, I promise."

"*Bom.*" Nuno nodded his head. "I have one more thing to ask. It is important. I need your help."

"My help?" Talia hiccupped awake from her half-daze. The woolen field of red carnations and white vines that spread across the oak planks restored to its flat state. "I'm not sure if I can help."

"It is that box." He pointed to the manila box in the corner.

"What box?" Talia asked, relieved that she could finally stare at it without suspicion.

"I know you have seen it," Nuno said. "It is for my friend in Fátima."

"What's in it?"

"I do not know."

A drunken man shouted after his friends outside the window.

"So when are you leaving?" Talia asked.

"Tomorrow. And I would like you to come with me."

"Oh." Talia's stomach whirling with anxiety or excitement, or both. "I don't know. I have to visit my great-aunt tomorrow and then head up to Porto. I don't have much time left here."

"We will go to Porto afterwards, I promise," Nuno said. "Come with me and I will help you find your uncle."

Talia didn't know how to react, not wanting to insult Nuno by suggesting she couldn't trust him. This was her first-ever one-night stand, so she had no experience removing herself from these types of situations. She thought of herself as a "flinger," preferring short affairs to fleeting nights. Nuno and Jared were complete opposites—Nuno understood her background, her childhood, without judgment or ridicule. His knowledge could be insightful, and it was better than traveling alone. "I suppose I could use the help. What do you have to do in Fátima?"

"I need you to drop off the box while I speak to my friend. It will not take long. I cannot do this myself because I have a reputation. I am not allowed to enter public places."

"Okay, now you're scaring me," Talia said.

"Nothing bad, but I must confess. I was a *cigano*. A long time ago, when I first moved here from Brazil. I had to eat. Fátima has a lot of tourists, *sabes*? When I got harassed by the police in one place, I moved to another. They banned me from all the public areas in the city."

"You were a *cigano*—a gypsy—in Fátima?" Talia sighed.

"Yes, but a long time ago when I was a teenager. I was young and stupid."

"I can't say this confession makes me trust you more."

"I want to be honest." Nuno stood, unblinking.

"Honesty is good," Talia said, pulling a nail off too close to the quick with her front teeth. "This friend of yours, is he trustworthy?"

"He is a good man," Nuno said. "I will also be going to Porto, to visit a friend. He does not mind if I bring a guest, so you will have a free place to stay while you look for your uncle."

"Is that the friend you've been speaking to on the phone?" Talia asked, seeing an opportunity.

Nuno seemed stunned at Talia frankness, but she knew deep down he wasn't as ignorant he pretended. It had been on the tip of her tongue since earlier that evening and she knew he could see it in her eyes.

"I'm sorry. You were pretty excited on the phone. For what it's worth, he didn't seem like much of a friend."

"Brazilians are passionate." Nuno raised his arms with a shrug of his shoulder. "We speak too emotionally sometimes."

"So, this guy in Porto, is he the same friend in Fátima?" Talia asked. "I would like to know who I'm going to be dealing with, if I'm going to stick my neck out for you. It's only fair."

Nuno exhaled. "You are right, Talia. Forgive me. My friend in Porto is a different man. My friend in Fátima is the one who has been calling me. We have, how do you say, a difference in opinion."

"I know the feeling."

"So you will come with me?" Nuno's eyebrows arched higher.

"Are you sure there's nothing in that box I should be concerned about?" Talia asked again, a shiver in her limbs. "You wouldn't put me in danger, would you?"

"Of course not. There is nothing in that box to be concerned about. *Nada.* It is true, Talia. I promise," Nuno said, placing his palm to his heart, a ring on his middle finger.

"I'm not a big fan of broken promises," Talia said. Like the promises she made to Jared? She was such a hypocrite.

Much like the wine she had been drinking, the plan was not settling well in Talia's stomach. Yet, the unlabeled manila box concealed in the corner, the size of a tall shoe box, piqued her curiosity, and her lack of sleep due to recurring nightmares kept her in a state of mild delirium. Regardless, Talia was no less clear on her intentions—to find the murderer and her uncle, especially if they are one and the same. Either way, she would at least return home with Vovó's jewelry box in tow. So far, all she found were more questions.

"What do you think? Will you be my companion to Porto? *Lisboa é praça de armas, Porto dos mercadores,*" Nuno pitched with an age-old adage comparing the former capital of Portugal with its current one.

His proposal enticed a desperate Talia, who was now two men down in her investigation, her trip budget shrinking. At that point, for a free place to say in Porto, a detour to Fátima seemed a fair price. She wanted to tell Nuno about Caryn, and enlist him to help find her, but she was afraid of how Caryn would react to her tryst.

If he's trustworthy enough to sleep with, he should be trustworthy enough to travel with. Talia took pride in being a good judge of character—able to read people as well as Freud or Jung thanks to Caryn, and a few classes in psychology and sociology.

Her instinct was to follow Nuno. "You do make a very tempting offer. I need to visit my Tia Maria's apartment in Alfama tomorrow morning before I leave Lisbon. My grandmother might have left something for me."

"I can help you get there tomorrow," he said. "*Depois*, you help me."

Talia wrinkled her forehead, but hid it with a bow of her head. "Who's this friend of yours in Porto?" she asked again, judging Nuno's reaction. "I should know a bit about him before I crash at his place."

"He is like family to me," Nuno said. "And he will be very happy to meet you."

ELEVEN

TALIA STOPPED to catch her breath. Resting her hands against her knees, she watched Nuno run midway up the steep and narrow cobblestone hill in Alfama that led to Tia Maria's apartment. Though she mapped out her route before she left, Talia drew a paper map of Lisbon from her pocket and glared through it, as if trying to read a novel in a language she couldn't understand.

An abrupt horn caused Talia to jump off the tracks. The vintage yellow Tram 28 had been rattling up and down those hills in the oldest quarter of Lisbon since the early 1900's. Before the metro was built, the Tram had been part of a vast tramway system that spanned the inner part of the city, most of which was now out of commission. She would have taken the trolley that time as she had many times before, its rickety climb as comfortable as a worn-in pair of jeans, had they not missed it by ten minutes.

Atop the hill stood *Castelo São George*, a Moorish citadel that overlooked the entire city, constructed as a fort to guard the villages bordering the Targus River. Pieces of its façade dated back to the eighth century, reconstructed with help from European crusaders, and then dedicated to the patron saint of England—a symbol of the strong bond between England and Portugal. It had accommodated many of Portugal's royalty, serving as a reception hall for famous guests such as Vasco de Gama, Portugal's revered explorer during the Age of Discovery, and extensively reconstructed by Salazar in the mid-twentieth century.

The Tram overlooked the eclectic buildings dotted in blue, yellow, and green across Lisbon's tallest hillside. Some buildings weren't painted at all. Instead, they were trimmed with *azulejos*— a Moorish term for the glazed blue tiles similar to frescoes that garnished the country, depicting scenes of historical events.

The frescoes filled Talia with the warmth of nostalgia, along with the scent of marinating *caracois* flooding the circling streets. Talia's mother would only have the delicacy—comprised of small snails, still in their shells, stewed in a sauce of garlic and local spices—in this part of town, where it originated. Her mother, a self-proclaimed connoisseur, declared no one else made a marinade that was up to par. Though not a big fan herself, Talia had to agree.

"Not sure if it's a right or left. I'm not good with directions," Talia told Nuno once he caught up.

Nuno looked over her shoulder and said, "*Esquerda,*" and then hiked the hill to her left.

Talia, surprised at Nuno's obvious certainty, had no instinctual sense of direction herself, so she trusted him without question.

"*Este?*" Nuno asked as he pointed at an enclosed staircase, worn down at the middle from frequent use, and two painted doors at the top left and right.

The left door was painted blue, but worn gray over many years; the right door was painted red with a black metal rooster as a door knock. An outdoor shelf in an arched recess in the wall in between held fading knick-knacks and a hand-painted red clay carafe holding wilted flowers at the center.

"That's it. The red door to the right," Talia said.

"Do you have the key?" Nuno asked.

Talia grinned as she yanked the keys from her pocket, and then tried each, one by one, on the chain. Three keys in, the door clicked open.

She tiptoed in, frightened to awaken her aunt too early from her night's sleep, all the while knowing the apartment would be empty. Many apartments in older parts of Lisbon are rent controlled, making it easy for those with less to keep their homes when they leave. Giving up their rental could mean the rent could rise above their means if they ever decided to return.

Tia Maria's apartment smelled musty from abandonment, but everything sat in place, not unlike Vovó's apartment back in Massachusetts.

The two were obviously sisters. Beyond their similar looks, save for a few small features and pounds, Vovó and her older sister had some of the same knickknacks showcased around their homes, many of which contained a painted rooster. In any Portuguese household, brightly painted roosters of all sizes and shapes were exhibited throughout to bring good luck—some made of glass, some painted on china, others carved into large wooden spoons.

In the legend of the *Galo de Barcelos*, a rooster from the village of Barcelos saved a Galician peasant who was on a pilgrimage to *Santiago de Compostela* from an unlawful hanging. On the day he was sentenced, the Galician announced the roasted rooster on the magistrate's table would come to life and crow when his day came to hang. Legend has it that on the day of his execution, the rooster did as the Galician predicted and reawakened to crow. The magistrate, realizing his error, hurried to save the Galician from his wrongful death. Luckily, a faulty knot in the rope had already spared the Galician and the relieved magistrate freed him without penalty.

Although most residents did not believe the legend literally, it had a common theme of justice, fate and miracle work often found in Portuguese literature. Throughout the country, wherever anyone needed luck, a colorful rooster was prominently displayed —on cash registers, cooking mittens, aprons, wine carafes, and even burnt into cheese boards.

The small apartment appeared more cramped than Talia remembered, though she hadn't visited since junior high. The main room was long and slender—cupboards, hutches, and bookcases lining every inch of every wall. A long Persian rug ran underneath the dining room table, which sat at the center, reserving less than a few feet on each side to maneuver around.

At the far end of the table, a narrow French door opened to a slim veranda overlooking the neighborhood's most popular restaurant bar. Everything from clothes to rugs to blankets and sheets draped off the tiny balconies of the tiled buildings across the street. A potted plant sat in a ceramic vase in the corner of the balcony, struggling to stay alive without human care.

A gust of wind entangled Talia in the sun-bleached curtains. They pulled her inside, and slammed the door after her.

"Is this you? You were always pretty," Nuno said, admiring an old picture of Talia from grade school hanging on the wall near the French door.

After a couple of long breaths, her heart still racing, Talia replied, "Liar."

"*Porque*? The glasses? They are cute. You look smart."

"Where were you in grade school?" Talia joked, the throb in her sinuses subsiding. "Oh, the hair, the outfit. There is so much wrong with that picture, I can't even."

"You were perfect." Nuno twirled Talia around by her shoulders, wrapped his hands around her head, and brought her in for a kiss. Talia blushed and kissed him back.

"Go have a look around, I need the *banho*," Nuno patted her butt as he walked away.

"It's on the left," Talia started, but Nuno had already discovered the bathroom.

She walked to the cupboard her aunt filled with special china and glassware, resting to the right of the French window. Talia pulled on the frail door handles. Locked. The iron keyhole appeared tampered with, but Talia blamed the dings and dents on its forty-plus years of wear and tear, as well as her aunt's failing vision. Talia removed the matching key from the chain, but there was nothing of much value left inside—a few mismatched dishes, teacups, and balls of dust. No jewelry box, or anything else of much importance, for that matter.

Talia then noticed a rectangular spot on the bottom shelf with a few less layers of dust than the shelving around it. Something had once rested there but had since been removed. Talia wiped her index finger along the darker grain, tracking with her a thin layer of dirt.

Talia leaned back in thought and almost knocked over the bookshelf she was balanced against. Everything rattled, but only one frame fell. When Talia picked it up, she noticed another photo behind the black and white one on display of her mother as a toddler, her tresses garnered in a polka dotted bow. She drew the picture out, avoiding a shard of glass.

Her great-aunt and grandmother must have shared photo albums as well, for the picture of Vovó, her grandfather, her mother, and the unknown boy she recalled seeing years ago in Vovó's bedroom drawer was once again in front of her. She almost called out to Nuno in a whirl of excitement, but refrained. After piecing the frame back together, Talia hid it behind a larger frame on the shelf, and then tucked the picture into her jacket pocket.

"Any luck?" Nuno asked as he walked out of the short hallway connecting the bedroom to the living room.

"*Nada*," Talia lied. "You?"

"This is not my business." Nuno waved his empty hand.

"You're absolutely right. I should be the one to do it."

"I will wait outside until you finish," Nuno said. "Remember, we must catch the train in a few hours."

"I shouldn't be much longer."

Nuno pecked Talia on the forehead.

"Where did you put that box while you were in there?" Talia teased.

Nuno clenched the manila box as he secured the front door behind him, ignoring her comment. Talia continued to search the room for another possible hiding spot. After ten more minutes of rummaging through cupboards and wheezing from disrupted dust, Talia gave up on her search.

Resting on a yellow chair in the corner near the hallway, Talia retrieved the picture from her pocket. For a few moments, she zoned in on the boy as if trying to read his mind, and then flipped the picture over. In faded chicken-scratched blue ink that reminded her of the handwriting on the lining of Vovó's dresser drawer, it read: "Familia Batista, 1974. Domingos, Tina, Carla e Carlos."

Her heart raced. The picture was proof. Her uncle did exist, and his name was really Carlos. Whether he was still alive and in Portugal, that was a different beast.

Talia tucked the picture back into her pocket and looked out the French door one last time before she bolted it shut. Nuno wasn't anywhere in the vicinity. For the first time since they reconnected at the café, she was alone, and she felt the urge to check her phone. The screen was cracked, only a few places on the face remained active. There were no messages, so she selected Caryn's name on her contact list. It rang three times before it went to voicemail.

"Caryn, where are you? I know you told me not to worry if you took off with a boy, but I just—it's been a long time. I'm going up to Porto later today. Please call me. Maybe we can meet up somewhere. I miss you. Call me okay? Me-a-vue."

Talia contemplated calling Jill, but what she'd found out about her uncle didn't quite correlate to the murder investigation. At least not yet. Jill was worried about Talia just as Talia was about Caryn, so she felt obligated to at least assure her she was alive and well. If only Caryn would do the same.

"Talia? Is that really you?" Jill asked on the other end. Her voice was shaking and a few loud cars passed in the background.

"I did something bad."

"Are you okay?"

"Yes, yes, I'm fine. Physically. Emotionally not so much. I cheated on Jared. We had a fight and I broke it off, so I didn't technically cheat, but I feel like I did. And Caryn. She's missing."

"Hold on. Back up. What happened with Jared?"

"It's a long story. I left him behind and now, I don't know. I slept with a guy I met yesterday. I don't even know why. It's not like me. I don't know what I'm doing."

Talia couldn't remember a time when she'd leapt into bed with a man so suddenly. Despite her determination to land a random guy at the end of many nights out with Caryn, she always ended up driving herself home after Caryn left with her flavor of the month. It wasn't that she couldn't find a suitor. As Caryn would put it, Talia just didn't *have the balls*.

"From what you've told me, you've been unhappy for some time. Don't beat yourself up over it. We've all been there. And what did you say? Caryn's *missing*?" Jill asked, shuffling the phone to her other ear. The background was quieter, as if she walked inside. Talia heard the ding of an elevator. Jill was likely headed home late the night before, she'd almost forgotten the eight-hour time difference.

"She took off with an older, creepy dude. She won't answer her phone."

"When was this?" Jill asked.

"Two days ago. Long enough to be a missing person."

"She's not missing if she chose to leave. Have you called the cops?"

"No." Talia's hands shook.

"Good. It may compromise your safety. I know you wanted to investigate this case, but I don't want you to get yourself in trouble, okay? Is this guy you're with dangerous?"

"I don't think so. Don't worry, I'm still investigating. I just got a little sidetracked. There's this underground crime lord who's into black magic. I think he may be behind the murders. He has ties to the girls. They're his cousins."

"Sounds like a lead to me."

"Yeah, I think so, too. He's hiding in Porto. At least that's what I hear. I'm heading up there to find him."

"Be careful, Talia. If this man has the power you say he does, he'll be very dangerous. If he knows you're on to him … I want the story, but not at your expense."

"I'll be careful, I promise. I gotta go. Thanks for listening."

By the time Talia made her way to the bottom of the steps, Nuno was flirting with a white-haired neighbor in front of a pink building a few doors up. Her stomach turned and for a moment she felt as if she'd have to rush to the bathroom. It was her chance to run, but she couldn't. The old woman, who wore black from the scarf on her head to the wool socks rolled uneven to her knees, giggled while placing her trembling hand on his arm, both with affection and for balance.

Nuno caught Talia's eye and whispered in the lady's ear. Nodding her head, she waved goodbye as he shuffled to Talia's side. Talia smiled at the lady and she waved back with a toothless grin.

"Did you find what you were looking for?" Nuno asked, his smirk loitering.

"Sort of," Talia said. "I think it's time I visited my great-aunt at the *Lar*. One last stop. I promise we won't miss the train. I can't stop in Lisbon and not visit. Who knows, maybe you'll sweep her off her feet, too."

———

NURSES RIVALING the age of their patients snickered like schoolchildren at the front desk of the rest home where Tia Maria lived. It took a few minutes for Talia to catch the nurses' attention after their gossip died down. Calming herself with the reminder that Europe worked at a slower pace, she waited. Nuno slinked into the corner, fidgeting.

"*Precisas ajuda?*" The broader of the gaggle wearing flowered scrubs offered to help.

"*Olá*. I am here to see *Senhora Silva*," Talia said in her best Portuguese.

"*Ora bem*, I will get her ready." The lady in the flowered scrubs marched to a back hall.

"Is she your grandmother?" one of the ladies asked.

"My great-aunt actually. My grandmother just passed." Talia frowned.

The remaining few women fawned and coddled Talia with a hug or a rub of the back. Talia wasn't much for the touchy feely with strangers, but at that moment, she welcomed as much comfort as the nurses intended to give her.

"She knows?" asked a nurse in pink scrubs and emerald-studded gold earrings.

"We've told her. Not sure if she remembers. I'm trying to find a man that may be her nephew," Talia said. "That's why I'm here. Also to see her since I'm not sure when I'll be back."

"I did not know *Senhora Silva* had a nephew," another nurse said, her reading glasses dangling from the gold chain around her neck.

"I thought she might not know either until I found this in her house." Talia revealed the photo she took from Tia Maria's apartment.

The women shared the photo, scowling and squinting to focus their failing eyes. "This is near my brother's house in Gaia," the smallest of the bunch said in Portuguese.

Nuno involuntarily perked at the mention of Gaia, as though curious himself about the picture Talia kept from him.

"Gaia?" Talia asked, aiming her back at Nuno. "I had no idea my family spent any time there."

"*Então*, she is waiting in the common room for you," the flowered nurse interrupted, pointing down the hallway she walked earlier.

Talia thanked the nurses and rushed to the visiting room. Nuno followed, but the nurses held him back, insisting only family could visit during off hours. Talia gave Nuno an apologetic smile and continued toward the visiting room.

She had forgotten how many years it had been since she last

visited Tia Maria. Her hair was now thinner and more silvery than in her memories, back slumped further, wrinkles folded deeper. Nonetheless, she glowed when Talia glanced through the doorway. She attempted to get up from her seat, but Talia eased her great-aunt back in with a kiss on the cheek.

"*Olá, Tia.*" Talia found some ease on the creaky chair next to her.

"*Olá,* Natalia," Tia Maria exclaimed with as much gusto as she could muster.

Tia Maria's dementia made it difficult to prolong a logical conversation. Sticking to family gossip kept her focused on the present, except for the occasional tangent about how she had to herd the sheep before her parents found out she was slacking.

Though Talia knew she'd feel guilty about it later, she used one of these regressions to her advantage, sliding the photo of her supposed uncle on the rickety table in front of her. "Do you know the child in this picture?"

Tia Maria leaned into the photo with a squinted stare for what felt like a century, but then a light brightened in her eyes. "Carlos," she whispered.

"So you *do* know him," Talia muttered to herself.

"*Pois!* He is your brother," the old woman stuttered.

"My brother? But I don't have a broth—" Talia trailed off. "Tia, who do you think I am?"

"You are always playing, Carla." Tia Maria beamed with pride.

Talia thought she looked more like her father than her mother, but she understood what her great-aunt meant. Now that she had physical proof and a confession from family, she could accept her suspicions to be true. Talia should have been excited. She had uncovered a family mystery, at least partially. Tia

Maria's testimony wasn't enough for a jury, but it was enough for Talia.

It was not as easy for Talia to acknowledge that her family had been lying to her for years. Not only her mother, but Vovó too, the person she trusted most. It shouldn't have surprised Talia, as it seemed to be the way her family preferred to live. If only she had known sooner, she could have saved herself a hell of a lot of grief.

Her uncle Carlos most likely died years before then. That was a logical conclusion. But Talia held onto the hope that she would find him and he would tell her everything she wanted to know about her family.

"Where is Carlos, Tia?" Talia asked her great-aunt. "Do you know where he is?"

Tia Maria appeared baffled as she stared at the dusty books on the shelves. Blinking her eyes, she then cocked her head to the tile floors that needed a sweeping, and watched a dust bunny creep underneath the chairs. She pulled the pilled blanket covering her legs up to her sagging chest, exposing her slouched hospital socks.

"Don't let him go," Tia Maria yelled, taking the room full of rambling old ladies in black skirts by surprise.

With her palm to her chest to calm herself down, her head pounding with her pulse, Talia reached over to take Tia Maria's hand to relax her before the nurses noticed.

"Your brother needs to stay in America with you, Carla," Tia Maria whispered in Portuguese, squeezing her hand so tightly Talia could feel her bones touch. "Something is not right with him."

TWELVE

"THE TRAIN to Fátima leaves in five minutes!" Nuno yelled.

He dragged Talia by the forearm a few yards out of the station doors before she caught up to his long-legged pace. Talia hesitated, leaning back with the weight of her backpack. In response, Nuno clenched his fist tighter and sprinted down the congested platform, pulling her sore arm with him.

"It's too late to turn back." Nuno's breath pierced through the crisp late afternoon air in short, visible gusts.

"Let's eat here, I'm starving," Talia hollered to compete with the Portuguese announcer crackling from the speakers.

"This is the last train today, *vamos!*"

Talia's red slip-ons had already chaffed her heels raw, but the hunger stung worse, hangover notwithstanding. As she chased Nuno into the train car parked at Lisbon's *Gare do Oriente* train station, Talia daydreamed about her last meal—the pastry at Café Suiça the afternoon before. Her head throbbed with hunger.

"Stop there!" a man shouted from behind.

Talia turned around to find a security officer, cladded in a camouflage suit and a green beret, towing a semi-automatic weapon the length of Talia's shivering leg.

"What is in that box?" he asked Nuno in Portuguese.

Good question. Talia would like to know herself.

"It is a gift." Nuno tightened his grasp.

"Let me have a look." The guard did not pause for an answer when he took possession of the box. Nuno had no choice but to comply.

The officer motioned to another officer, who held a leash to a dog wearing a blue apron. The black and tan beagle waddled its way to the package in the officer's hand and then waddled over to Nuno, but the dog wasn't interested in either. The officer handed the package to Talia with a tip of his beret, and the two resumed their haste to the train. Once they settled into a pair of private seats towards the back, Talia reviewed her checklist.

Wallet? Check. Passport? Check. A manila box Nuno's been obsessed with since Talia met him? Check.

Nuno snatched the manila box from Talia before she could examine it further, but she had managed to gather as much information as she could short of opening it. It was heavy, unlabeled, and tightly packed. Thanks to the guard, it was definitely not something dangerous.

She buttoned the hidden inner pocket of her jacket against her chest. The reflection in the fingerprinted window multiplied the tar pits beneath her eyes. She rested her forehead on the cold seat in front of her in an elongated sigh, and watched the remaining passengers board in slow motion as though choreographed within a muted music video.

She couldn't rid herself of the conversation with Tia Maria earlier that day. Her great-aunt was clearly not in her right mind, yet Talia believed her claim that her uncle Carlos did exist.

Whether he was still alive or in Portugal was yet to be discovered. Although the nurses insisted the picture was taken at a vineyard in Gaia, it wasn't proof of where her uncle lived once he returned. But it was a starting point.

What did her great-aunt mean when she said her uncle wasn't right? Was he unhealthy or mentally unstable? She begged her mother not to let him go. Go where?

Talia watched as the smoke from the train moved the shadows along the buildings they passed. How credible a witness could her great-aunt be if she was commanding a grade-schooler to stop her teen brother from leaving town? That's a lot of pressure to put on a child.

According to the date on the photo from her great-aunt's apartment, her mother would have been too young to have any say in her older brother's departure. She was barely old enough for fourth grade. Talia wondered if her mother missed her brother deep down, underneath her defensive mask. She now understood the heavy burden she must have carried all those years.

Pai Paolo warned her that her uncle lived, and that Vovó sent him letters to an address in Porto. Another clue that led north. Worst of all, if Jared's bookstore encyclopedia was right, and they were the same Carlos, her uncle may well be a notorious felon. It explained why Vovó banished him from the family and their memories.

Still, he couldn't be the only Carlos Batista in the whole country. Carlos is a common Portuguese name. Talia tried to convince herself that it could be just coincidence. Problem was, she didn't believe in coincidences. Everything happens for a reason.

The train quaked into motion, driving farther into the distance the slatted triangle awnings that hung like open parachutes above *Gare de Oriente*. Designed by Spanish architect

Santiago Calatrava in time for the opening of the Expo '98 world fair, the Gothic transportation hub located on the eastern side of Lisbon is one of the world's largest stations, serving over seventy-five million travelers as a high speed rail, subway, and bus station. Housing the rail to major cities in the country, such as Coimbra, Braga, Faro, and Porto, Talia expected to visit the station at least once during her stay.

She sat in quiet awe at the way the lights illuminated the modern structure, a broad wave of warm yellow beaconed in the center of the starless sky, begging her to return before it was too late, though she knew it already was. She feigned sleep to observe Nuno's reflection nestling into the seat behind her. He had slotted the box between himself and the window, laid his jacket on top, and leaned his elbow against it.

Talia saw Nuno's green eyes close, waited a minute to be sure, and then snuck out her phone from inside her backpack. Fiddling with the cracked screen, she managed to get to her messages.

Jill had left her a voicemail. "Please be careful. This guy would kill two innocent kids. Do *not* think he won't harm you. Please call me if you need *anything*."

There was still no word from Caryn.

THIRTEEN

HIS HEAD CROWNED WITH A FEDORA, the old man rests his stout frame on the throne coring the sanctuary, its yellow posterior facing the main entrance.

On the cement floor surrounding him, red candles trace the lines of a chalked daisy sigil, the tip of each petal showcasing assorted pictograms. Young boys and girls lie above them, yellow petals sprinkled across their white linens, eyelids fluttering, limbs restless.

In the chalk flower's eye, bowls of fragrant violet holy water lie at the old man's bare feet. To his right and left burns urns of incense, their aroma identical to the hallways of a Catholic church. He stoops his head into a silent prayer, a moment of pause enlightened by the slow roar of hand-beaten drums drifting from the dark corner.

The old man raises the copper cup from the edge of the throne's armrest, guzzles the distilled rum inside, and adjusts the empty vessel near the candles at the base of his throne. A clay ashtray holds cigars and a pack of wooden matches.

The old man strikes a match against the concrete, ignoring the strips lining the sides of the matchbox. The flame erupts as he tugs from the opposite end of the cigar, puffing several times before a plume of smoke escapes his chapped lips. He steals a few drags, exhales with purpose, and then extinguishes the smoldering nub into the ashtray.

After a minute of wheezing, he clears his throat and mouths a prayer. His whispers ascend, inaudible, but with the shake of a stadium speaker. The room pulsates with the breath of his words, the currents of sound palpable. As the waves pass through his audience, they plunge into a trance, the pain lifting from their tense faces, their bodies suspended in mid-movement.

The children lie paralyzed, no longer shifting in their chalk petals, sweat beading on their necks and foreheads. Then a hand twitches. Then two. Then all at once, the children convulse into seizures, the strength of their spasms lifting their torsos into the air as the old man builds his chant into a thunderous undertone.

Facing his palms to the sky, the old man lifts himself from his throne with a grunt. As if lifting the weight of a car, he levitates the children with a stroke of his hands, the children's convulsions quieting in mid-air. With each creak of his aging back, the children climb higher until over six feet of air separates their languid bodies from the floor.

The old man repeats the chant in a roar, his arms outstretched above his head, his toes nudging the concrete. The whites of his eyes glisten in the dungeon. With his mouth agape and pointed to the ceiling, he releases smog from his lungs like a ghost from his chest. He falls to his knees, bones cracking against the stone, his arms stationary. A tear swells in his eye as he holds in a cough.

Not of their own free will, the children outstretch their arms and link hands, forming a reflection of the drawing beneath them, their loose robes and tussled hair dangling in the atmosphere in between. As their fingers touch, the flames inflate with crisp energy. The swell elevates the children farther, and then plummets them four feet, their limbs brushing the cement.

Dropping his hands, the old man slumps over panting onto the cold slab. Releasing their interlocking fingers, the children crash onto the concrete, the gust of their fall warping the chalked symbol and diffusing all the burning candles across the room.

FOURTEEN

THE CONCENTRIC COLONNADE paved with cobblestone mosaics led up to the *Sanctuario de Fátima* and much resembled its sister church, the Vatican, but on a smaller scale. Although the first stone was laid in 1928, the basilica that towered above the colonnade was not approved by the Roman Catholic Church for another two years. Atop its 200-foot bell tower, an illuminated bronze cross pierced into the heavens, and rose high above the bronze statue of the Sacred Heart of Jesus, who receives followers into the sanctuary.

Nossa Senhora de Fátima or Our Lady of Fatima, is a loving name for the Virgin Mary, commemorating a series of events in 1917, when the Virgin Mary, accompanied by angels, allegedly appeared to three shepherd children near the village of Fátima on the thirteenth day of each month for six consecutive months. During these encounters, the children performed rosary prayers and confessions, but the mystery rested in Fátima's secrets, a three-part message of which only the first two parts had been publicly revealed for decades.

The first secret included a prophecy of a typical hell scene of fire-scorched caves and enslaved sinners writhing in pain. According to one of the children, Sister Lucía, the Virgin Mary pleaded for the consecration of Russia in hopes that it would absolve them of their sins during the First World War, and that the war would end once society ceased offending God.

The third secret had been buried in the Vatican's annals throughout the twentieth century. Some speculated the Vatican kept its vaults locked to conceal the prediction of chaos in the Catholic Church and the loss of many of its faithful followers. Talia recalled the barrage of news stories back in the States about moral and legal troubles in the Church and wondered whether those rumored predictions might have come true.

In 2000, the Vatican revealed the third secret, a prophecy of the failed assassination attempt of Pope John Paul II, in May of 1981, and the pope thanked Fátima for his survival. Many continue to believe the Vatican held back a one-page document that prophesied the impending apocalypse, but the Vatican maintained its position that the entirety of the text for the third secret was revealed that day.

The controversy didn't discourage many, as devotees continued to visit. Over 70,000 people pilgrimage to the basilica every year in May and October. Barefoot mothers and old ladies crawled the dirt path along the edge of the grounds, praying their sacrifice would be enough for Fátima to grant them their one request.

Sheltered underneath the curved path that traced the colonnade with pillars, Talia noticed a tall blond man wearing a blue shirt with sleeves that hugged his biceps. He looked like Jared from behind. She felt compelled to shadow him, but as she edged closer, a little brunette girl ran into his arms. Talia frowned. It wasn't him.

"Do you believe in *Nossa Senhora?*" Nuno asked.

Discussions about religion irked Talia. She found herself limiting contact with her paternal uncle to only special occasions due to this overwhelming aversion. The conversation always began innocently enough and then, just before Talia could squirm herself out, her uncle asked if she had ever read *The Book.* Talia politely tried to remove herself from the conversation without admitting her true beliefs—of course, not before listening to a ten-minute sermon claiming Jesus saved his life.

"I believe in the power of positivity," Talia said, crossing the wide courtyard that on special days can hold over a hundred thousand visitors.

"*Uma Portuguesa* who doesn't believe in God? I cannot believe it is true," Nuno said, walking beside her with the box still tucked under his arm.

"Clearly, you believe," Talia said.

Nuno nodded, his chest raised.

"My dad thinks he failed me because I don't believe." Talia adjusted her necklace. "I told him I don't need religion to know how to be a good person."

"*Claro,*" Nuno said. "Believing in God does not make you good. There are many who believe in God who are not good people."

"Exactly," Talia said. "I just don't feel the need for organized religion in my life. It doesn't give me anything I don't have already. I guess for some it provides a sense of release and hope. I can understand why they'd want that."

"The world can be a terrible place."

"I do love the architecture, though. Churches have some of the most beautiful architecture. You could even say they're divine," Talia said. "But I think the power of prayer lies in the belief that their prayers will work, not that a god answers their prayers. The power of positive energy."

Talia marched up the stairs to the modern sanctuary, a minimalistic and airy beech room with a yellow mosaic wall set as a backdrop to a gold modern impression of Jesus on the cross hanging behind the altar. "I suppose I believe my great-grandmother was trying to speak to me through visions of bees, and that my cousin could have cursed me with the evil eye or a hexed meal, but I'm not sure about the rest."

Nuno stood by her at the base of the sanctuary aisle. "Do you not have to believe in God in order to believe in the devil?"

Talia had never considered religion in that way, but it is a yin and yang. You must endure evil in order to appreciate good—the balance of energy in the universe. Talia couldn't say she was an atheist, like Jared. She was more agnostic. She believed there was something at work, just not anything man has conjured up so far. The power of opposing energies seemed a more plausible story.

Nuno huffed, transferring the box to his opposite arm.

"Should I carry that for a while?" Talia asked.

"No." Nuno tightened his grip.

When they arrived back in the colonnade, Talia was overwhelmed by a strong urge to urinate and convinced Nuno to accompany her to the bathroom building near the pilgrimage entrance. While in the stall, Talia multi-tasked in order to check her phone. She didn't know why she didn't want Nuno to know she checked her email, or find out about her contact. Talia attributed her secrecy to the fact that journalists do not divulge their sources, but it wasn't a convincing argument.

Having not received a word from Caryn or her source, Talia decided to call Jared. When his photo displayed on her cracked phone, Talia's heart sunk. How could she explain that she was spending their trip with a man she spent the night with, a man that Jared had already been jealous of since their first meeting? He was right to be. Talia hung up and composed herself. Alone in the bathroom, she washed her hands in one of the scuffed sinks. There was no mirror to check herself. She wiped her forehead with the dampened paper towel she used to dry her hands.

When she walked out, Nuno was not where she left him. She scoured the perimeter but he wasn't in sight. Concluding that he must have taken the path that zigzagged around the grounds and ended at the stairs leading to the most replicated Fátima statue, Talia started her own pilgrimage.

Having completed this path many times before, she didn't stop at the smaller statues and plaques scattered along the way. Nuno was not anywhere on the trail within Talia's line of sight, but once she arrived at the stairs, she felt obligated to climb them. She wasn't fond of leaving things unfinished.

On a stone plinth a foot high sat the four-part white statue of the Angel of Peace preaching to the three children—two sisters and a brother—kneeling in prayer before her. Talia stood alone atop that hill, studying the awed but calm detail in their faces. The pathways were vacant at that moment, which Talia assumed was due to the mass being held at the church.

She was startled to witness from the corner of her eye one of the statues of the girls wobble, searching for a more comfortable kneeling pose. The little girl stood up, jolting Talia back with horror. Her sister followed, and Talia rubbed her eyes in disbelief, inching backwards.

The hallucination of the girls, who were now playing in the field around their own statues, made Talia wonder if someone had spiked the *Prego*, a Portuguese steak sandwich, which she devoured when she arrived in town with Nuno that afternoon. Talia found a tall stone to sit on, hoping it would end her paranoia. When she looked up, the little girls morphed—headbands instead of scarves draped on their heads, their dresses resembling the matching set her cousins wore in photos from the crime scene. Talia gulped.

The girls jerked their heads and gaped at her as they floated closer, their mouths moving silently. As they neared, their whispers grew louder. Transfixed by her curiosity, Talia suppressed her instinct to run and instead attempted to translate what the girls repeated. Curiosity always trumped Talia's desire for safety—not a terrible or unique trait in a reporter.

Her cousins traveled fluidly, now hovering a foot above the ground, at Talia's eye level, a few feet in front of her.

"Prima," the girls repeated in unison. "We are waiting for you."

Talia screamed and ran towards the church, almost tripping on the way down the hill. While looking back to be sure the girls weren't following her, Talia crashed into Nuno.

"What is wrong?" Nuno asked as he held Talia's arms to calm her.

"Nothing. I'm fine. I'm fine." Talia ran her shaky hand through her hair. "Where have you been?"

"I needed to make a phone call. Are you ready to go?"

Talia had been ready for hours.

———

ONE OF FÁTIMA'S sixty-two church bells rang seven times in the misty distance, stirring the scattered fog engulfing the main bell tower. The slivered moon crept behind the trees before its bright rival set for the evening.

A small white ambulance zoomed past them, its blue emergency lights spinning beams through the trees. Talia traced the beams to a dim driveway less than a block ahead of them. The dampened parking lot at the end of the driveway sat vacant, minus a beaten car and two windowless yellow vans rusting together to the far left of the front entrance. The only working sconce at the front door flickered to poorly define a pathway in the evening haze.

For efficiency, the more rural parts of Portugal offered their residents small clinics and pharmacies as part of the country's free healthcare system. Though the small medical facilities are open 24 hours a day, only a telephone and a phone number are posted at night outside the darkened entrance. A doctor or pharmacist was always on call. It typically took them around fifteen minutes to arrive.

Talia recalled an instance when she experienced this for herself. After spending the day pulling weeds from her cousin's garden, drawing a few nicks to her skin, her entire body broke out into a rash, one limb at a time, until even a cold bath in calamine lotion didn't soothe the itch. In need of drastic measures in a rural town, Talia's mother drove all over searching for the nearest pharmacy. A phone call and thirty minutes later, Talia was prescribed a shot of miracle antihistamine and a large tube of prescription-strength hydrocortisone to rub on her skin. By the next morning, the rash was gone.

We are waiting for you, the girls' lilting whispers echoed in her skull. Jared would think she was losing it. She also needed to stop thinking about Jared.

"Are you sure I should do this?" Talia asked. "Maybe you would be better for this job. It's your friend in there after all."

Nuno leaned over to hug Talia, who flinched at first. Her tight shoulders loosened as she inhaled Nuno's familiar scent of cloves and lavender.

"Drop the box at the front desk. The nurse will know what to do."

There was something about that manila box that Talia was attracted to, as if it had some pull over her the way it did Nuno. Whenever Nuno wasn't looking, she'd find herself staring at the box, trying to find a way to open it without being caught. It seemed impossible with packing tape lining its every seam. Without some kind of replacement tape on hand, and Nuno being distracted for at least ten minutes, she didn't see how it could be done. He never let the box out of his sight.

Nonetheless, Nuno was an asset to Talia's search for the murderer. He could help her maneuver through the world of occultism in a way Talia could not do alone. He knew the ins and outs of Portugal and even offered her a place to stay in Porto, an invitation any poor college graduate on vacation would have a hard time declining. Plus, he was nice to look at.

Her stomach turned. Talia so easily moved on after Jared. How could she just leave him in a foreign land to run off with a handsome European? When did she become one of *those* girls?

Once she solved the case, Talia hoped to reunite with Caryn and Jared to beg their forgiveness for deserting them. Jared would claim Caryn left them first, and he was right. But Talia could only blame herself for walking out on Jared. Fortunately, Talia had plenty to occupy her mind at that moment, which helped her not to dwell on her long list of past mistakes.

"*Ora bem.* I will be here between the vans. Tell the nurse it is for *Senhor Pedreira.* Say it for me, *por favor.*"

"*Olá, isto é para Senhor Pedreira,*" Talia repeated, no longer disguising her fluency.

"Perfect. *Boa sorte.*" Nuno wished her good luck.

And there it was, in her hands, the box she'd been eager to hold since she saw it in Nuno's hotel room in Lisbon. She wanted to rip it open like a present, to laugh and cry when she finally saw what it held inside, but Nuno's vigilance did not waver.

The walk to the dilapidated building couldn't have taken more than a minute, but to Talia, it might as well have been an hour. She focused on every crack in the asphalt to divert herself from the fear multiplying in her gut. One of the automatic sliding glass doors rattled open to display the hospital's familiar interior. It was not just any hospital. It was the hospital in her dream two nights before.

Her prophetic visions had never been sharper than since Vovó's passing. It was as if Vovó was able to spiritually connect with Talia more in death than in life. Vovó could have been warning Talia about this hospital. In her dream, Caryn called for help, meaning Caryn could be in there and in trouble.

She trudged on with a heavy step. Smaller than she remembered, the hospital was home to ten rooms and a few offices, not the infinite expanse it had been in her mind. No one manned the front desk to the left, and no one sat in the mustard pleather chairs lining the waiting room to the right. A black and white television mounted in the corner above the seating broadcasted a modern Portuguese novella.

Talia bent her knotted shoulders back with the box still in hand, and then inhaled a long breath through her nose. Her hands trembled and her stomach twisted at every step, stricken by the dread of stepping back into the nightmare that remained so fresh in her mind. Talia censored the urge to scream out Caryn's name in the hope that she'd answer, mimicking her nightmare.

Concerned about leaving the manila box unguarded at the front desk, Talia tiptoed down the hallway she had previously sprinted in her mind. She crept to the first door and peeked into an empty hospital room with beige curtains, concrete windows, and crisp white bed linens. Tiptoeing further into the hallway, Talia heard a faint woman's voice escalating in the distance. Her instincts rushed her into the next open door, the box still under her arm. That nurse was most likely the nurse Talia owed the box to, but she couldn't give it away just yet. Not before she figured out what was in it.

The musty storage room lay unfurnished, aside from a rusted file cabinet sitting in the far corner. Talia held her breath when she heard a woman's footsteps pass, and then pulled open the bottom drawer, too warped to fit back into its hole. It was crammed with piles of dusty pictures, letters and forms filled out by hand in Portuguese, all wilted, caked with mold, and gummed together.

Talia placed the manila box to the side and shuffled through the pile of stationary, searching for any office supplies, when she saw, to her surprise, a familiar picture. It was of Caryn and herself in Belém, eating their pastries, the day they last spoke. Talia noticed something else about the picture—at a tall table in the far right corner of the photo stood Pierre, shadowed by the sun. He spied on the three of them while drinking a *bica*. The picture was taken at least six hours before they met.

Jared took the photo with his vintage Holga camera, which always left a few burned spots where the sun snuck in through the left corner. No matter how many ways Jared duct-taped it, the spots could not be removed, yet he was always anxious to play with the contraption. He said it gave the photos character.

Talia seized the Holga photo and a few of the folded forms and letters surrounding it in a fistful, shoved them into the outside pocket of her backpack to accompany Vovó's watch and a few travel cords, and then zipped it.

Nothing in the room could be used to open the manila box. Its packing tape was too secure to tear without a sharp object. She picked at the corners of the tape with her short fingernails, but it must have been sealed with hot glue, it wouldn't budge. At that point, she lost concern for getting caught, too consumed by curiosity. Maybe another room would have a pair of scissors or a knife.

Balancing the box, she ducked her head through the door-jamb. When the hallway cleared, she sprinted toward the sliver of light escaping from a half-open door at the far end of the hall, and crouched behind the gurneys along the walls. For an empty clinic, there sure was a lot of equipment hanging around. The hospital looked more like a front for a drug ring than an institution of health.

Caryn was nowhere in the building. In fact, there were no patients at all. There was only an office at the end of the hall. Its modern industrial style resembled offices found in the pages of an interior decorator magazine, and was unlike any other room in the building. The white walls exhibited colorful abstract paintings. One Jackson Pollock-esque painting set the conference area apart from the rest of the office. There, a set of leather seats encircled a mahogany coffee table.

The large wooden desk nearest the doorway displayed rows of frames, a few still holding the sample photos they came with—stock stills featuring a staged family with a rental pet, all too content with life to be real (except the dog—he was always happy to be there). Some frames still wore the price label on their backs. One of the desk's file drawers was left ajar, with a briefcase wedged into it.

A discussion between men arose in the office. Talia slid in closer for a better view. It was Nuno, arguing in Portuguese with a thin man hidden in the shadow.

"I told you I did not want her in here," the man said in Portuguese. It was a voice Talia recognized.

"What was I supposed to do with her?" Nuno said. "I needed to preoccupy her while we spoke, since you insisted I visit. I told you I had this under control."

"And you think she can be trusted?" the man asked. "What if she sees something? She is not stupid, Nuno. She was suspicious of me, and if you keep acting this way, she will be suspicious of you, too. We cannot have that happen."

"She thinks I am waiting outside," Nuno said. "I needed to make sure you had everything you needed to proceed. She is already having visions. I knew she would be the one."

"Where is the box?" The shadowed man's voice trembled.

"I had her give it to your nurse," Nuno said with a twitch in his throat.

"*És maluco!* What if she opened it?" The man shadow wavered in and out of the light.

"*Ó pá,* calm down. She would not do that," Nuno said as he fidgeted with his watch.

"How can you be so sure?"

"I will handle her." Nuno casted his hands to his sides.

The shadowed man stepped halfway underneath the green tiffany lamp to the right of his desk, highlighting a pair of sockless penny loafers. Though it was a strain, Talia identified him as soon as she caught his eye, and not a minute sooner. If Pierre was there, where was Caryn?

Pierre launched a flood of French and Portuguese curses, waving Nuno towards the opposite side of the room, where Talia assumed he must have entered. Nuno scrambled to calm the man, but it only succeeded in snowballing the tantrum. Pierre's sudden madness created the perfect ruse for Talia's escape without being caught.

Talia couldn't deduce what Nuno meant by her being *the one*, but it was clear she was at least the one who caused Pierre's roars. Nuno seemed to have no idea why his French friend became enraged, and Talia planned to keep it that way. As she turned to make a run for it, she ran into a woman twice her size wearing gray scrubs storming down the hallway. Her dark hair, streaked with burgundy, wilted at her shoulders. It was the nurse. It was too late to run, so Talia took a deep breath to compose her thoughts.

"What are you doing?" the woman asked in Portuguese.

"*Boa noite, isto é para Senhor Pedreira,*" Talia recited without forethought. She handed the woman one of the old letters she stole from the supply closet instead of the manila box as she had promised Nuno.

The nurse gave Talia a perplexed look and said, "Give me that box, little girl. Don't waste my time."

Talia smiled at the impatient nurse and scampered towards the front door, pretending to be an ignorant American who didn't understand her language, but the nurse wasn't fooled. She didn't allow Talia to leave until she handed over the box. Talia had no choice. She planted the box in the nurse's hands. Before Talia could change her mind, the nurse ripped it away. Pleased with herself, a grin broadened across the nurse's face as if she had discovered the Holy Grail.

"*Agora sai daqui.*" The nurse motioned for Talia to leave, her creepy grin lingering.

The nurse's vigilance reflected in the front window as Talia wandered through the sliding glass door. When she looked back, the nurse raced towards Pierre's office.

"How did it go?" Nuno asked, out of breath. "Did you give the nurse the box?" He paced, running his hand through his hair every few seconds.

"Yep. All done."

"You were in there a long time." Nuno looked at his watch.

"No one was at the front desk. I had to wait," she lied. "Did you see what all that commotion was about?"

"Shh," Nuno said.

"Guess not," Talia whispered.

Nuno pointed at a man in a green uniform moving through the parking lot. The security guard surveyed the clinic with his cupped palms against the window, passing over Talia and Nuno, who were hidden behind the vans to his left. Not finding anything suspicious, he walked in the sliding door.

"*Vamos!*" Nuno wrangled Talia behind the building. Once clear, they sprinted toward the train station until they ran out of breath.

"Okay, that's it." Talia panted as she slowed down, finding a tree to lean against.

"*Sim*, we are far enough." Nuno rested against the tree next to her.

Talia wet her lips. "I thought I heard your voice in there."

"In the clinic?" He straightened his posture.

"Yes. I thought I overheard you talking with someone." She resisted the urge to tug at one of her ragged fingernails.

"*Não sei*. Someone must have the same voice. Very strange." His cheeks flushed.

"Yes, very. I thought maybe you decided to talk to your friend after all." Talia cleared her throat, conscious of not sounding frustrated. She didn't want to scare him off.

Talia wanted to ask Nuno outright whether he was conspiring with Pierre to con her friends, but she couldn't come up with a good motive to back her argument. She had nothing but far-fetched theories and doubt. Nuno may not have been the safest companion to Porto, but abandoning him then would be rash. If the duo were indeed planning a con, Talia's awareness gave her the upper hand, and she planned to use it to stop them before they succeeded.

"I wish, but I could not take the risk. I stood outside waiting, like I told you," Nuno said.

Talia's head throbbed. She knew Nuno was lying, but she couldn't say anything just yet. She shifted her weight from one leg to the other, her eyelids heavy. "I need a nap."

"We can sleep on the way to Porto," Nuno said. "Stopping is dying."

FIFTEEN

THE DAMP FOLIAGE grazed Talia's ankles as she raced barefoot across the rows of barren vines in search of a place to hide. A reflection from the amulet bouncing around her neck blinded her on occasion, causing her unsteady footing as she trampled the farmlands. Her heart thumped in her throat, her breath erratic.

It was too late.

A masked man hooked her arm and wrenched it back, bucking her knees and twisting her ankle. The musky scent of sandalwood swamped Talia's senses as the man fastened her wrists behind her back with rope. The echoes of her screams pierced her eardrums.

A welcome drizzle cooled Talia's cheeks, but she could not tell whether the water had come from the breeze that rose from the river, or the fog suspended above her.

A sort of sunrise emerged behind her, warming Talia's back. She jerked her head back to an angry mob trailing behind her. They wielded torches, farm tools, and copies of *The Old Testament*.

Their howls were hard to interpret until they were so close that Talia could smell the ends of her hair singe.

"*Bruxa, bruxa!*" the throngs of bloodthirsty Christians chanted in unison.

The sky was as bright as day, and Talia noticed the pile of branches stacked in a teepee form in front of her. She panted. Digging her bare heels into the grassy field, she unsuccessfully deterred her captors, who continued to tow her toward the heap.

"You don't understand. I'm not a witch!" she cried.

Beyond the fields, she caught a glimpse of a circular building with an illuminated gold dome, a brass cross staking its tallest point.

Before she could react, she was tied to the pole that arose from the stack of branches. The flames mounted and a bead of sweat gathered behind her ears. Talia searched the herd for a familiar face in hopes of stirring enough sympathy to save herself.

A face appeared in the crowd as if sent by God himself. It was Jared, his eyes cold and his expression hard as he raised his rake above him. He didn't holler like the rest, and despite his stoic appearance, a tear swelled in his left eye. As it rolled down his face, it stained his cheek with a crimson smear.

"Jared," she screamed, contorting her body in an attempt to free herself. "I deserve this, I know I do. I realize now what I've done. Please forgive me, Jared. I'm so sorry. Please get me out of here."

Jared followed the masses, shaking his head, ignoring her cries.

The flame only scaled higher, so Talia focused on accepting her fate with dignity. But when the inferno lapped at her toes, she resumed screaming, with the smolder of her own charred flesh choking the air from her lungs.

SHRIEKING and gasping for air after her latest nightmare, Talia found herself stretched out on the cold floor of the train station in Caxarias, the closest station to the Fátima shrine, over fifteen kilometers away. The tiled floor felt cool and refreshing to Talia, having just escaped a cave of fire in her subconscious. It was no longer a foreign feeling to awaken to a sea of concerned faces.

"Are you okay, Talia?" she heard Nuno ask.

"This is why I hate sleeping at the station," Talia croaked.

"*Então*, you saw what you wanted to see, now leave!" Nuno shouted at the spectators, then tended to Talia. "Are you sure you are okay, Talia?"

"Yes. I'm fine." Talia lifted herself up to rest on the chair she recalled sitting on earlier that night, Nuno hovering over her as if spotting her at the gym. "What time is it?"

The rising sun slipped through the windows of the small, unimpressive square building, its weak rays not yet heating the concrete structure. A couple of hours remained before the first train to Porto departed in the morning. Their rush the night before proved useless, as the last train had already departed by the time they reached the ticket booth. Without a place to stay or much money to spare, Nuno and Talia resolved to sleep on the benches of the station until their train arrived four hours later.

"Was it another of your prophetic dreams?" Nuno asked, almost fascinated.

"I think so," Talia said, unwilling to elaborate.

"It was bad, *sim*?"

She could still feel the flames on her neck. "Yes. How did I get on the floor?"

"You fell off the chair, but you looked so comfortable I let you sleep. Then you started to kick and scream, and everyone came over. There was not much I could do to stop them. *Desculpa*."

"It's not your fault. I've had these nightmares long before you came along. As my grandmother used to say, it's my cross to bear."

It was true. Nuno hadn't caused her latest nightmare, or the ninety before then. He was, however, the source of her growing anxiety. She couldn't deny his actions since she met him the day before had been suspicious. There were the angry calls, the unlabeled manila box, and then there was Pierre. Nuno told Pierre she was *the one*, which was never a good omen. *The one* always has to sacrifice something, and Talia wasn't willing to give anything up.

Maybe she already had, though. Caryn disappeared. Talia didn't find her at the clinic, which was a relief, but she was still missing. More than ever, she needed to hear Caryn's voice, but she felt uneasy making the call in her current company.

Talia bit her lip, the taste of iron on her tongue. What had she gotten herself into?

———

THE DESERTED CENTURY-OLD *São Bento* train station was congested with passengers arriving along with Talia and Nuno that early morning. The sun peeked through the grey clouds dotting across the arched skylights as Talia and Nuno debarked their train.

It had been years since Talia visited Porto, but the station remained the same architectural wonder. Floor to ceiling, twenty-thousand complex blue and white painted *azulejos* lined the walls, depicting historical scenes such as the Battle of Arcos de Valdevez, or Prince Henry the Navigator conquering Cueta, Morocco.

Magnificent arched windows hung below the tall ceilings, and chiseled pillars divided the tiled scenes.

Throughout her youth, Talia had always been fascinated with Lisbon, planning a visit for a few days at the head or tail end of her trips, but as she aged so did her appreciation for Porto, the lovely old port town sliced by the Douro River. Known best for its eponymous Port wine, Porto has managed to keep its old world charm with its bright buildings and cobblestone streets. Its rolling hillsides bed the fertile Douro River, its distinct vined hills cutting across the top of the country.

Cultivating grapes from as early as 2000 B.C., Porto constitutes the third oldest environmentally protected wine region in the world. Akin to the French cities of Champagne and Bordeaux, laws prohibit wines not produced in this region of the Douro from being officially named Port. Only locally-grown grapes aged and fortified with *Aguardente vinica*, a neutral grape spirit similar to Brandy, give the sweet dessert wine its world renown.

Talia hardly considered *Aguardente* a light spirit, regardless of its innocent grape composition. In America, southern slang terms the liquor, often made from undrinkable wines, as *firewater*. At harvest season, its distillation saturated the atmosphere of her father's hometown village with a harsh stench that stung Talia's throat and eyes. *It will put color in your cheeks*, Talia recalled her grandfather saying, his cheeks frequently rosy.

As usual in Porto most times of year, the skies threatened to leak. An ominous cloud crept overhead. Talia drew her jacket in tight to shield against a draft that slapped her hair across her cheeks.

Though eager to begin her journey around the city to find the killer who could be her uncle, she didn't know where to begin. The clues she obtained in Lisbon were limited. The nurses at her great-aunt's resting home were convinced the picture of her uncle was taken in the Gaia, the town right across the river from the city of Porto, home to all the Port wineries. Pai Paolo suggested her uncle might live at an address with the number 1209, yet Vovó suggested a time of 12:09. Talia didn't know who to believe.

Weaving through the throngs of passengers, a herd of cattle were ushered to their inevitable demise, and a flashback of Talia's nightmare sent her gut into a rollercoaster loop. She kept the paranoia at bay as she watched the green country landscape dash past her train car window earlier that morning, but her grasp on sanity had slackened since her arrival in Porto. The air thinned around her. She couldn't catch a full breath.

Talia hadn't yet digested that one of her night terrors had come true when she visited the hospital in Fátima at Nuno's request the night before. It was the first time since Vovó's passing that a vision had become reality. The frosty hallways, the grimy fixtures, even the black and white vintage television bolted to the wall: all of it appeared in her nightmare two days prior.

Jared was wrong. Her nightmares do come true. What she didn't anticipate, besides the small size of the clinic, was the appearance of Pierre. Where had Caryn gone now that he was in Fátima?

Caryn and Jared could have met up in Lisbon after Talia left. Why hadn't either of them contacted her? Jared had every reason to be angry at Talia, but Caryn made her choices. She didn't deserve Caryn's silence. Just because she was not at Pierre's side didn't mean he had done something with her, but Talia couldn't think of another reason why she wouldn't have reached out to her by now.

Until then, Talia had no reason to suspect that Nuno and Pierre knew each other. Nuno admitted the friend in Fátima was his frantic caller the first night she spent with him. The photo from Jared's Holga camera exposed Pierre's spying on the three of them at the pastry shop in Belém. She also met Nuno the afternoon before, at the restaurant on *Rua Agusta*.

It appeared the two men aimed to separate the group. What they intended to accomplish was still a mystery. Pierre said there are a lot of places to hide in this country. It seemed Talia found Pierre's hiding spot. He didn't look pleased.

The new turn of events didn't sway Talia into distrusting Nuno any more than she did already, having known him for less than three days. Her lack of skepticism was unusual—lesser events would have typically worried her—but Nuno could help find her uncle and the murderer, be they one and the same; he knew the scene. Since initiating this investigation, no one else has been as willing to support her quest, except perhaps Caryn.

A hunched old woman in a black shawl almost knocked Talia into a trashcan when she found her grandson, her excitement fueling a surge of adrenaline strength. Though fuming, Talia held her tongue, respecting the old woman's family. The incident brought to mind the ghosts of the girls floating from the statues of Lucía and her sister on the grounds of Fátima the day before, their pale faces coated in disappointment. Talia was unable to escape their eerie murmurs.

We are waiting for you. A swell of nausea rushed her esophagus like a punch to the gut. She was unable to discern from their whispers whether little Lucía meant they were waiting for Talia to solve their murders or to join them in the afterlife.

"Where do you want to go first?" Nuno asked.

Recognizing that Nuno was not proposing a journey to either heaven or hell, Talia replied, "I need to check my messages," and directed Nuno through the masses to the tram headed to the *Bolhão* district of the city.

The Café Majestic, one of the Europe's top historical coffee-houses, did not always bear that title. Its original name "Elite" was replaced shortly after the Art Nouveau building's grand opening in 1921. Located on *Rua Santa Catarina*, a pedestrian-only avenue that is home to many local shops and restaurants, Café Majestic was once a hot spot for bohemians, intellectuals, and the glamorous cultural elite of *La Belle Époque* in the roaring 1920's.

Due to financial troubles, the historic coffeehouse shuttered its doors from 1983 until its grand re-opening in 1994, two years after the government released ownership. Just as the country had envisioned, the ornate Art Deco architecture was restored to its original glory, a treasured landmark in Portuguese history.

Its peach interior was juxtaposed with lavish mahogany arched mirrors that striped the walls, with a pair of cheerful marble cherubs brandishing every column. Brass chandeliers draped low under the coffer ceilings, the marble tabletops emulating their glow. Talia and Nuno were led to a table at the far end of the café. The upholstered leather seats, bolted with brass to an engraved mahogany base, enveloped Talia in old world comfort.

Reasoning that she had resisted a pastry the morning before and had been running around the country burning calories, Talia allowed her sweet tooth to win the battle for breakfast that morning. She indulged herself on a *Cimbalinho*, the local nickname for a shot of espresso which is almost identical to the *Bica* in Lisbon, and *Rabanadas*, a Porto style French toast smothered in an egg custard sauce. It's a Majestic favorite.

Had it been later in the day, Talia may have instead ordered another local favorite, the *Francesinha*. Translating to "little French girl," the decadent sandwich is reminiscent of the French *Croque Monsieur* and is only available at restaurants in the Porto region. Instead of ham like its French counterpart, the locals used roasted meat or *linguiça*, a spicy Portuguese sausage, coated in melted cheese topped in a tomato beer sauce to be soaked up by the sliced bread.

Nuno didn't appear as ravenous as Talia, ordering a *Pingo*, a shot of espresso with a drop of milk, and a *pastel de nata*.

While she waited for her coffee, Talia tapped into the WiFi and downloaded her latest messages through the screen cracks, trying to be discreet.

"What are you looking for?" Nuno asked, just as Talia had expected.

"Work stuff," Talia said. "Maybe one of my contacts can give me something to find the killer. I sent them what I've found for certain so far. We'll see what they say."

"I thought you were looking for your uncle," Nuno said.

"I am, but I also need to finish my story. My editor is trying to get in touch with me, no doubt. She rarely lets this much time go by without checking up on me."

She wasn't exactly telling the truth. Talia fretted over her job, but her heart was fixed on avenging her family. She had to assume now that Nuno had been apprised of whatever Pierre may have learned from their conversation at the bar in Cascais.

Whatever was revealed in that short conversation, Talia knew it was Caryn who did so, her inhibition limited due to the devilish draw of the *Caiparinha*. The issue concerning Talia was what Caryn told him after they left. She was already spouting things to Pierre she shouldn't have, revealing more than what Talia was comfortable divulging to a stranger. What else did she say once they were alone?

Talia looked at her screen. Another cryptic message from her contact appeared. It read: *Diamond Jubilee*. Baffled, Talia tapped the words into her phone, but it resulted in a list of historical events surrounding the Queen's Diamond Jubilee in Canada in

1952 to commemorate the sixtieth anniversary of her ascension to the throne.

That can't be it.

The waiter swung by with their order. The *Rabanadas* were still as delicious as the nostalgia surrounding them.

Talia sipped her coffee and pondered. "Sorry, I have to do this." She hated people who spent an entire meal glued to their devices. At that moment, however, it was a necessary evil.

Attempting to narrow her results, Talia added "Porto" at the end of her search string. That seemed to do the trick. Diamond Jubilee was a *Colheita*, a single-harvest tawny Port aged over six decades in an oak barrel. Graham's cellars had exclusively produced this particular Colheita. Talia assumed her contact had suggested she visit the Graham's winery near the river. It was the only real lead she had.

"Want to go wine tasting?" Talia asked.

"We should finish eating first," Nuno said.

"Of course. We need a good base," Talia said as she rubbed her belly.

Nuno chuckled, smiling at Talia a beat too long.

Talia wolfed down her French toast, gulped her *Cimbalinho,* and requested the check when the waiter passed. Nuno barely finished his custard tart before Talia counted the tip.

"Have patience, *gatinha*," Nuno said.

"I'm patient, I just don't have much time." Talia smiled at her unintended play on words. "I'll be leaving town in a few days and I can't go back empty handed."

"I think you will find what you are looking for."

"How can you be so sure?" Talia saw the opportunity to get some answers.

"You are the type of girl that gets what she wants," Nuno said.

"Am I?"

Nuno nodded with his eyes closed.

"So then tell me, what was in that box you were carrying? You know, now that it's no longer in your possession. What was the nurse supposed to do with it?"

"That is history, Talia," Nuno said.

"It was yesterday," Talia said, grinding her teeth. "I promise not to tell anyone."

"I already told you, I do not know what is in the box. I just do as I am told."

"Okay. How about … Pierre? Do you know a man named Pierre?"

"*Desculpe*, who?" Nuno asked, poorly bluffing innocence.

"The guy who ran off with my friend, Caryn. His name was Pierre. Just wondering if you knew him."

"Why would you think I know him?"

"Just a hunch I guess." Talia sank her shoulders.

"Still worried about your friend, I see."

"Yeah, and the last person I saw her with was this guy Pierre. If you knew him, well, it sure would make my life easier. Thought it was worth the try."

"*Desculpe*," Nuno apologized.

"Did you talk to your friend at the clinic? Did he get the box?" Just like a journalist should, she tried a different tactic to get the answers she sought. Ask a question in diverse ways and maybe one of them will be the lucky winner.

Nuno paused. "Oh, *sim*, yes. *Obrigada*."

"No problem. I'm glad you were able to finally speak," Talia said. "I thought he may have been the one calling you. Whoever it was seemed frantic."

"We were able to discuss the issue."

"So what was the issue? I'm sorry. I've told you so much about my current situation, it's only fair I listen to yours."

"It is a long story," Nuno said.

"I can make time. After all, you have been more than accommodating this whole trip. The least I can do is listen."

"He is an old friend, from my days as a *cigano*. He is almost shameful for me to speak of. But I owe him a few debts I must repay."

"Debts as in money?"

"Much more than that." Nuno stirred his empty cup. "He saved my life."

"Really? How?" Talia asked.

"It is hard to explain," Nuno said. "We were young."

"So you're still paying off your debt, huh?"

"It would seem that way, yes. I owe him my life, but he is not an honest man. He asks too much of me. My debt will never be repaid."

"You could say your life is priceless."

Nuno laughed. "*Sim*, I could."

The two stuffed themselves and their bags into a green and black Mercedes taxi headed for the Douro River. When they arrived as far down *Rua São João* as cars were allowed, the two piled onto the sidewalk.

The busy street on which they stood was named after Saint John the Baptist, who as written in the Bible, saw the sharp edge of a guillotine after a bargain to dance with a princess had gone awry. The citizens of Porto have such a special affection for *São João*, they organize an annual citywide celebration in his name on the night of June 23. The centuries old festival is one of the largest in Portugal, which speaks volumes about a country that loves to celebrate its districts throughout August with fairs and live music that carry on until morning.

The festival of *São João* was rooted in an ancient pagan courtship ritual. The ritual consisted of knocking the one you desire on the head with a garland of garlic—or the inflatable hammer sold on every street corner today—to show your interest. Every *Bairro,* or neighborhood, decorated their streets and alleys weeks in advance, each with its own history and distinct style.

Visitors flocked into the streets as soon as the shops opened and carried on drinking and dancing until long after the fireworks burst above the *Ponte Dom Luis* bridge at midnight, their streaks of color reflecting like a prism in the dark river. There was no bad seat in the city.

The *Praça da Ribeira* was bustling as usual, the large courtyard teeming with an eclectic mix of tourists and locals dining and chatting in the open air. Bordering the northern coast of the Douro River, the boardwalk at the *Ribeirinha,* or Little River, housed two levels of shops and restaurants that were sculpted into the hillside—serving fresh, locally-caught fish with a variety of Portuguese wines, or selling knickknacks to tourists. The area had endured as the commercial epicenter of Porto since the Roman Empire, when the port, which became the city's namesake, was constructed.

The sky deepened. Nuno and Talia had just stepped onto the boardwalk when the first drops of a short-lived downpour hit her forehead. Well-versed in Porto's gloomy weather, the locals took shelter in the caves and restaurants that were already teeming with customers. Though Talia wasn't as vigilant as the locals, she managed to grab a dry spot in the tunnel, which cut through a half dozen restaurants, before the tourists caught on.

Nuno struck up a conversation with an older couple visiting from the Alentejo region of Portugal located in the middle of the country—an area comprised of farmlands and a few wine varietals. The couple struggled through their introversion to engage, so Talia chimed in to further ease their timidity. By the time the rain stopped, the four were cackling at the wet world around them.

Ponte Dom Luis I, the metal arch bridge connecting Porto to Gaia, towered behind the *Ribeirinha* boardwalk, clearing the fog in its way. Constructed in just five years, *Ponte Dom Luis I* became the longest bridge of its kind at time of completion in 1886. Its namesake, King Luis I, whose son became the slain King Carlos I, preferred the sciences to politics. Investing in oceanography, he established one of the world's first aquariums, *Áquario Vasco de Gama*, which today continues as a home to a large collection of marine life in Lisbon.

Though it was originally designed to carry road traffic on both levels, the top level of the *Ponte Dom Luis I* had been converted to a metro line and pedestrian walkway—the walkway Talia planned to climb in order to visit the wineries in Gaia on the opposite side of the Douro River. Although the clouds scattered, the puddles and slicks caused by the storm's urgent force had yet to dry. Climbing the bridge's many metal stairs to the top daunted her.

She spotted the Graham's cellar building across the river, the one her contact had hinted she visit in her latest cryptic message. Talia pointed to the winery. "There it is. That's where we need to go."

A path cut through a poverty-stricken area of the city and led up to the bridge. Brightly clothed elderly women leaned out of their iron balconies, their smocks clashing with the rainbow hues of their rundown bungalows. Towels and shirts pinned to clotheslines extended from poles posted along the side of the buildings, the air perfumed with sautéed fish and stone-baked bread.

Talia always played tourist when she wandered through those

paths, guilt-ridden for treading upon an already trampled community. Talia smiled with a lowered head at the mothers flashing concerned brows as she passed.

Views of the Douro River and the two cities that bordered it were spectacular from atop the bridge, even through the haze that danced around them. The fog enchanted the riverside, its gothic influence peeping through the spaces in between the early afternoon sun and the hovering storm clouds.

To the left of the bridge, the hill peaked with a round church, its gold dome crowned with a cross. Talia recognized the building from her most recent nightmare, or at least she thought she did. As she slow-roasted on the stake, Talia had focused on the church, watching it fade away with the thickening of smoke. It was the last thing she had seen before her death. In her nightmare, the building glowed in the dark sky, but it looked exactly like this one, though not at the same angle. All she could remember was looking up to it.

Though tempted to trail her nightmare to the church, Talia convinced herself it was more logical to follow her contact's lead to the winery. To the right, among the many wineries of Gaia, stood a giant shadow of a caped man, brooding over the buildings that climbed the valley. It would have spooked Talia had she not already known it was just a billboard cutout logo for a popular winery, *Sandeman*. As intended, it succeeded in increasing Talia's thirst for *Vinho do Porto*, the official name of Port wine.

The wine industry in Portugal originated in the twelfth century, when wines from the country first shipped to England. Due to its cold climate, England was forced to import wine. The more convenient the commute the better, as the demand was high. In 1386, Portugal and England signed the Treaty of Windsor, forging a financial and diplomatic bond between the two countries enduring throughout the tumultuous centuries since.

From the time of the treaty, Portuguese grapevines grew beyond the Douro region, near the mouth of the Tagus River in Lisbon and in the northern province of the Minho, which produces the semi-sparkling white wine, *Vinho Verde*.

The history of port, Portugal's most popular wine variety, is a matter of some debate. Some speculate that when Britain outlawed the sale of French wine due to ongoing political and military conflicts, they sought a new vendor. Portugal was easy to reach by sea, but it was a longer journey, causing the wines to spoil by the time they arrived in England.

A pair of brothers accidentally invented Port wine in the late 1600's by adding brandy to the bottles in hopes of maintaining wine quality during shipment. Since then, British companies perfected the process, which is why wineries in the region sport names of English and not Portuguese descent. The wine may be produced by these centuries-old English wineries, but the vine-yards, or *quintas*, on which the grapes were grown, were largely run by generations of local Portuguese families.

The bars and tasting rooms lining the Gaia side of the Douro River swarmed with tasters undeterred by the early hour and the frequently inclement weather. W.J. Graham's Port, established in 1820 by the blending of two families, is a known favorite of Winston Churchill and Queen Elizabeth II. The tasting room was built in 1890 and located on the far end of the boardwalk. Its stone walls and wood furnishings accented the style, along with a hint of an industrial flair in the light fixtures suspended from the high rafter ceilings. Behind a windowed wall, oak barrels stacked into pyramids laid on dirt floors to keep cool, their movement confined between long four-by-fours.

"Do you think the clue's somewhere on the bottle, or was the hint just to get me here?" Talia asked as they found a place to stand at the bar, but Nuno didn't answer. Talia searched the wine tasting menu for the vintage her contact suggested, Diamond Jubilee, but none of the four years it was released were listed.

"I do not see it here." Nuno flipped through his own wine list.

"Neither do I," Talia said. "Maybe the bartender will know."

Once he finished introducing the next tasting to the couple on the other side of the bar, the bartender wandered over to Talia and Nuno.

"*Boa tarde.*" The young bartender wished them a good afternoon, his short brown hair parted to the side and slicked back to match a tucked-in appearance like a sommelier at a Michelin-starred restaurant.

"*Boa tarde. Falas Inglês?*" Talia asked.

"*Sim.* Yes, I speak English. How can I help you?" the bartender asked, his thick accent elongating every syllable.

"Do you happen to have a bottle of one of your Diamond Jubilees?" Talia asked.

"*Desculpe*, we do not have those in this tasting room. It is too special. You will have to rent a private tasting in the Vintage Room."

"Do I have to actually taste it? I only need to see the bottle. I'm looking for—I'm on a scavenger hunt. A friend of mine told me to look for a clue on a bottle."

"Ah, *sim*. I have heard of that," the bartender said. "The museum is next door if you want to visit. I believe they have a bottle there you may inspect."

"Yes, thank you. *Obrigada*," Talia said, a skip in her step.

Nuno nodded his head at the bartender and followed Talia out the door.

"You lie well, *gatinha*." Nuno bowed his head.

"Is that supposed to be a compliment?" Talia asked. "You say what you have to say to get the right answers in my business. I guess it comes naturally now. You think he'd help me if I told him I was investigating a murder? I can assure you he wouldn't."

The museum was the size of a large banquet hall. A long wooden table with inlaid glass compartments, encasing the winery's many historical artifacts, split the center of the hall like a dining table in a royal manor. Encased in one of the narrower walls, a line of vintage Port wine bottles were on display. Talia was pleased to see the oldest Diamond Jubilee from 1952 on exhibit. Only the front of the bottle was visible, and there was no easy way to get into the case to turn it. Nothing on its front label provided Talia with any clues. Another dead end.

"*Desculpa*," Talia said to one of the clerks, proceeding to ask the woman if it was possible to remove the wine bottle for inspection.

"*Não é possível*," the woman declined with an irritation in her tone. It didn't surprise Talia—if she had been the clerk, she would've felt the same.

"Well, I've hit a dead end," Talia huffed as they walked out of the museum. "We're back to square one."

"*Desculpe, gatinha*. I wish I could help." Nuno watched as Talia paced in circles. "Want some wine?"

"I could use a drink," Talia answered. "At least we won't have to go far."

It had been over thirty minutes since their last visit, but the bartender at the tasting room at Graham's Lodge greeted them with a smile. "Did you find what you were looking for?" the bartender asked, wiping rings of wine off the counter.

"Not exactly." Talia pouted.

"You did not find the bottle?"

"We did, but it didn't have the clue we're looking for." Talia plopped her elbows on the bar.

"*Desculpe*," the bartender said. "Is there something else I can help you with?"

"I'm not sure there is," Talia said. "At least not with any of the clues I've gathered. But you certainly can help with some *Vinho do Porto*."

"That I can do," the bartender said, cracking a grin.

"What are you looking for?" Nuno asked.

"I don't even know. Anything."

Nuno frowned. Talia could tell Nuno wasn't enjoying her investigation.

"There's still one more lead I can follow," Talia said, tapping her fingertips. "Remember my nightmare at the train station?"

"I cannot forget."

"I saw a building in my dream, a church, and I think it was the Santa Clara."

"The church on the hill on the other side of the bridge?" Nuno asked, pointing in what Talia assumed was its direction.

"Yeah, I think so. I'm not sure what angle I was looking from, but that dome looks so familiar. I think I want to go visit it. What time do we have to meet your friend?"

"Whenever we like. He will not be in town until tomorrow."

"He doesn't mind us coming by when he's not there?" Talia asked. "I didn't realize he wasn't going to be there."

"He has a very big house and I am always welcome there."

"Okay, fair enough," Talia said. "Do you mind if we stop at the church first?"

"If you think it will help."

"I have no idea if it will help, but it's all I got."

The bartender looped back with their final tasting, a vintage tawny port of twenty years.

"Maybe you *can* help me," Talia said to the bartender.

"Anything," he said, wiping the clean glasses in the sink with a black dishrag.

"Do you know a man named Carlos Batista?" Talia asked. Nuno wasn't the only one that kept information on a need-to-know basis.

"Talia, what are you doing?" Nuno asked, his eyes wide.

The bartender didn't blink, he just gawked at Talia with his bottom lip drooping, gripping the glass so tight she was afraid it might break. "Why would you ask me that?"

"I– I just thought someone around here might know who he is." Talia had nothing else. It didn't seem as if her informant wanted her to find the bottle of Port, and if not, she pointed her to Graham's for a reason.

"Everyone knows who he is," the bartender said, "but I am not his friend."

"I didn't think you were," Talia said. "I just wanted to know if you had any idea where he may be, where he was last seen. What's the word on the street? You're a bartender. People talk when they drink."

"You never told me his name," Nuno whispered, smiling apologetically to the bartender.

"I didn't think it was important," Talia said. "Unless you know him?"

"Of course not." Nuno stepped aside.

"I know I sound crazy, but please, can you tell me anything you may know about this man?" Talia shook her clasped knuckles at the bartender.

"He no longer calls himself Carlos," the bartender whispered after he took a look around the tasting room.

"I figured as much," Talia said. "Anything else? Do you know the name he uses now?"

"*Não*, I do not know anything." The bartender leaned in closer. "But I know someone who does."

———

TALIA AND NUNO had an hour to kill before the arranged meeting with the bartender's confidante on the grounds of the Santa Clara church. Thanks to Talia's quick thinking, the schedule worked out perfectly—they could visit the church from her nightmare while they waited.

Having never revealed her uncle's name to her contact, Talia wondered if this was her intent all along. Maybe Talia grasped at nothing, craving to connect her uncle to the crimes so much that she always found a way to do so, as Jared had accused. He would say she put herself in danger by following a notorious criminal. In fact, he had already said as much. Caryn, on the other hand, would support Talia's decisions and willingly come along for the ride. Talia wished Caryn was there to help her get into her uncle's head.

"Are you sure you want to do this? This man is very dangerous." Nuno tried to keep up with Talia's stride, but this time, he was the one who lagged behind.

"He is also family," Talia said, out of breath and stomach mumbling.

"You do not know if this man values family." Nuno placed his hand on Talia's shoulder. "You must be careful."

"You're starting to sound like Jared. I can take care of myself," Talia said as they found the arched entranceway to the gothic church. The onyx doors were warm to the touch from when the sun had briefly resumed its place in the sky that afternoon.

Dating back to the fifteenth century, the Santa Clara church was unassuming at its completion, the stonework façade not installed until a couple centuries later. Its meek stone exterior does not prepare a visitor for the extraordinary wood carvings encrusted with gold leaf padding its rotund interior. Gilded cherubs and saints had been carved into the walls and pillars. Archeologists estimated it required over forty-four hundred pounds of gold to complete the elaborate baroque masterpiece. Talia felt as though she were marching up to the throne of a queen, not the aisle of a cathedral.

"This is proof of how rich Portugal once was," Nuno said.

"It's luxurious, that's for sure. I feel like I'm underdressed," Talia said, dusting off her jacket. "I think I'm going to walk around the grounds, see if I can find a clue to where I was in my nightmare."

"It is getting late, I should go with you," Nuno said.

The hedges and buildings guarding the church were too high for either of them to find a decent view of the city. Talia even climbed halfway up the walls, worrying the many tourists who passed them by. They often stopped and gossiped before they continued on their way. Once the guard returned from his rounds, Talia feigned innocence.

"It's impossible unless you're a giant on a ladder," Talia huffed.

"Ten *minutos*," Nuno said, checking his watch.

Talia lost track of time. "Thank you for reminding me, I almost missed it."

Talia kissed an unsuspecting Nuno on the lips. He smiled in a state of bliss as she ran her fingers through his hair.

"*Tem cuidado, gatinha*," Nuno said.

"I'm always careful," Talia said with a wink. "You stay here while I talk to the guy. But please keep an eye on me. You know, in case."

"I will not let anybody hurt you," Nuno said.

"*Obrigada*," Talia sighed in his ear, and then kissed him on his prickly cheek. His musk calmed her nerves.

What harm could happen on a well-lit and well-guarded plot of public property? This was the biggest breakthrough in her investigation thus far, there was no room for fear. Somehow she trusted Nuno to protect her, even though he'd given her plenty of reason not to. Either way, it was a chance Talia needed to take.

Nuno suggested a central area in the courtyard, a place with plenty of exit routes in case she needed to make a run for it. Talia could no longer spot Nuno from where she stood, and she hoped he was hiding in the darkness somewhere, watching over her.

A surly man strolled in her direction. He seemed the type the bartender would know, so she prepped herself for the encounter, but the man continued past her. Talia assessed every person who walked by as a possible contact, but it was not until the courtyard had cleared when the man she was scheduled to meet had finally emerged from the shadows like her own personal FBI informant. Talia tried not to stare at the older guy, wearing a scruffy beard and a torn leather jacket. There weren't too many bikers in that part of the world, so it took her by surprise.

He positioned himself at her side, head high, as if they were both at a gallery admiring the same painting. In a scratchy accent he murmured, "Are you the American who is searching for someone?"

Talia cleared her throat and whispered, "Yes, that's me. Do you know where he may be?"

"A little bird told me he has returned to town," he said, widening his beady eyes. "He is looking for someone, too."

"Do you know who that someone is?" Talia struggled to hide the tremble in her voice.

"His niece," the man said. "Are you her?"

"No, but I may know who she is," Talia lied. "Where would she find him? If, of course, she wanted to meet him."

"When he is ready, he will be found."

"Are you saying you won't help?"

"I am saying he will find you," the man said. "Or as you say, your friend. And whatever *she* may be keeping from him."

"Keeping from him?"

"There is a rumor that his niece holds the key to unlock the other side."

"The other side of what?" Talia said.

"Life," the man said. "I must go. You will not see me again."

And just like that, the man crawled back into the obscurity that bore him.

Talia stood there perplexed, uncertain of what to do with the information she was just given, or whether she should tell Nuno what she'd found. She holds the key to the other side of life? She couldn't tell if it was a metaphor or a physical key. Her uncle was already looking for her, so he must know she's in the country. She hoped she didn't just give herself up.

A wave of nausea struck her belly, her heart fluttered into her throat. Talia had never feared for her life before, and the paranoia was hard to control. Even when she helped convict criminals, she would hide in the background while the police did their job. She never had any serious enemies or hung out with shady crowds. This was a new feeling, and she wasn't a fan.

Nuno snuck up behind Talia, causing her to jump in place.

"*Desculpe, gatinha,*" Nuno said, caressing her arms. "What did he say?"

"I'm not sure if it's good news or bad news."

NUNO FOLLOWED the thread of passengers waiting at the taxi stand near the Dom Luis bridge in Gaia, but continued past them to a black Mercedes sedan parked ahead of the rest. A suited man with a black driving cap on his graying head motioned for their bags, but they both refused his help with an apology in Portuguese. Winking to the driver, Nuno followed Talia into the backseat. She grilled them both for details, but neither revealed their destination.

"Are you sure you know where you're going?" Talia asked Nuno as they bounced around the hills lining the Douro River.

"*Claro que sim*, Talia," Nuno said. "It was once my home."

"When?" Talia asked, her jaw agape. "Why didn't you tell me this before?"

"When I was young. He is a good friend. He saved me from a terrible fate and offered me a warm home to rest. I like to visit him when I am in town."

"May I ask what he saved you from?"

"That is for another time and place," Nuno said, motioning to the driver.

Talia sighed. Another dodge. He was not an easy one to crack.

The starlight wasn't enough to illuminate the green and purple vines that cascaded along the countryside. Before she got the chance to ask, the private car hooked into a blind driveway and crawled around a wide, unpaved path dividing two crops of grapevines. A quarter mile down the dusty road, the fields of ripening vines cleared, the path smoothened into a paved cul-de-sac, and a modern castle-inspired mansion arose beyond it.

A young maid all in white drew open the grand entrance door to greet them when they parked. Her thin tan removed a few years from the faint lines edging her dark eyes. She looked overworked and exhausted, but undeniably under thirty.

The driver rushed around to open the passenger door for Talia, who already had it open. Talia offered Nuno an impressed smile and he took her hand, steering her past the maid and into the foyer. Flustered, as if she hadn't received company in years, the maid paraded them up the master staircase to one of the many themed suites on the second level.

Portraits of familiar-looking people lined the hallway. One painting hanging near the bathroom reminded Talia of her great-grandmother, a similar photo could have sat on Vovó's dresser, her hands clasped at her crossed knees in a bulbous dress and a forced smile. Locked vitrines exhibited the sorts of strange pagan relics Talia studied while researching Macumba—ornate jewelry, wood-handled cleavers, leather bound books written in Portuguese and opened to pages explaining the use of menacing round symbols.

The maid presented Talia and Nuno a room far more ornate than expected. It had its own white stone fireplace with a small leather sectional arranged near it, a four-post bed, and its own master bathroom with marble tiles and a two-head shower.

"Are you sure this one's for us?" Talia asked the maid.

"This is the room he requested." The maid's hands clasped in front of the bleach white apron tied around her patterned dress, her head low to avoid eye contact with Nuno.

The maid's panty hose, visible by their reflection in the direct indoor light, cinched a small fold in her waistline and tucked into her pearly sneakers. Her large bust balanced her healthy birthing hips and childlike smile. Square-rimmed glasses nestled on her small nose, her thick dark tresses tied back in a bun, pinned on the sides where a few strands had already escaped.

"*Obrigada.*" Talia turned to Nuno as the maid bowed out the door. "Wow. This place is crazy nice. Is this a working vineyard?"

"Yes it is. It produces a few different varieties of Port," Nuno said as he peered out the window that overlooked the grounds. "My friend will not be here until tomorrow afternoon, which is good. We need to rest. Let's go to bed. *Estou cançado*."

"Yes. Bed. Please."

Nuno's suggestion to crawl into the cloud of pillows piled on the bed before her rolled a sense of tranquility throughout Talia's feeble body. But it did not suppress the desire to steal a moment alone with her phone. She hadn't yet heard from Caryn.

Talia wasn't keen on games. Being an only child of immigrants, she had the choice of playing games alone or spending hours teaching her parents how to play them. It wasn't long before she passed on the latter to avoid the frustration. If her uncle was behind the disappearance of her friends, did that mean Pierre and Nuno were his men? Talia couldn't believe it. They were con artists for certain, but kidnappers sounded a bit extreme. Greed makes people do crazy things.

Talia assured herself that while Pierre seemed capable of kidnapping her best friend, Talia was very much with Nuno of her own accord. No one forced her to stay in this gorgeous vineyard estate with him. There is where she chose to be.

Talia gave in to Nuno's many advances, resisting her fatigue, but as it intensified, her guilt resurfaced. She went through the motions with Nuno, a kiss here, a moan there, but deep down she wondered where Jared and Caryn could be, and if they were safe. Talia regretted leaving them now, and not being more wary of Caryn's disappearance, even through Jared's attempts to convince her otherwise. She squeezed her eyelids, conjuring the memory of being in bed with Jared in Lisbon, but when she opened them, Nuno hovered above her, eyes sealed and mouth gaping.

"*Te amo*, Talia," Nuno moaned as he fell back into bed.

Talia's stomach turned. She didn't know what to say. She loved Jared. That was still true, no matter how he may have hurt her. Nuno was a fling, a pastime, a rebound. She never even considered loving him. It had only been a few days.

After an elongated silence, Nuno asked, "*Estás bem?*"

She felt his breath on her skin. "I'm sorry. What?"

"Is everything okay?" Nuno asked again.

"Of course. Why wouldn't it be?" Talia mustered a smile and wrapped her arm around Nuno's chest, nestling her head into the hollow underneath his collarbone. She had made a terrible mistake. She needed to explain this to Jared. He needed to know.

"Are you worried about meeting my friend?"

"I'm more worried about *my* friends," Talia said.

"Your boyfriend," Nuno said, a finality in his tone.

Talia felt his heartbeat rush and pulled away, leaning on her elbow for support. "I haven't been able to reach my friends since I left Lisbon, and I'm worried."

"Do you miss him?" Nuno asked.

"Who, Jared? We aren't together anymore, and it's more than just him I'm worried about." Talia lifted herself up and wrapped the white sheet against her chest. "I'm sorry. This is obviously the wrong time for this conversation. I shouldn't have said anything. I've just been off tonight."

"There is nothing to be sorry about. We should rest for tomorrow."

"Yeah." Talia stared at a painting on the wall.

"Come here." Nuno tapped his chest.

Talia loosened her grip on the sheets and settled next to him. Nuno glowered at the walls, deep in thought. Drained and jittery, Talia cursed herself for her consistent bad timing, but she couldn't stop thinking about the hospital in Fátima. So many of her nightmares already came true. Then there was Jared. Her mind always boomeranged to Jared.

Nuno snored for ten minutes before Talia caressed his arm to see if he was unconscious. Satisfied with the results, she crept out of bed, eying him while she reached through her bag for her phone. Nuno tossed and turned on the creaky bed, and Talia held her breath until he resumed snoring. No one called, but there was one text message from her contact that read: *See you at the house.*

SIXTEEN

LINGERING in the limbo between sleep and wakefulness, through the stained glass that separated her from reality, Talia watched with one slit eye as Nuno reorganized her backpack, placing each piece in its proper position, then rushing to her side. His reentrance shook the bed, forcing Talia's eyelids to widen.

"*Bom dia, gatinha! Dormiste bem?*" Nuno asked.

"I slept a little better," Talia croaked. She should have asked him why he was in her backpack. She should have but she didn't.

"*Outra* nightmare?"

"As usual. I have a headache. Do you think you can get me some aspirin? I want to feel better before I meet your friend."

"*Tá bem, gatinha.* I will ask the help," Nuno said and then left the room.

Talia's headache wasn't painful enough to be medicated, but the excuse permitted her some alone time. Nuno hadn't given her much time to herself since she reconnected with him at *Café Suiça* two days prior. She examined her backpack leaning against the leather couch.

The canvas bag wasn't zipped as tightly as Talia had trained herself to do, so as to avoid being easily robbed. It came second nature to Talia to check and recheck her belongings to make sure she theft-proofed them as much as possible. She remembered running through her typical routine the night before. She opened the large pocket first. Her journal sat on top, but she remembered packing it below her jacket. Talia kept a photo of Jared and herself as a bookmark, taken with the rest of the Holga shots from their first day in Algarve. She flipped the pages to the last entry. Jared's photo was missing.

She flicked through the book and found it stuck in a different page with a fingerprint smudging the bottom left corner. She extended her finger against it, and found the print could not be her own—not just because she was careful not to leave marks on her photos, but because the finger that created this print was twice the size of her own. Talia skimmed the bookmarked entry, written moments before she met Nuno at Café Suiça:

Did I do the right thing? I'm not sure Jared even understands me, or this gut feeling. I have to trust my instinct and keep focused. I hope one day he understands why I had to do this.

Talia frowned. So much had happened since that entry, so much that Talia wouldn't know how to explain to Jared if she ever got the chance. Staring at the photo of the two of them on the beach, happy and peaceful, Talia noticed a tear on the corner, ripping off the head of man in gray flat-front slacks similar to those Nuno wore at the restaurant where they first met. When she searched through her jacket for the other letters and photos she stole from the hospital, they were missing.

Talia yanked at the seams of her inner pockets in hopes the pictures would pour from the stitching. Nuno must have taken them to destroy evidence that he was planning something with Pierre. It was the only logical explanation.

Voices echoed outside the door. Talia pulled out her clothes for the day and stuffed the journal back into her bag, zipping it all the way shut. She checked it twice and waited.

After a few moments of silence, Talia opened the smaller pocket to discover the strings of the velvet bag untied. Her stomach dropped. The pouch revealed Vovó's watch in decent condition except for one thing: the back was loosened. Talia chose a blade on the miniature Swiss Army knife she always carried and finished the job.

A thin gold key escaped from within the watch's gears and plinked onto the floor. Talia swiped it before it made another sound and examined it in her palm. It was small enough to open a luggage lock or … a jewelry box. Talia chuckled at her complete ignorance. Unlock your inner being, of course. Deep Throat was telling the truth, she *was* hiding a key.

Talia should have suspected the inscription was more than an inspirational quote. Vovó wasn't the type. Even Nuno wasn't fooled. It was clear now that Vovó gave her the watch because she placed the key to her jewelry box inside. This was further proof that Vovó feared her heirloom might not reach its proper owner at her demise. Now all she had to do was find the box it unlocked.

Talia almost forgot about her inheritance from Vovó in the wake of uncovering her notorious uncle, who her family had disowned. The discovery of a key didn't bring her any closer to finding the jewelry box it opened. Talia was a sitting target, and she knew that whoever stole her heirloom would be searching for her next.

I am saying he will find you. Her FBI informant may have been right about the key, but what did he mean about *the other side of life?*

Murmurs drifted from the hallway. Talia snapped the backing onto the watch and placed it in its bag in her backpack. Instead of tossing the Swiss army knife with the watch as it had been packed originally, she placed it in her pocket and slid the key into a fold of her bra as she hustled into her clothes. Nuno burst in as she finished adjusting herself on the bed.

"*Ai, gatinha, que chatice.* Here is your aspirin," Nuno grumbled and nestled next to Talia on their bed.

Talia took the glass of water and the pill from Nuno's palm. She threw her head back with her hand over her mouth, all the while keeping a firm grip on the tablet still embedded in the creases of her palm. When Nuno looked away, she tucked the pill in between the overstuffed mattresses. She didn't really need the medication, and she wasn't certain of Nuno's intentions, or the extent of his con. Talia was raised better than to accept a pill from a man she didn't trust.

"I could sleep for days." Talia yawned. "What time is it?"

"Eleven o'clock," Nuno said.

"Yikes. I guess I was tired. Sorry about that."

"*Não faz mal,*" Nuno said. "I slept a lot too. We needed the rest."

"I guess so. Will we get a chance to tour the grounds today? This place is so beautiful, I would love to get a closer look."

"I will see what I can do. My friend will be pleased you are interested in the property."

"Is he looking to sell?" Talia asked. "Not that I could, in any way, afford this myself."

'Oh no, he is just very proud of his accomplishments."

"Well, he should be. I'll need to thank him for his hospitality myself. I couldn't have asked for better accommodations. I should not have been worried. I'm such a worry wart." Talia shook her head. "Forgive me."

"You are always forgiven," Nuno said, pulling her in for a kiss on the neck, the scent of cigarette smoke in his hair. "I will go see what I can do about the tour."

She was able to manipulate Nuno more easily than she expected. Across the room, Talia gazed out the window that overlooked the Douro River and the boundless rows of vines sandwiched in between, the saturated sky as surreal as a brushed canvas landscape. The main house in which she stood extended far into the distance to the right. To the left, a clearing made way for a humble stone ruin with roof in tact, the lone building on the grounds that wasn't renovated. Behind it, the green cliffs plummeted hundreds of feet into the river. Talia wondered if anyone had ever fallen off, never to return, like the tourists at *Boca do Inferno*.

There was a rustle. A birthday-card sized white envelope, sealed and unmarked, launched from the crevice underneath the door. In a rush to grab it before Nuno returned, Talia tore open the envelope to reveal a hand-penned note with no signature. It read:

We've been waiting for you.
The truth lies underneath the books.

The message read too similarly to those of her contact for it to be coincidental. The doors in the hallway repeated for miles. Anyone could be living there without Talia's knowledge. She stuffed the note into her backpack and opened the door to the suite, but on the other side stood Nuno.

"*Olá, gatinha,* where are you going?" he asked.

"Oh, I just thought I'd take a look around, see if there were any other guests in this massive house."

"No one is in this house but us," Nuno said.

"Your friend could have a lady friend in town with him."

"He has very few friends, and no lady friends."

"If you say so. You seem a little frustrated, what's up?" Talia asked, rubbing his back.

She feigned concern while Nuno complained. "I hope he received the package. He has been very anxious to get it."

"I gave it to the nurse, just as you asked. I promise." Talia held back a wince as she crossed her heart.

"Domingos will tell me when he arrives. I will just have to wait."

"Would your friend know?" Talia asked. "The one you visited at the hospital?"

"That is the problem, I cannot reach him. He has not answered his phone."

"Ah, the tables are turned," Talia said. "Maybe he's living it up with a girl he just met, just like you did. We girls can be very time-consuming. Maybe you've even met her before and didn't realize it."

"Yes, he is probably busy," Nuno said with an urgent tone.

"I am sure your friend came through for you like you always have for him," Talia said. "Is Domingos your boss?"

"He is my client, *sim*, and he is the owner of this house," Nuno said.

"Oh." Talia was at a loss for words, an issue she rarely encountered. "If you knew you were going to see him, why didn't you just bring the box yourself?"

"It is complicated," Nuno said, shirking the question.

"I get it," Talia said, annoyed that she wasted another opportunity with her directness. "So did you end up getting us a tour of this gorgeous vineyard?"

"I am sorry, no. Security has been very strict and the guards would like you to meet my friend before they show you around."

"Can I at least get a tour of the inside?"

Nuno exhaled. "I am sorry, not yet."

"Well, I tried," Talia sighed. "So why the heightened security? Did something happen? Should we leave?"

"No, no. This always happens when my friend is in town. He is, what do they say, paranoid. I will make it up to you, *eu prometo*." Nuno wrapped Talia in a warm embrace of sandalwood and smoke.

Talia wanted to recoil, to deny his advances and call him out on his indiscretions, but she sensed a strange connection to him that was hard to explain, a sort of kinship that lasted through lifetimes. If she could get him to admit the truth about Pierre, she could let the rest slide and forgive him.

"When do you think your friend will be here?" Talia asked.

"Soon," Nuno said.

We've been waiting for you. The ghosts of her cousins also repeated that simple phrase throughout Talia's hallucination at Fátima. Were they foreshadowing the note that was just slipped under her door by a stranger, or was it the other way around? The people behind the note could have also been haunted by the apparitions of these girls, or by the spirits of their ancestors.

The truth lies underneath the books. As she rested her chin on Nuno's shoulder, she examined the suite for paperbacks, notebooks—anything with words in it—to make sense of the note's final line, but the room didn't even have a bookshelf. Whatever truth the people behind that handwritten note wanted Talia to discover was not located in that suite, and she was beginning to sense that Nuno would prefer if she never left.

If what Nuno said was true and no one else occupied the house, the maid could have been the one who sent her the note. She had access to their room and knew Talia was in there alone. It was a bold move for a woman who couldn't muster the confidence to look Nuno in the eye, but not an impossible one. Caryn would call her passive aggressive.

Someone knocked at the door and startled Talia.

"*Desculpem a interrupção*," the maid apologized. "*O patrão* is ready to meet you."

SEVENTEEN

TALIA LOOKED THE PART, but wasn't ready for the role. With the tip of her stubby fingers, she tugged at the sides of her skirt, which did little to hide the thumb-sized black tattoo of an Ouroboros on the inside of her left ankle.

Talia tightened the top button of her blouse and combed her fingers through her hair with one last glimpse into the gold-trimmed mirror hanging in the hallway. She didn't usually bother with perfecting her appearance, but it was a sign of respect to dress well for a gracious host, who offered her lodging she could never dream of affording on her own.

The maid beamed with pride as she suggested the two of them wait in a large office on the first story at the back of the house. Engraved French doors opened to a panoramic window that encompassed the widest wall and overlooked the vineyard. The Douro River pushed through the hills surrounding it. The mountains beyond the valley hid behind a shroud of murk reaching as far as the horizon, the stubborn late morning sun bleaching scattered patches throughout the sky.

On the wall adjacent to the window, a built-in bookcase showcased literary classics from Byron to Voltaire translated into Portuguese, and the entire collection of Pessoa's published works. One shelf held Portuguese encyclopedias exploring mythology and religion. Snuggled against a leather copy of *The Old Testament* like an old friend was *The Great Book of Saint Cyprian*, a volume many devout Christians consider a sin just to touch. They believe reading this occult book from back to front can summon the devil incarnate, and bookshops that dare carry it keep it chained in a box away from public consumption.

The office furniture evoked nineteenth century Portugal with hand-carved wood and ornate brass trimmings. The pair of mahogany chairs on the receiving end of the desk spiraled like volute banisters, upholstered with worn leather that was bolted by dozens of fasteners, reminiscent of those at The Majestic Café.

Not a single piece of technology could be found in the room. It was an office without a means to communicate outside its walls, fit only for private in-person meetings. A rush of butterflies filled Talia's belly.

On the opposite end of the desk sat an antique credenza with one of its doors unlatched. Stowed inside was what appeared to be an unmarked manila box with an uncanny resemblance to the box Nuno had been carrying around with him in Lisbon—the one Talia handed to the nurse at the clinic in Fatima.

The office door creaked open. The maid, grinning at Talia, held the door for Domingos' arrival. Nuno rushed over to shake his hand with vigor, but Domingos smiled and took his hand by force of habit, all the while making his way toward Talia.

"*Olá, Senhorinha Braga,*" Domingos said as he removed his hat and approached Talia to kiss her on each cheek.

Nuno's friend was smaller than Talia had expected, and

much older. He stood a few inches taller than her, but wider, his bald head reflecting the white clouds radiating sunlight through the window. Although he may have appeared unassuming in Nuno's six-foot shadow, the man's confidence towered above him. He wore a gray suit that appeared custom made, his face shaven to a thick mustache he must have nurtured for years. He reeked of cheap French cologne and shoe polish, the latter likely originating from his freshly shined loafers.

He stepped back from Talia, and flipped the fedora back onto his head, leaving behind the fuzz that still sprouted around his ears and neckline. The man placed both his hands onto Talia's shoulders, expanding his chest with a gold-spotted grin.

The cuffs of his white, starched shirt were fastened by gold cufflinks to match the ornate ring on his chubby finger. The opening of his sleeve widened just enough to reveal the Ouroboros tattoo on his inner wrist. His tattoo matched the one on Talia's ankle. Above his tattoo, his forearm was wrapped with gauze badly in need of changing.

"You are a very pretty girl," he rasped.

"*Obrigada.*" Talia smiled politely. "*Muito prazer, sou Talia.*"

"You speak well, Natalia. How have you not been married yet?" Domingos lifted her left hand for a closer look at her ring finger.

Blood rushed to her cheeks. Talia resented the typical concerns about her marital status, as if wearing a wedding ring meant she achieved success in an old-world Portuguese society. The aggravating inquisitions often triggered memories of her aunts and uncles teasing her at family gatherings. *You're the last one,* her aunt told Talia at her cousin's wedding the year before. Lifting her eyes to the ceiling, her aunt continued, *I hope I'll still be around when it happens. Se Deus quiser.* Talia was certain God didn't care one way or another if she'd marry or whether her aunt would be there to see it. He had bigger cod to fry.

"Nuno has told me a lot about you," the man said.

"I hope it's all been pleasant." Talia recollected a few moments during the whirlwind of the last few days when Nuno could have slipped away to make a call—while he waited outside her great-aunt's apartment or when he vanished in Fatima. It must have been then.

"He has nothing but kind words." The man stared out his window and wheezed. "My name is Domingos."

"So I've heard. Nice to meet you, Domingos. This is a nice place you have here."

"I have done well for myself," Domingos said.

"That's apparent. How does one acquire a vineyard? I ask because I wouldn't mind having one of my own one day."

"If you believe hard enough, life can give you all you desire," Nuno said.

Only if you believe, Jared whispered in her head.

"I guess I don't believe enough yet." Talia smiled, twiddling her thumbs, hoping she wouldn't have to employ any of the evasive maneuvers she used on her Evangelical uncle. "Do you believe in all the occult relics you have lying around or are you just an art collector?"

"A bit of both. It is a fascination I have had my whole life," Domingos explained, running out of breath. "I see you wear the *Figa.* Do you believe?"

"My parents do, so I guess I do somewhat. It's too ingrained in me to not believe some of it at least. But I can't say I believe in anything completely."

"Better to be safe than sorry." Domingos winked.

"Exactly. Your English is outstanding, by the way. Have you spent a lot of time in England or the U.S.?" Talia asked. His accent was almost too perfect, his inflections in the right places, the ease with unrolling his R's. Even her parents, who lived in the United States for over twenty years, weren't able to drop their thick accents so effortlessly.

"I have not been to either country. I have a lot of American friends," Domingos said.

Talia nodded. She didn't believe a word, but she understood the power of pride.

"So how do you two know each other?" Talia pointed at Nuno. The manila box caught the corner of her eye, but she tried to block her curiosity, which could cause suspicion if she wasn't careful. "Nuno didn't tell me much."

"We met on the streets of Lisbon," the man said, his eyes fixated on Nuno. "He needed help and I gave it to him."

Talia shivered. "I didn't realize you lived in Lisbon, Nuno. I thought you spent most of your time in Fatima?"

"It is true," Nuno said. "I traveled to Lisbon after I was kicked out of Fatima. Lisbon is a big city, I was not used to it. But, *Senhor Domingos* found me when I needed him most, when I was lost."

"And now you are found, my son," Domingos rasped, patting Nuno's back.

———

AFTER GREETING Talia in the hallway outside the office with an awkward grin, the maid walked her to the room while Nuno stayed behind to chat business with Domingos. With a wink, the maid abandoned Talia at the top of the staircase, opting to disobey Domingos's request to escort her.

A burning sensation wrapped Talia's left ear. It wasn't a good sign—the left ear meant someone was speaking ill of her. Talia wished the badmouthing came from her friends, whom she'd abandoned in a strange land. That would be the best scenario.

Despite not knowing the maid's motives, Talia didn't waste the opportunity to snoop for clues. It was her favorite task in a reporter's job description. Never an opportunity lost to look inside a suspicious door or eaves drop on an interesting conversation.

Jared and Talia were nearly expelled from college due to a suspicious door. Jared never enjoyed the hunt for the story, being the head sports writer at the *New Falls University Tribune*. Everything he ever needed to report on was right in front of him, on the field or court, and he possessed the looks and manners that could charm the ball out of a goalie's hands.

Talia enjoyed pressuring Jared into strange situations. The aforementioned door stood near the elevators at the top of an abandoned building next to their dorm in college, rumored to have been haunted by a suicide the decade before. It was always locked, except for one early Sunday morning. The two were near the elevators after a big football game, when Talia got the urge to try the door. The knob turned and the door popped open. Talia spun and blasted a devilish grin at Jared, who creased his brow.

Ignoring Jared's disapproval, Talia stepped in and found a hidden stairwell leading to a forgotten attic three stories high. The first story preserved vintage school desks that could be found overpriced online, dusty school books haphazardly stuffed onto sagging shelves. She climbed and climbed, neglecting her partner in crime, not resting until she reached the top level of the building. From a grimy half window at the top, Talia found the most glorious view of Boston she had ever seen, complete with the Citgo sign and the crown of the Prudential Center both glimmering in the starless sky. There were so close she could touch them.

The janitor screamed into the doorway and Talia carried all the blame, swearing on her grandfather's grave that she would never trespass again. The next day they both received a written warning, one of the three needed for expulsion. Jared nagged her about it ever since, but Talia had no regrets.

Talia scouted her surroundings in Domingos's gothic manor and then tiptoed back down to his office, almost knocking into one of the African statues that lined the dim hallway. A conversation in Portuguese between Domingos and Nuno seeped through the sliver in the doorway.

"It is in her watch." Nuno's voice juddered with his pace.

"Her watch?" Domingos lit a thick cigar with a match and a series of long puffs, the plumes curling from his lips.

"She told me it was a present from her grandmother," Nuno said. "The inscription on the back was my clue. I was not able to open it before she woke, but I know it is there."

"She is already asking too many questions. You are running out of time," Domingos said. "I have no patience for stupidity."

"I speak the truth. You will have what is rightfully yours soon," Nuno said. "She will do as you wish. I made sure of it."

"*Pede á Deus que sim*," Domingos warned.

Nuno faked a courteous smile, observing the smoke swirling around Domingos's nose, and stomped towards the door behind which Talia hid. She dashed down the corridor to the next empty alcove and, in her best posture, pressed her body flush against the wall. Paranoia rose in her chest despite her constrained respiration. She couldn't be the only one who heard the thumping against her rib cage, the rumbling against her eardrums, she could smell their energy.

Nuno marched the opposite way, shadowed later by Domingos and the maid, who cozied in the assumed privacy of each other's company. When the hallway cleared, Talia slunk to the credenza, the door still ajar, and opened it with a bent finger. Inside the cabinet, the box Talia gave to the nurse in Fatima rested on its side. It was no longer sealed, the packing tape sheared and lifted at its ends as if peeled off and then reapplied at half its adhesive strength.

Talia equated this find to one of the gifts her mother unsuccessfully wrapped, with the bumpy packaging failing to conceal the identity of the item inside. Those were always the easiest to take apart and put back together without anyone being the wiser, providing she could keep her poker face steady at gift time. Talia could hardly maintain her composure with the box before her then, a Cheshire cat grin spreading from ear to ear, channeling the joy of a less curious child on Christmas morning.

She stripped the tape from the box and separated the folds. What was placed inside took Talia by surprise. The mahogany jewelry box, which matched her grandparents' bedroom furniture, sat unscathed on a pillow of bubble wrap. Talia raised the heavy jewelry box to eye level and gawked, its dark wood burned with dots and swirls, its legs bowed into curls. How did Nuno get this? And why would Domingos want it?

Talia raised the small chest against her right ear and jiggled it. Something heavy tumbled inside, a velvet-lined bed muffling its movement. The lock on its face had been dented and wrenched out of place. Talia removed the key she recovered from Vovó's watch from within the lining of her bra and stuck it in the lock on the jewelry box. A click and then the lock released. She surveyed the room and then lifted the top.

Therein, underneath her uncle's birth certificate, rested not a photo of the brooch Vovó had shown her, but the actual polished jewel itself. The picture didn't do justice to the delicate hand-craftsmanship of the gold frame, nor the brilliance of the sapphires, amethyst, and emeralds encircling the large jade gemstone set at the heart. Encrusted into the jade, a cameo of a soft face and the detailed topography of her crown, from her flowing hair to the tip of her nose.

Talia's eyes swelled as she exhaled through a wave of emotion as it passed. She pinned the brooch into the waistline of her skirt next to the Swiss Army knife in her pocket and wrapped the box to its original state, brimming with pride as she placed it back into the cabinet like new.

Just then, Domingos's voice resonated down the hallway, the tap of his loafers multiplying. Talia scrambled to find a place to hide. A strange iron handle protruded through the hardwood floors in the far corner, underneath a small Persian rug hidden in the shadows near the bookcase. Talia almost knocked herself unconscious with the door, which released too easily when she tugged on the handle. She climbed into the dungeon and pulled the door closed above her as quietly as possible. *The truth lies underneath the books.*

Nuno joined the incoherent commotion and joined it as it dissipated. It was her chance to escape. Smoothing her hands against the dank walls, Talia lit the two sconces hanging opposite each other with the lighter stuffed into her pocket, imprinting her unaccustomed eyes. Through the rings of light burnt into her retinas, she tripped across the tomb.

Half-melted crimson candles sagged around bowls of dried herbs and statuettes of Fatima, Jesus, and a topless black woman in a long rainbow skirt, which Talia recalled from her research to be the *Pomba Gira*, also known as the Mistress of the Devil, a deity in the Macumba religion. Coagulated beads spattered the sawdust floor underneath the crude altar, a deeper red than the dripped wax nearby. In between the sconces and above the statuettes, two metal hooks dangled from the ragged wall.

It was a place of worship and … sacrifice. Someone had been

hanging by the wrists there recently. It looked as though Domingos had more than just a fascination. He was actually practicing voodoo.

Ten minutes later, assuming from the silence that she was clear to go, Talia climbed the dungeon walls. But unable to find a nook to grasp for balance, she slid back onto her hip. After a moment of silence, Talia grabbed the Swiss Army knife from her pocket and stabbed the longest blade into the soft, dirt wall. It was just enough to leverage her through the hatch door, but as she climbed out, she was ambushed by a couple of brute security guards, the knife still lodged into the wall.

"Let me go!" Talia shouted, unable to wrangle free from the guards as they dragged her up the stairs.

The taller guard directed her by the elbow with a creepy grin. "I love when they put up a fight." He dragged Talia in for a kiss on the cheek, and then shoved her into the room with a violent smack on her backside.

Nuno sat on the leather couch near the window, immersed in Portuguese soccer stats printed in the local newspaper, a photo of world-renown Cristiano Ronaldo in his red *futebol* jersey slapped across the front page. Nuno looked up and then jumped up, a rookie goalie prepping for Ronaldo's deadly kick.

"*Donde fostes?* You said you would be back thirty minutes ago," Nuno scolded. "You are not *that* bad at directions."

"Actually, I am. Doesn't seem like you were too worried." Talia shuffled her feet. "This place is huge."

The words she spoke came from a subconscious part of her psyche, a place she didn't control. Talia always assumed Nuno was up to something; she wasn't blind. But how naïve she must have been, assuming their meeting was just a happenstance along the way, and fate that they would meet again. It was clear to her now that Nuno and Pierre had been stalking them in Cascais, and they stole the evidence that proved it, dumping it in a file cabinet in the closet of an abandoned building to cover their trail.

They were always after Vovó's jewelry box. It sat right next to Talia the whole time and she was too blind to see it. Worse yet, Nuno delivered an allegedly powerful amulet into the hands of an occultist, or so it seemed from the many relics in Domingos' collection and the dungeon underneath his office. The drops of blood she saw in the dungeon must have been from a human being, the one that once hung from the shackles.

Talia had the sudden urge to run to Porto, no turning back. She should have known it would be too good to be true that a sexy guy would invite her to a gorgeous vineyard out of his newfound love for her. She had been used. The sight of Nuno sickened her. Her stomach tightened as he approached.

"What is wrong, *gatinha?*" Nuno rubbed his palms on her shoulders.

"Have you ever visited my great-aunt's house before yesterday?" she asked, reminded of the strange dust patch in her great-aunt's cabinet. It explained how Nuno knew where her great-aunt's bathroom was. He'd already been there.

"*O que?*" Nuno's eyes widened.

Talia fought the urge to mention the brooch, knowing for certain Nuno would force her to return it. There were so many questions she wanted to ask him, like what Domingos planned to do with such an infamous relic in black magic, but she had to stay silent. For now. Talia needed to figure out her next course of action before she admitted to knowing his plans. As long as Nuno continued to believe Talia's ignorance, she kept her final move, whatever that may be.

"Never mind." Instead, Talia rebelled against Nuno by blatantly searching her backpack, determined to check her messages in front of him without hesitation, but her phone was missing. The front pocket, the large pocket. She even checked in the secret pocket in the back, but it wasn't there either. Talia panicked, her heartbeat irregular. "What did you do with my phone?"

"*O que?*" Nuno shifted his gaze, unable to look Talia in the eye. "Are you accusing me of stealing? Why would I steal anything from you? I have everything I need."

"Do you, now?" Talia stalled while she gathered her thoughts. She vowed to contain herself but it wasn't getting easier. She looked around and noticed the room didn't have a phone, or any other means of communicating with the outside world. Her chest tightened.

"Talia, I am on your side," Nuno said. "You know me."

"It's only been a couple of days. How can I really know you?"

"I do not know where your phone is, *eu prometo*."

Talia frowned at Nuno's promise. He could have been telling the truth, but she caught him rummaging through her backpack earlier that day. The thought of losing her connection to the outside world terrified her. She was no longer allowed to leave their suite for any reason, and the walls were asphyxiating her, imprisoning her in one of her nightmares.

Nuno, either ignorant or defiant, crept up from behind and kissed Talia on the neck.

"Stop." She slinked from his moist breath on her shoulder.

"I am trying to relax you," he said.

"It's not working," Talia said. "I need to find Jared."

"Jared? Jared left you." Nuno tightened his embrace.

"No, I left him." Talia twisted her torso to release herself.

"Why didn't he come find you if he loved you so much?"

"How could he find me? I'm in the middle of nowhere with people he doesn't know."

"If he loved you, he would have found you." Nuno caressed Talia's arms.

Hiding her frustration was proving impossible. Then an idea came to her—she needed to act fast.

"No one has ever made me feel the way Jared does. I'm sorry." She leaned back against Nuno's shoulder. "Sometimes I miss him. We've never been away from each other this long."

Nuno stopped caressing Talia's arms, then resumed intermittently. It was working. She leaned her shoulders back into Nuno's chest and rested her eyes. "You can't just stop loving someone, you know? It takes time."

He dropped his hand to his side and walked away, causing Talia to trip a step back on the rug for before she caught herself.

"How can you love him? He has not asked for you once. How can you love a man that can easily forget you?"

"Asked for me? When did he not ask for me?" Talia placed her palm at the base of her throat to calm her thumping chest, as her mother did when she was a child. "Do you know where he is?"

"He has not tried to contact you," Nuno said.

"No, you said he hasn't *asked* for me. When would he have had the chance to ask you about me, Nuno?" His name stumbled out of her mouth in a high-pitched screech. Her heart pounded in her throat.

"That came out wrong. My English, you know," he stammered.

"Yeah, your English." Talia's sarcasm, a predominantly American cadence, didn't translate well throughout the rest of the world. Nuno furrowed his brow, misunderstanding Talia's remark.

She caught sight of a security guard in the window, balancing a tray of food while marching towards a dilapidated building near the edge of the cliff. It was unlike the rest of the buildings on the estate, which have been updated. This building looked to be abandoned, like the rustic cottages in her grandfather's hometown, deserted by younger generations of farmers who wanted a chance at an education and to explore the world, while their few fading relatives labored to keep the village alive.

"I can help you forget Jared."

Talia played a smile to distract him. "How about I freshen up and we'll talk this out when I'm done?"

Nuno released his shoulders and winked. "Take your time."

He smacked Talia's behind, which added to the sting from the guard's previous whacking. She turned to simulate another smile, then wandered into the adjoining bathroom. The slender window above the toilet was not as prominent as the one in the room. Talia started the shower to create white noise, and then stood on top of the bowl to secure a view of the grounds.

It was a trek through the vines to get to the structure on the other side of the field. The security guard walked out, now with an empty tray. From the second story window, Talia observed the guard sneaking into a concealed doorway to her right. Due to her angle, she couldn't tell where it led. Jared and Caryn could have been in there, but there was only one cup.

She fiddled with her skirt for the brooch and exhaled when she found it unharmed, pinned to the inside waistline of her skirt, where she left it. Talia inspected the room for a way to escape undetected and found a three-foot square doorway at the bottom of the plumbing closet. She opened the door and saw a piped ladder leading down in between the walls. The space was wider than the void space in a normal wall. Talia suspected she was about use the passageway as it was intended, and much like Alice, she crawled into the rabbit hole.

She descended the brittle ladder, rung by rung, her path illuminated by the cracks of the closed door above her until she felt the dank cement on the soles of her feet. The passageway opened into a larger room.

Squinting to adjust to the lack of light, she spotted a doorway on the opposite wall by the sunlight trickling in through its cracks. The rays cast a dim spotlight through the dusty air onto a workbench in the far corner, a tall cabinet to its left. The cabinet shelves overflowed with muddied trinkets and tools. A pocket-sized metal flashlight caught the light and Talia snatched it. To her surprise, it shone a bright beam when she flicked the switch. She directed the beam around the cabinet to find anything that could be useful, but unless she wanted to trim hedges or replace bicycle gears, she was out of luck.

Something scuffled in the room. Talia spun around, slicing the flashlight like a machete through the dark, but she was unable to find the source. An empty cabinet obstructed a sealed doorway. Someone tried to cover up a hole where the knob should have been with putty and many coats of black paint, but the concave area was shrunken and cracked.

Talia heard a nagging drip beyond the door. She backed into the cabinet, using her weight to push it along the wall and out of the way. A draft from underneath revealed a two-inch gap between the door and the concrete floor. She bent her knees to peek underneath and jerked back at the stench of vinegar and mold.

Another scuffle nearby alarmed Talia again. The noise drew closer, the flashlight more a distraction than any assistance. At that instant, a rat hurried across Talia's foot, leaving behind a wet track. Talia stifled a scream and wrinkled her nose in disgust.

She shoved her fingers in the space underneath the door and

pulled with all her might. It loosened. Talia aligned herself in a pulley position and yanked harder, this time with both hands. The door dragged, stymied by something unknown. After stealing a pair of pliers from the shelving, Talia stabbed them through the putty hole, smashing it into sand. She stuck her hand through and discovered a latch on the other side. With a few snaps of her wrist, the latch released.

Talia gripped the cavity and dragged the door until it offered just enough room for her to squeeze through. The flashlight illuminated an old cellar similar to her grandfather's back in the States, down to its large green vat and three oak barrels. A leak from the middle barrel had caused the inch-deep puddle of burgundy in which Talia was standing. It was likely the source of the vinegar odor from the other side of the door. Talia could no longer tell the difference. The stench had already seared her sinuses. Straight ahead, a rusted medicine cabinet hung on the wall, and underneath it, a pedestal sink.

A rush of blood hit Talia's temple and with it, a flood of flashbacks to her nightmare. Terrified to see her own face in the mirror, she swung herself and the flashlight towards the large vat and stepped back until she bumped into a pole in the middle of the room. Talia didn't want to look, but she had no choice. She needed to know what was in there, and the sooner the better. She was unsure of how much time had elapsed since she left—surely enough to cause Nuno some concern.

Talia forced a step toward the eight-foot-deep vat, and then another. She placed her fingers against its side for balance. It was damp from condensation, or at least Talia had hoped. Stabilizing herself with one hand over the edge and one holding the flashlight, she climbed a few feet and peered over.

No amount of forewarning could have prepared Talia for what she saw next. In the spotlight, amidst thick clumps of torn red grapes, Caryn's face floated, puffed, pallid, and stained with a purple ring. Her eyes gawked at Talia in cold distress, devoid of the life and love they radiated only a few days before. It was the face she saw in the mirror in her nightmare, except this time it was not her own.

Talia screamed and the room screamed back. Scrambling to grip the vat wall after losing her balance, she slid off the side of the sweaty concrete tank and smacked the back of her head against the metal pole, the impact reverberating across the wet floor in waves.

The room spun into blackness.

EIGHTEEN

IT TOOK a moment for Talia to recall why she woke in a puddle of spoiled wine, propped against a pole in her grandfather's basement, skirt hiked to her thighs. She rubbed the back of her head and found the bump that caused her to fall unconscious. Examining her fingers, she was unable decipher between her blood and the wine dripping from her hair onto her new blouse.

It's only ketchup, her mother used to remind Talia when she caught something a little more violent on television than was expected. Her mother was a cop drama lover—if a detective was the main character of a television show or movie, she'd watch it. Cop shows come with a large amount of blood, which had frightened Talia before her mother comforted her with the ketchup excuse. Later she discovered it was actually high fructose corn syrup mixed with red food coloring, but the result was the same.

"Another great outfit destroyed, that's what you'd say. You picked this damn outfit out," Talia said to Caryn's body floating in the vat. "Why did you have to run off with a stranger? Did Pierre do this to you? Did he kidnap you for their freakish occult ceremonies? And Nuno, was he sent to take care of me—to seduce me into his schemes?"

The eerie fact that Domingos had an exact replica of her grandfather's gritty basement hidden in a secret room in his mansion sent a chill down Talia's kinked spine. She was lucky no one found her while she was unconscious, and luckier still that she didn't die there, fermenting with her dearest friend since grade school in a syrupy grave.

How would Domingos know what her grandfather's basement looked like? Of course. Even her possible concussion couldn't mask what was so obvious to her then. Domingos was not just Nuno's friend and employer. He was also Talia's uncle. She had her suspicions, but this was proof. There was no other explanation for why a complete stranger would have replicated her grandfather's wine cellar, the sanctuary where he spent years drinking to avoid his family. Domingos was even her grandfather's given name, which was appropriate for a man who was obsessed with his father.

Domingos's affinity for the occult fit the description Jared read about Carlos Batista at Livraria Bertrand in Lisbon. The logical conclusion: Nuno and Pierre had been sent by her uncle to separate Talia from her friends and deliver both her and the amulet to him. It was obvious why he'd want the amulet, given that he practiced voodoo, but Talia couldn't figure out how her friends fit into his plan.

The flashlight shone from halfway underneath a puddle, and Talia crawled towards it on her scuffed palms and knees. She dragged herself up to the sink to clean up, but the faucet offered no water. In a rage, Talia threw the flashlight at the mirror, the shards crashing into the sink and plunking into the puddled floor. The flashlight cracked on the cement and its glow cut out, leaving Talia in the dark.

"Forgive me, Caryn. I never meant for this to happen. I've made some unforgivable mistakes. I wish I could take them all back." Talia rubbed her forehead with her sticky fingers, her head pounding and gut spiraling. "I'll come back for you, I promise. I'll give you a proper cremation, like you deserve."

Talia blew a kiss and grabbed the door handle. "Me-a-vue."

The setting sun beamed less brightly through the door's cracks than when Talia first arrived. Squinting through the gaps, she surveyed the grounds for security guards and a safe route. The guards made their rounds along the far perimeter of the property. Talia waited until they were out of view, observing the stone ruin that now appeared so distant.

One fact kept Talia on track: from the window, the security guard fed one prisoner. If Jared was, in fact, being held captive, he could still be alive in that building. She wished she could say the same for Caryn.

The base of Talia's skull throbbed and her stomach turned as she headed into the dimming light. A wave of blood orange flooded the room. She looked both ways and limped into the fields. The landscape melded together, no vine any different, no path but the one in front of her. Her uncle wouldn't go this far over an old legend. It didn't make sense. It was just a piece of jewelry. But as Caryn would say, obsession is rarely logical.

According to *The Book of Cyprian*, a copy of which her uncle kept in his office, Queen Maria Padilha was a very prominent witch in Macumba, often invoked in many chants and rituals involving nurture and protection. Commonly called *Pomba Gira* and the Queen of Fire, she was most popular among the Gypsies. To a former Gypsy and member of a faction as she believed her uncle to be, finding an amulet that had been blessed by the *Pomba Gira* would be as life-altering as an Impressionist art collector finding a lost Claude Monet.

If only Talia had discovered a lost piece of art instead of the grape-stained corpse of her best friend. The image of Caryn's bloated purple face would haunt her to her grave, a permanent reminder of Talia's worst regret. How could she have let this happen?

Talia hunched her shoulders, snapping back when she caught a whiff of her clothing and gagged. She reaffirmed the brooch was still pinned into the lining of her skirt. Not only was it hanging there, it had left quite an impression on her pelvis. Her fall must have smashed it against her abdomen, tearing her skin in a few places in a twisted new branding. Talia couldn't feel it, even as she sat there touching the blisters with her sticky, purple fingertips.

When she finally touched a part that burned, the haunting image of Caryn's bloated face reflected in her eyelids, like the crackle of a black and white horror movie.

Take care of your best friend, her father reminded her before she left. It was an inside joke of sorts, a reminder that no one can be a better friend to her than herself. At first, Talia scoffed, claiming it was an excuse to be a terrible friend. After years of heartbreak and toxic relationships, it became her mantra, a reminder to never forget to put your own well being first, to be selfish when necessary. The saying didn't help Talia now. It didn't feel as if she could take care of anyone at the moment, let alone herself.

Her best friend was dead because of her, and she was trapped in the estate of her psychotic uncle, kilometers from the nearest neighbors. Another of her nightmares had been executed. Talia had feared it was her own demise her dream foretold, and in an odd way it was true. A piece of her died with Caryn in that wine cellar, leaving a hole in her heart she could not heal. What could Caryn have done to deserve this fate? A stolen piece of jewelry was surely not enough to provoke such a terrible end.

Talia sobbed in the twilight, awakening the stars one by one, the cool breeze compelling her eyes to shut. She couldn't stop, until a rustle in the leaves frightened her into silence.

Before she had the chance to look, the smarmy guard from the house leapt from the vines and tackled Talia into the dirt. Another guard, fresh-faced and thin, trailed closely behind, flaring a floodlight into Talia's corneas as his partner pinned her down.

"Escaped your cage, *ó pintainha?*" the guard asked, straddling her with his thick thighs. His mouth almost touched hers, the occasional spittle flicking onto her upper lip. His rancid breath stank of onions and moonshine. Talia vomited a little in her mouth but swallowed it down. She struggled to free her legs, but the guard, now inebriated, hadn't lost any of the strength he flaunted earlier that afternoon.

"Looks like we have some time alone." He restrained her wrists above her head with one arm, his moist uniform as pungent as his breath.

Talia freed her arm for a fleeting moment and punched the guard before he twisted her wrist back into place, his face unharmed. It was worth it.

With the tip of his finger, the guard popped open the top three buttons of Talia's blouse, exposing her bra. When his filthy finger landed on Talia's bottom lip, she bit down with all her might. The guard cried out, tightening his calves around her thighs to keep her writhing to a minimum. She could taste his sweat and blood on her tongue. Intending to choke her with one hand, Talia took advantage of the guard's lack of motor skills by aiming for any vital organs. She stabbed the guard's hand with any sharp objects within her reach, but it didn't faze him—self-medication numbed his senses. She needed to try something different.

"Are you guys taking turns?" Talia asked, a shiver in her throat. "Because you know, if you are, I think I'd rather have him first." Talia pointed her restrained hand to the thin security guard holding the spotlight.

"What did you say to me?" The oaf guard, suffocating her with his weight, jerked back like an insect hit by repellant.

"You heard me. I want that one first." The air circulated back into Talia's abdomen, her voice sturdier. "Don't I get some say in this?"

"*Pronto*! Let me in there, Luis," the thin guard said in a reedy tone. "You heard the girl."

"She is mine, Marcelo. I claimed her," the oaf guard slurred, swinging his arm like a caveman. "She does not get a choice."

That quieted Marcelo for a time, kicking the dirt like a kid on a time out while Talia struggled with Luis. Then Talia caught Marcelo's eye again.

"You heard her, Luis," Marcelo demanded, stepping closer. His tone toughened. "She wants me. That makes me first this time."

Talia winked at Marcelo, blowing him a kiss. He raised his shoulder with pride, but then shied away, too embarrassed to meet Talia's gaze now that she had admitted her interest. His collar neat, his stance unyielding, Marcelo was not as inebriated as his colleague, and hopefully not as unreasonable. Talia had suspected it wasn't their first ambush of an innocent girl, intoxicated or not. In fact, she banked on that assumption, and that the one on security duty would be the pawn. Taking advantage of his lack of confidence was Talia's only move. Luckily, it appeared to be working.

"*És louco, Marcelo. Desculpa, pintainha*, I don't take requests," the guard said. He bit into Talia's exposed shoulder, his incisors breaking through each layer of her skin, one by one. She screamed in agony. As he moved his head, Talia craned her neck to get a good angle on his earlobe, ready to rip it apart, but then he changed positions.

Although revolted, Talia winked again at Marcelo. He blushed and made a move towards her, but something stopped him in his tracks. Luis took one end of Talia's skirt and tore its slit up to her bikini line in a ferocious whack. Talia screeched, fighting him off in violent torrents of fists, elbows, and stiffened knees.

"Please stop! You won't get away with this. My uncle will have you killed," Talia pleaded, but none of her excuses worked. He reached his hand up her skirt. "No, please stop!"

Finally mustering the nerve, Marcelo smashed the spotlight on Luis's forehead and threw the first punch to the back of his head, knocking Luis's face into the dirt. Luis held his cheek in his hand with a blaze in his eyes, and raised his fist to Marcelo in a raging growl. The two guards crashed into each other, battling egos with knuckles, while Talia liberated herself from underneath the scuffle, grasping at rocks and torn vines for leverage.

Once Talia crawled behind a row of vines, she stood up and ran as fast as she could, underneath grapes and through irrigation trenches, running into the fields until she was certain the guards could no longer find her. By then, she was also unable to figure out where she stood. Too short to peek above the vines to get her bearings, and with no safe place to climb unobserved, she had no idea where to go next. She fastened her blouse a hundred different ways in a mild temper tantrum, but it persisted in falling open, exposing more of her bra than made her comfortable. Talia cussed in frustration. Her only navigation rested in her intuition, which only added to her anxiety. It was as if she was cursed to run through these vines for eternity, like a lost soul in the deepest levels of Dante's Inferno.

A beacon in the dark sky, the Santa Clara church poked above the landscape, in between the swaying trees, its angle exactly how Talia had pictured it in her nightmare. It was a sign. She held her blouse shut with a clenched fist and followed her gut down the path. When she saw an opening, it was near the side entrance of the main house, with its unpainted concrete block walls. She stood a mere one hundred feet from where she started running. Nuno emerged from the courtyard and caught Talia cursing in Portuguese into the night.

"There you are!" Nuno yelled. He jogged over to Talia, who was disheveled and fraught. "What happened? Your clothes are all ripped, and … purple. Did you go swimming in wine?"

"I got assaulted." Talia tugged down her skirt.

"*O que?*" Nuno asked, his skin flushed and limbs fidgety. "Who did this?"

"Apparently, I need guards for the guards." Talia grunted.

"I thought you were in the bathroom. After an hour, I started looking for you. It has been almost three hours! Don't worry, I did not tell Domingos. Where did you go?"

"Does it matter?" Talia asked. "I'm here now."

"You are a feisty one, *gatinha*," Nuno said. "I am going to tell Domingos about this guard. Look at what he did to you."

"I don't need to see it, I feel it," Talia said. "Don't bother telling him. He won't care."

"Of course he will," Nuno said. "He is a reasonable man."

"I'm not so sure he is. Not after what I found."

Nuno stopped. "What did you find, Talia? Where were you?"

"My friend is dead in your friend *Domingos's* basement. He killed her."

"Excuse me?"

"You heard me." Talia could feel the blood rushing back into her cheeks.

"I do not understand. What basement?"

"Thanks to your friend, Caryn's floating in a vat of spoiled wine down there." Talia pointed to where she thought there was a door, but it was no longer visible.

"What door, Talia?" Nuno asked.

"It was right there. I was just in there. Maybe the door is camouflaged or something. I know what I saw."

Nuno nodded and directed Talia towards their room with his hand pressed against her lower back. Talia stalled with requests for bathroom breaks or finding something she'd lost in the fields, but Nuno didn't allow for excuses. Somehow, someway, she needed get back to the shack on the other side of the field that night or there was a good chance she'd never see Jared again. She already lost Caryn, she'd be damned if she let her uncle take Jared, too.

To what extent was Nuno involved in her uncle's crimes? Was he truly just a messenger, ignorant of his employer's plans? Talia found it hard to believe that Nuno wouldn't know something was off after having lived there for years.

Nuno was carrying Talia up the stairs when the maid rushed down, yelling Portuguese cuss words and shooing Nuno away. "Where are you taking her?"

"*O Patrão*, he will kill me if there is wine on the white rugs." The maid dragged Talia with her. "Come to the laundry room. *Vamos!*"

"Okay, but hurry, *por favor*." Nuno's shouts trailed.

Talia chased the maid across the courtyard, through a paved corridor shaded by a pergola, and then ending in the laundry room. Its grimy walls narrowed at the horizon. Two fogged basement-sized windows on the right wall let in some of the moonlight through their iron bars. Washing machines lined the left wall of the dusky room, dryers to the right, and at the far end, she found a pile of folded clothes.

"Your clothes are on the washing machine in the back. *Boa sorte*," the maid mumbled, and hurried off.

"Good luck with what?" Talia asked, but the maid had already vanished.

Talia peeled off her sticky garments with a series of relieved sighs. Freezing in her stained purple skin, she bounced around to dry off and warm up, and then slipped on the freshly dried clothes. The chemical aroma of lavender and lilies soothed her nerves, if just for the length of an inhalation. The black jeans and t-shirt were more her style than any skirt, and they fit pretty well. The maid knew her size.

Talia nearly overlooked the envelope sneaking out from underneath the pile. Heavier than normal, she ripped the letter open with a less-than-sane curiosity. Inside were a folded piece of notepaper and a gold key.

A detailed hand-drawn map of the grounds was scribbled on the note. On one end a big red "X" marked where the building near the cliff stood and on the other, a red stick figure marked the equivalent of a "You Are Here" dot on a directory board. The fluorescent light shone through the piece of paper revealing writing, similar to the note slipped under her door, on the other side of the map.

> Repeat.
> May the arm of Zambi restrain
> Whoever wishes to do me harm.
> May my enemies be paralyzed whenever they
> Harbor evil thoughts against this sinning
> > daughter.
> – Padilha

Her signature. It proved the maid and her informant were one and the same. The maid clearly wrote the note. How would she know her contact's name otherwise? She went out of her way Talia's whole stay, risking her job to assist her in ways only her contact would understand. Her last text even said she'd see her at the house. It all made sense. But why would she be helping Talia if she works for her psychopath uncle?

Whatever the maid's intentions, Talia had little choice but to follow her instructions. As much as she'd like to pretend, the map was her only chance to discover who was captive in that building. She slid the key into her pocket and slinked out the back entrance as the maid's drawing suggested.

The vineyard was easier to navigate with a map in hand. Talia lamented her lack of directional sense while she counted her way through rows of vines to the east and west, chanting Padilha's poem under her breath with blind faith. It was strangely relaxing.

The fruity dew gathered on the leaves, splashing Talia's cheeks as she shuffled through the vines. Although mounds of wax dotted the grounds surrounding the building, only a few candles glowed at the front entrance.

Talia hugged the concrete wall along the side of the building facing the river to avoid being seen. Just then, a dragging sound followed by a loud crash came from within. Talia could feel the rumbling underneath her feet.

Someone was still in there. Talia fought the urge to scream Jared's name out loud, afraid it might awaken her captors. She anticipated a reaction for what felt like ten minutes, until she hadn't heard so much as a breeze, and then ran towards the front corner.

The closest candle was still too far for her to blow out, so she tore a leafy branch off a nearby vine and fanned it toward the entrance. She swung harder and harder until a steady breeze tickled the flame close to extinction, but nothing changed until a heavy wind hurtled through the vines, snuffing all three candles in one fell swoop. Talia thanked the universe.

She scurried to the front door but it was locked. A blue and white *azulejo* plaque affixed to the left of the front door read "Raposo" in hand-brushed cursive. She recalled the note the maid left for her and shoved her fingers in her front pocket. With the moonlight to guide her, she tinkered with the keyhole. Another gust of wind swung the door wide open before Talia had a chance to remove the key.

She had been in a room like this before, a temple with a stone altar littered with red candles and multiple statuettes of deities. It was a larger version of the dungeon in her uncle Carlos's office. The weathered pews adorned with red and white embroidered linens scattered around the perimeter. To outsiders, *terreiros* like these are rural temples located on large farms or plantations, far outside the vigilance of the city. To believers in these cults, it is not just a place of worship, but a sanctuary for their spirit hosts— to sing, dance, celebrate, sacrifice, and mourn together.

A moan echoed from the corner.

Talia spotted Jared tied to a rusty pole to the far right of the hall, and ran towards him. "Jared. You're alive!" she yelled, unable to silence her relief.

Jared moaned again, biting at the monogrammed handker-chief tied around his mouth.

"I'm so sorry, Jared," Talia cried as she pulled off the hand-kerchief. "I didn't know this would happen. You have to believe me."

"I do believe you," Jared rasped. "I'm the one that should be sorry. I should have listened to you. I should have taken you seriously."

"Shh." Talia held his cheeks and kissed his lips. The scent of his sweat, the taste of his skin, warm and comforting.

"Caryn is dead," Jared said.

"I know. I saw her."

Jared creased his forehead.

"I don't have time to get into it right now," she said. "What matters is that you're alive. I love you so much."

"I love you, too, baby. Now untie me."

"I need to tell you something," Talia said as she fumbled with the knots, her hands trembling like Vovó's did near the end, hard to control.

"It can wait. We need to get out of here first."

"It can't wait. Jared, I did something I regret. I hope you can forgive me."

"If you're going to say you killed someone, I would say under these circumstances, it's excusable." Jared rubbed his unbound wrists.

"It's worse than that. You see, I met —"

"There you are, Talia! Again you slip through my fingers," Nuno exclaimed as he burst into the building. "I see you have found Jared."

"So, you *did* know he was here. You bastard," Talia said.

"Have patience, *gatinha*," Nuno said. "I just found out."

"You're the guy from the restaurant in Lisbon," Jared said as he lost his balance and slipped onto the stone floor.

"I don't believe you," Talia said.

"You should, after what we have been through." Nuno forced a kiss onto Talia's lips.

Talia shoved Nuno away. "What are you doing?"

"What is he talking about, Talia?" Jared loosened the noose around his ankles.

"If you continue this way, Jared, I will have to leave your girl-friend here with you."

Jared stopped, a figurative gun pointed at his head.

"I can explain," Talia said. "I was trying to tell you this earlier but—"

"She has not told you she found someone new?" Nuno asked with a grin.

"It's not what it sounds like," Talia said, but Jared looked away.

"It is exactly what it sounds like. I comforted her when she left you, Jared. She needed someone and I was there for her. I understand her."

"Why are you doing this? Haven't you done enough already?" Talia asked. "You lied to me. If I had known, I would have never let you touch me. You violated me."

The two guards walked into the room and tied Jared back up, but not without resistance.

"Leave him alone, you rapists!" Talia shouted.

"*Desculpa*, Talia, but Domingos is looking for you. You must come with me."

"I'm not leaving without Jared."

"I am afraid it is not a choice. You have to come with me or Domingos will not be happy with any of us, and then how will you save your *namorado*?" Nuno asked.

"You can help me. If you cared for me at all, you *would* help me," Talia begged. "You can't just leave him here."

"I have no choice. He must stay or we all do."

"I'm staying then." Talia stomped her foot.

"No, Talia, go," Jared said. "I'll be fine."

"Are you crazy? No, you won't. I'm not leaving you."

"You have no choice, Talia," Nuno said. "Come with me and we can convince Domingos to let him go, together."

Talia shuddered. The guards slobbered at her as she tripped past them, but Nuno glared at them until they stepped back in unison.

"I'll be back for you, Jared, I promise. I love you."

Jared didn't respond.

"Get your hands off me!" Talia yelled at the guards as they escorted her to the room.

"Domingos is going to have both of our heads," Nuno said, leading the pack up the stairs.

"I can't believe I left Jared there," Talia said, her eyes sunken.

Luis kissed the air as Talia slammed the door in his face.

"You had no choice. Even I am not able to stop the guards."

"You didn't try very hard. You were too busy acting like a teenage boy."

"*És maluca*," Nuno said.

"I *am* crazy, crazy for trusting you. You knew all along where my friends were. One of them is dead now. I should never have let you touch me." Talia paced the room, dodging Nuno's gaze. More than ever, she craved a glass of wine, but she couldn't let her guard down for one moment.

"Dead? Who is dead?" Nuno asked.

"Don't play games with me now, Nuno. I'm over the games," Talia said.

"*Te amo*, Talia."

"You're absurd. How could you love me?" Talia scrunched her nose. "You don't even know me. I'm positive I don't know you."

"I love you anyway. One day you will see what I have done for you and you will love me back, *sem ajúda*."

Talia paused, mouth agape, digesting Nuno's possible confession. "Without help? Are you admitting to luring me into your trap so you could hand me over to my uncle? I know what you've been up to."

"So you know about my friend?" Nuno asked. He forced a smile, and a fire raged through Talia's body, raising the hair on her freckled head.

"Of course I know. It wasn't hard to figure out with the familiar photos and his fascination with the occult. The creep even has a replica of my grandfather—his father's—wine cellar," Talia said. "Why did you bring me here? Was I part of the package he paid you to deliver?"

"I am loyal to your uncle because he was there for me when I had no one else. He is like a father to me. You will see him the way I do. He is a good man," Nuno said. "He only wants what is best for his family."

"Our definition of a good man differs."

The stone building haunted Talia from the window. She should be there, freeing Jared. This was her fault. No one else was to blame. She stumbled into her uncle's plan, seduced by his gopher boy. She was the fool who led her friends to their kidnappings. She abandoned them, left them for dead in a foreign country, to pursue a dangerous criminal straight into his trap. She was a fool for thinking it could end any other way.

"Please trust that I meant you no harm. I had no idea what your uncle had been planning. He asked for a favor and I, of course, agreed. His intentions were harmless. He rarely spoke of his family, so when he mentioned you, I was, how do you say, intrigued."

"You lied to me," Talia said, approaching Nuno's face by mere centimeters.

"Not about my feelings for you. *Nunca.*" Nuno grabbed Talia's hand. "Please, forgive me."

A lock of Nuno's mane tickled Talia's nose and she inexplicably longed to kiss his scruffy cheek. He drew her in, and intoxicated by the smell of lavender and cloves, she kissed him back. But when he fiddled with her *Figa* necklace, she snapped out of her trance.

"What are you doing?" Talia cracked her forearms on his chest.

"Your necklace tangled. I fixed it." Nuno raised his hands in the air like a fugitive.

"All I want is to shower and go to bed."

"Your escape route has been locked. They came to fix it while you were gone."

"They wouldn't have known unless you told them."

"I was worried. It was getting dark, and I know how violent those guards can be, what they tried to do to you." Nuno shook his head.

"Violent doesn't cover it." Talia shivered, thanking the universe once again for allowing her to escape before the guard could do any real damage, the kind of damage that was done to Caryn. She assumed Carlos had been informed of Talia's revelation. This gave him ample time to conjure his next move, leaving Talia with no card to play. But it was worth everything to find Jared.

The moon hid behind the white sky that evening, and Talia's wet head collided with her pillow. Nuno caressed her back. Her exhaustion did not help her sleep any easier, as she could not shake Nuno's unwavering watch. She had, however, managed to fool him into thinking she was in deep sleep.

Nuno placed something scented with lavender, vanilla, and ginger under the pillow near her nose, sang a few words under his breath, and left the bed. Talia slit her eyelids to be sure Nuno had indeed gone to take a shower. Underneath her pillow rested a small burlap satchel, handmade of herbs and tied at the end with a blue satin ribbon. Was it some sort of love potion?

It was not a potion, as it was not in liquid form, but the believed end result was the same—to force someone to love you. Talia had seen these before in Wiccan shops, and if she recalled correctly from her research, the scents of lavender and vanilla open hearts to new lovers; ginger keeps them faithful.

In Portuguese-speaking countries, these satchels are called *bolsas*, or pockets, and they can also contain ground bones, hair, and skin from various sacrificed animals or humans targeted for love or revenge. She had found a similar satchel at her cousins' crime scene, the one Pai Pedro claimed was evil.

Talia scrubbed her upper arms through a chill. All those different scents Nuno wore, they weren't part of his cologne, but rather, intoxicating herbs to control her.

Jared would never take this as a credible excuse for her misbehavior. She knew the consequences of her actions, yet a part of her was drawn to Nuno, compelled to be near him. She thought it was fate. After all, Nuno's eyes didn't wander like Jared's, and he supported every move she made. Now none of Nuno's actions over the last few days felt genuine.

Neither scenario alleviated the shame of being lured into an affair by a man who neglected to mention her sociopath uncle raised him, or to forget the years of laughter she could have experienced with her best friend. Talia gazed out the window to the *terreiro*, now cordoned, her goose bumped arms dangling at her sides. What had she gotten Jared into this time?

Timing herself against Nuno's shower, Talia dumped the satchel contents out of the window and replaced them with the mix that Pai Paolo gave her earlier that week in a tin canister, zipping across the room to bed and back to the window before Nuno reemerged from his steam bath.

"Everything is worth it when your faith is not small," Nuno said, quoting Pessoa once again. "You will see Jared again, *gatinha*, I promise. You do not need to worry."

As he kneaded Talia's shoulders, she curbed a wince, well aware that playing along may be her only hope to save the man she loved. And yet Nuno's aroma was tough to resist. She felt herself sinking back into his bare chest and then halted, her head bobbing as if she had fallen asleep in class. She could not, would not waste another minute listening to Nuno sweet-talk her into his duplicities. She needed to focus.

NINETEEN

THE DRAPERY COVERING the dining room windows fooled Talia into thinking it was evening rather than late morning, and a yawn caught her off guard. Carlos sat at the opposite head of the long dining room table, its polished grooves reflecting the dim radiance of the chandeliers.

"I hope you do not mind. I am sending Nuno on an errand. I thought we should talk." Carlos adjusted his fedora with a nervous tick. "Alone."

It was a far distance for an intimate talk.

"I will speak to you later, Talia." Nuno excused himself and walked out the front door, avoiding eye contact.

"Wait, Nuno, don't go," Talia said. Jared's musk still emanated from his Red Sox sweatshirt, which Talia wore as a quiet form of solidarity that morning.

Hovering around his chair, not quite ready to sit, her uncle continued, "Nuno has done well for me. I have been looking for you for some time. He tells me you already know who I am."

The room chilled. Talia searched for clues to her uncle's identity to corroborate her theory. None of the metal-framed photos lining his desk were recent. Most were torn and yellowed. Talia recognized one of the pictures, though it had aged more than the one she stole from her great-aunt's house.

"I think you know more than that," the man said, holding back a wheeze.

Talia could not believe she hadn't seen the resemblance before then. He was oddly familiar, like an old photo of her grandfather in the army that her mother carried around in her wallet. He was even balding in the same places.

Talia couldn't blink, nor did she dare try for fear of showing weakness. "Are you Carlos Batista?"

"I have not been him for many years," the man said, staring out the window. "My name is Domingos Raposo now."

The sun peeked through the curtains, stinging Talia's eyes. "I know who you are," she said, picking at her nails. "You're my uncle." As her words spilled out into the air, she felt their terrible truth solidify. Her stomach turned.

"From what I hear, you were also looking for me. Seems we have found each other," her uncle said. "I knew you would come to me once my mother passed."

"I loved her very much." Talia dropped her head.

"As did I, selfish as she may have been." Carlos leaned on the table with his knuckles.

"I'd hardly call her selfish." Talia clenched her fists at her side. "She was everything a grandmother should be."

"I can see why you think so highly of her." He charred a cigar and puffed three times before inhaling. "She did not cause you the pain she caused me."

"What pain could she have caused you? You seem to have done well for yourself from the looks of this place."

"You could not understand."

"Then explain. I have nowhere to be. You have me trapped here."

"You are a passionate girl, Natalia, but you must learn patience." Carlos shook his head. "I suppose it is time you knew the truth, after being lied to by our family your whole life. Your grandparents, my parents, ripped me from the only place I called home and took me to a country I despised. I had to leave everything right before I was about to graduate and start a life for myself."

"You mean moving to America?" Talia asked. "They were trying to give you a better life, like all good parents do."

"What *they* considered a better life. But it was not better to me. Should I not have a say? I was almost an adult. Five long years I spent trying to make friends, fit in, and even go to college. But the people were unfriendly and angry. I worked at a local garage to make money, when I could have been training to run a business in my home country. So I returned."

"You can't blame them for reaching for the American dream. Most things don't work out the way you plan," Talia said. "It's called life."

"They did not try to stop me," he continued, unfazed. "I had to fight all my battles alone. My father was a brutal, unreasonable man. He never ceased to remind me of my place in the family."

"That's tough love. My dad was the same way. He probably thought you could use the extra layer of skin. He's been dead a long time now, you know. You should really move on."

Carlos's eyes reddened with fury.

"I'm enjoying the family therapy session and all, but why am I here? You didn't bring me out here to the middle of nowhere just for a family reunion."

"What makes you think I have another motive?" Carlos pursed his lips. "I wanted to meet my niece."

"You could've sent a letter or called. But instead, you had one of your *friends* come fetch me," Talia said. "I think you owe me the truth about why I'm here, Carlos."

"My name is Domingos," her uncle said. "And you already know the truth."

"Maybe you think our bloodline makes us telepathic, but I have no idea what you're thinking." Talia pointed her index finger into the air with flushed cheeks and a clenched jaw. "Why don't you just tell me and save us both the drama?"

"We have much to talk about, but not on an empty stomach. My maid will be here any minute now to serve lunch. Please sit down."

Her newfound uncle exhaled a plume of cigar smoke, and then sat in his seat, muffling a cough. She hesitated, but without the words to reply, Talia cleared her throat and sat down.

"Natalia is such a pretty name. Do you know where it came from?" Carlos asked.

Talia nodded her head and tightened her grip on her glass of *Vinho Verde*. "After the patron saint of my grandfather's hometown."

The legend of *Natalia de Alva* had been told in her household hundreds of times since her youth, so Talia had no need to hear it again. Natalia de Alva was an innocent young girl, loved by her father's small village of Alva just outside Porto six decades before her father was raised there.

As is the nature of any story passed down by word of mouth alone, the dates and details surrounding the girl were vague. What was known for certain is she was not yet an adult when she died of an unknown illness, a common occurrence in the rural mountain farm villages of Portugal, which rarely housed a doctor.

To save space, the Portuguese government excavated the

dead who had been buried for over five years, after they have decomposed, and placed them deeper into the ground in order to bury a new body above them. This practice shocked Talia when she first heard of it, but it was an essential part of the legend of *Natalia de Alva,* who was also unburied when her time had come.

To the grave diggers' surprise, they found her body unscathed, and her cheeks flush. These are signs of sainthood. Her casket was exhibited at the church for decades; her name was worshipped with an annual festival in August consisting of a procession, large feasts, and live music playing into the late night hours.

"It is a beautiful and sad story," Carlos said. "Do you believe it?"

"It's hard to know what to believe." Talia preferred to avoid small talk.

"Would you like some Port? We do make our own here." He stalled. "I am sure you have seen the vineyards."

"Oh, I was up close and personal." The scent of the guard's breath still lingered in Talia's nostrils. "I would much rather hear *your* explanation as to why I'm here."

"Very well," Carlos said. "You were right to assume that I brought you here for a reason. You have something special of my mother's that is rightfully mine."

"And that would be?" Talia asked in an attempt at ignorance.

"You are far smarter than you show, Natalia, but you have not fooled me. My mother, your grandmother, left you a jewelry box of great importance to me. One she promised to me long before you were contemplated in your mother's mind. You are not as clever as you may think, Natalia. You left behind evidence."

"You're not making sense," Talia said, her heart quivering.

"The jewelry box, my dear. You forgot to lock it when you stole my amulet."

In all of Talia's delight, she forgot the one important part of snooping—leaving everything as you found it. She put together the manila box, but she forgot to lock the jewelry box that was in it. A rookie mistake.

"I don't know of any amulet," Talia said, her throat clenching. "Your mother told me once of a brooch that belonged to Maria Padilha."

"*Rainha Maria Padilha*," Carlos corrected. "There will be no disrespecting the *Pomba Gira* in this house, my dear niece."

"I am well aware of your undying loyalty to the Mistress of the Devil," Talia said. "I am also not your family. In fact, I don't even know you. And at this point, I'm pretty sure I don't like you either."

Carlos grunted, and began a retort, only to be interrupted by a clambering food cart juggling a large silver pot. A stack of white bowls leaned next to it. Talia smiled as the maid ladled the steaming soup into the first bowl and placed it on top of the plate already on Talia's placemat. The maid smiled and steered the cart towards her uncle's side of the table to repeat the same task.

Talia hadn't much of an appetite, regardless of her love for Portuguese kale soup, thickened by potatoes and salted by *linguiça*, which the maid had served. It's one of the signature dishes Talia craved when visiting the motherland.

When the maid stood at a safe distance beyond the exit door, Carlos continued, "Where is it, Natalia?"

"I don't know what you're talking about," she said.

"I know you have it. You have not fooled me."

"You keep saying that, Carlos," Talia said with a nod, "and I may actually believe you one day."

"My name is Domingos. Who raised you to be so impolite?"

"Your mother," Talia said. "Forgive me, but in what culture is it polite to invite someone to your home under false pretenses?"

"It is also not very polite to steal."

"According to your mother's will, the jewelry box is mine, so therefore, you're the one trying to steal it from me. Rather unsuccessfully, I might add."

"Arrogance does not suit you. There is more at stake here than you know, my dear niece." He sipped soup from his polished spoon. "I have been following you since you arrived in the country. One of my men met you the other night."

Talia stirred her soup, watching the kale swim in between the potato crumbles like seaweed. She had almost forgotten about the bartender's friend, her FBI informant.

"Not much of an appetite, I see," her uncle said. "My cook makes the best *caldo* in Trás os Montes. I bet your friends would have loved it."

A lump the size of a brick dropped in Talia's stomach. She jerked up, her spoon clashing against the tiled floor. "I know what you've done to my friends. They had nothing to do with this."

Her heart raced further, her eyes threatening to well up with fury. She counted to five.

"*Paciência*, Natalia. Have you lost your sense of humor already?" Her uncle patted down the ends of his mustache with the tips of his stumpy fingers.

"You think killing my best friend is funny?" Talia's shout echoed across the room.

"I did not kill anyone," her uncle said. "I gave them a place to stay."

Talia shook her head. "My friend Caryn is dead. She is floating around in a concrete vat in your creepy wine cellar. A wine cellar that looks exactly like your father's back in the States. Freud would have a field day with you."

"I do not understand." Carlos shook his head and looked down like an innocent suspect, but Talia had no intention of giving him the benefit of the doubt.

"What did Caryn do to deserve to die? Was she too feisty? Did she try to escape? I can't imagine she'd die without a fight."

"Your friend Caryn was living here with us. Fine girl," Carlos said. "I do not understand. She left a couple days ago."

"Oh, she left alright. She left this life, thanks to you." Talia's pitch escalated. "Did you use her as part of some satanic ritual you held in your dungeon? I saw your secret lair. What kind of monster are you?"

Luis marched into the room, reporting for security duty, evidently not removed from employment for being a serial rapist.

"Ah, perfect timing. I'm afraid you'll be confined to your room, Natalia," her uncle said. "This man here will make sure you stay there until further notice. Your pranks last night cost you and your boyfriend a great deal of freedom. I hope it will be worth it."

The desire to smack the smirk off her uncle's face overwhelmed Talia, and she struggled against Luis's firm hold to do so, but it was no use. Luis, with his dark eyes and an expressionless jowl, was far larger and stronger than Talia, as she had already witnessed the night before.

"Jared is alive, I saw him. I'll find him again and you'll pay for everything you've done. You have my word on that, Carlos!" Talia screamed as Luis dragged her away.

"Empty threats, my dear," Carlos said. "I commend your delightful spirit. I see a lot of my mother in you."

Talia spat at Carlos, but it landed just short of his fancy shoes, inspiring him to laugh so heartily he shed a tear. Now sober, the guards chaperoned Talia to her room while still in her uncle's sight.

"You know where to find me if you change your mind." Luis winked and then slammed the door behind him, just in time to dodge Talia's shoe, which cracked against the handle.

Talia flipped him off as he fiddled with the lock on the other side. "I won't be changing my mind, you rapist!"

"Hey, hey." Nuno yelled at the guard. "What happened?"

"Like you don't know." Talia straightened her wrinkled blouse.

"*Não sei, pá.* Did you get caught doing something again?"

"I'm on to you. I know what you and my uncle are up to and I'm going to stop it."

"I don't want to hurt you. I like you very much, Talia. *Já te disse.*" Nuno dug his fingers into Talia's waist to draw her in.

"Get off me," she said, and then slapped his cheek. "You're as much of a liar as he is. What have you done with my boyfriend?"

"*Now* he is your boyfriend?" Nuno asked, his pitch higher than normal. "*O coração, se pudesse pensar, pararia.*"

"I don't have time for semantics, Nuno," Talia barked, ignoring the quote from Pessoa that Nuno recited. The poem declared that if the heart could think, it would stop.

At that moment, she wished his would. He had succeeded in manipulating her by quoting heartbroken verses from her favorite Portuguese poet, but she was no longer misled.

"Why did my uncle kill Caryn and take Jared prisoner? I don't understand why Caryn needed to die."

"Your uncle is not as bad as you say. He does things different than other people. There is a good reason why you think you saw your friend."

"I *know* I saw my friend, drowned in a vat of spoiled wine. *Your* friend is so amazing he ordered a brute guard to prey on his own niece and laughed as he fondled her up the stairs. After he attempted to rape her hours before, of course. I'd call that different. If you think he's a great guy, you're either ignorant or in on the master plan. Which one is it?" Talia folded her arms against her chest.

"I do not know what Domingos is thinking, I just do as I am told," Nuno said.

"His name is Carlos and ignorance is not an excuse," Talia said.

"We all make mistakes."

"This is a bit more than a mistake, Nuno. Someone died, someone I love. If you say you care about me, how are you allowing this guy to hurt me like this?"

"I do care about you, but I cannot control what your uncle does. He is his own man."

"He'd listen to you if you told him to let Jared go." She placed her hands on Nuno's chest and whispered, "Let him go and we can be together."

"It is not up to me, Talia," Nuno said. "I would do anything for you, *tu sabes*. But you have seen your uncle's power. I am no match for him. Both our lives are at risk."

"Power? You mean his money. I can see his money," Talia said, looking around the room. "But money is not infinite. It won't save him when his time comes."

"It is more than money. Do not lie to yourself, *gatinha*. We cannot play games with this man. *Isto é sério*."

"I'm well aware of how serious this is. What else do you know? What other lies have you told me? Lies are like cockroaches, Nuno. When you find one, expect a dozen more."

"*Sim*, I lied, but I care about you. I thought I was doing the right thing. I was bringing a family together," Nuno said. "You must believe me."

"Is that what this is to you, a reunion?" Tears welled in Talia's eyes. "What reunions have you been attending lately? Do yours usually involve murder, kidnapping and attempted rape? Because mine sure seem to."

"This is not what your uncle intended." Nuno's lips curled downward.

"Then what did he intend? Did he intend you to drug me with your herbs and spells? Did he intend you to seduce me into getting trapped in his estate? Which part of this nightmare did he intend?"

There was a knock at the door.

Talia grunted. "Can't I have a moment to think here?" Talia nibbled her fingers, pacing around the bed.

"I think you need to rest. *Estás maluca.*"

"I'm not crazy, Nuno. You've been using me." Talia tripped over her words. "I can't do this. I need some time alone."

"After what you did last night, it is lucky you are still here with me," Nuno said. "*Senhor Domingos* has plans for us tonight."

"I refuse to do anything that man has planned for me." Talia felt woozy, the air thinning and her throat constricting.

"He is your blood, *não*? Maybe you can help each other."

"Taking your niece's boyfriend hostage is not the best way to get to know her, I can tell you that," Talia trailed off. "I don't feel well."

"You are very special to your uncle," Nuno said. "To both of us."

Talia leaned her hip against the bedpost, no longer able to carry her own weight. An unusually calm Nuno offered his balance, but she refused, swinging her fists in the air, her vision blurry.

"What have you done to me?" Talia slurred as she felt her knees smack the floor.

TWENTY

THE DIM WORLD hastened past Talia, her limbs paralyzed and jaw clenched. The journey through the hallways ended with her cheeks cooled by the breeze that rustled the leaves in the distance.

In an attempt to rub her eyes, her arms bent back, bound behind her as she twisted herself on a stiff but mobile chair. She jerked her shoulders but couldn't break away. A pair of callus hands freed her from the handkerchief that blinded her, yanking with it strands of her hair. The rays of the setting sun burned through her slivered eyelids.

"*Desculpe*. The way you have been acting, I had to take precautions," Talia heard her uncle Carlos say.

"What did you give me?" The curve of Talia's neck tracked her uncle's voice. "You … you drugged me."

"Not exactly, my dear niece," he said. "Our boy Nuno knows a trick or two. He should demonstrate for you sometime."

"He already has." Talia struggled to loosen her ankles.

"*Paciência*, Natalia, you will not be leaving. I promise."

Able to clear her vision with a few blinks, Talia realized she and Carlos were not alone on the veranda overlooking the vine-yards. To her uncle's left stood the maid. She offered him a tender glance and scampered inside.

Plumes of smoke wafted from behind Talia to the right. Unable to turn her head, she was still certain it was Nuno. A half-empty box of cigarettes rested on a glass table peeking out from the darkness, the same brand Nuno smoked.

Talia wiggled her torso to find a more comfortable position, as impossible as it seemed. The rope that kept her bound to the metal chair dangled around her wrists. Until Nuno walked into the light, she couldn't escape, even though the urge to do something irrational was nearly overpowering. "Was this necessary?"

"I am afraid it was," Carlos said. "*Claro*, I could not trust you to attend our important event tonight on your own. You are the star, you must make an appearance. *Tem que ser*."

"The star of what?" Talia asked, fearful that these were the plans Nuno spoke of earlier. "What kind of event?"

"You will see," Carlos said, drawing a drag off his cigar, and then erupting into a chronic wet cough. He drew a yellowed hand-kerchief from his pant pocket. It was the same monogrammed handkerchief Jared had tied around his mouth the night before. Opening it at his face, her uncle released a ball of phlegm that sounded as if it had been accumulating in his lungs for days.

Her grandfather used to cough like that. He passed away years before Vovó, after a long bout with emphysema. Even after many years smoke-free, her grandfather carried around mono-grammed handkerchiefs into which he regularly coughed up pieces of his already sliced lungs.

"You sound like your father," Talia said. "He died eight years ago, but I'm guessing you already know that. Looks like you're headed for the same fate."

Reacting as Talia had hoped, Carlos pounded his fists on the iron railing, unable to stifle another cough. "Fate is a funny thing, Natalia," he said, his throat scratchy.

"Is Jared going to be at your event tonight?" Talia asked, a rasp still noticeable in her voice. "If I'm the star, I assume Jared will be a part of this event of yours. I know he's in that stone building near the river. I saw him there."

"Is this true?" Carlos waved his stubby fingers toward a rumbling in the dark. "Was she indeed in the *terreiro?*"

Talia did not turn to look. "Of course it's true. I'm a terrible liar. Tell him, Nuno."

With a clear view of the stone building below, she searched for any sign of Jared. An ominous swarm of clouds shadowed a round wrought-iron sign with a triangle symbol that had been staked into the soil near the entrance. Various colorful figurines, such as Fátima and Jesus, guarded the open doorway.

"I told you she was hard to fool." Nuno strolled into view, forcing out the last drag of his cigarette and throwing it off the side of the balcony.

"Well, you got me this time." Talia sneered at Nuno as she yanked at her chaffed wrists and ankles, tightening the knots further. "You got what you wanted. Congratulations."

"It did not have to be this way," Nuno said. "You are—"

"You are too determined to tame, Natalia," Carlos interrupted. "So we took stronger action."

"By poisoning me? Gee, thanks. Your sense of family really warms the heart." Writhing in her seat, Talia managed to stand, but with her arms and legs fastened together, she could not maintain her balance. Twisting her ankle, Talia tumbled backward into Nuno's arms. "Don't touch me," she said while recoiling from Nuno's grasp.

Nuno steadied her hips on her bound feet and refused to let go as Carlos walked closer.

"I see you have Batista blood, Natalia." Carlos squeezed her shoulder with his free hand, a plume of smoke seeping out his nose and encircling her face. "I like your passion. Your friend had that passion."

Talia's heart tightened. Attempting to step on Nuno's toes as another escape tactic, she almost lost her balance and again he caught her, wrapping her in his tobacco and sandalwood musk. She hated herself for the desire she still carried for him, whether real or induced.

"I apologize for the brute of my guards," Carlos said. "It seems they do not know their own strength. I had no idea your friend was missing. I assumed she left, but it turns out my guards got a little out of control."

"The *guards* did that to her?" Talia shivered. She hadn't considered the guards suspects, even though she knew she wasn't their first victim. The guards succeeded in doing to Caryn what they tried to do to Talia, and then hid the evidence. Her stomach curdled. "You knew they did this and they still work for you? You do know they tried to do the same to me?"

"I heard about your scuffle and they were reprimanded accordingly." Carlos huffed from his cigar.

"Accordingly would be to fire them or throw them off the cliff," Talia said. "You stationed them a hundred feet from my bed as I slept. Do you get pleasure from tormenting me? Am I part of some kind of sick vendetta—a child punished for the sins of her grandparents?"

"You are no child. You act as if you are sinless, as if you have not committed a crime against me." Carlos breathed heavily, his cheeks rich with blood like his father when he took one drink too many. "This is not just about my parents. You are here to help your family."

"You are hardly family," Talia said. "Families don't drug each other. Families don't tie each other to chairs."

"We do what we need to survive, Natalia. When you are older, you will understand."

"I will never understand this. I'll never understand the death of my best friend. You let those guard dogs take her from me."

Carlos closed his eyes and pursed his lips. "Why did you wear that *Figa* necklace if you do not believe?"

Talia inspected her chest for the necklace. It was missing. She also no longer wore the outfit she put on earlier that day. Instead, she wore a red embroidered dress resembling the doilies her mother crocheted to protect their furniture from her collection of knick-knacks. A fresh set of tooth prints peeked from underneath her shoulder pads. A hand-braided gold belt cinched her waist. Talia scrunched her nose in disgust for the outfit and her twisted theories for how she got into it.

Nuno had once again invaded her privacy. A cramp spanning the length of her arms up to her neck displaced the burn on her hip where the amulet had once rubbed. She could feel the amulet's weight lifted, its lingering chafe a reminder of Vovó's last wishes.

"What did you do with my necklace?" Talia asked. "And where's the amulet? Why was it so important that you had to kill my friends to steal it from me?"

"I believe I have spotted a hypocrite," Carlos said, the tap of his fingers reverberating throughout the iron railing.

"Yes, you're right. I'm the biggest hypocrite on this balcony," Talia said. "I wore the *Figa* because my mother—your sister— gave it to me for protection from people like you. Isn't that why you took it? You remember your sister, right? She believed it worked. A lot of good it did me."

"I am sure your mother barely remembers my name," Carlos said without blinking. "She had no problem letting me go."

"She was a *child*. She was too young to protect you. She needed her older brother to protect *her*. That was *your* job."

"And it was my parents' job to raise me in my homeland, and they failed," Carlos said. "We cannot be everything to everyone."

"Who have you been but a disgrace to our family?" Talia asked, fearful of the nerve she may have pinched in her uncle's unstable mind. Maybe she was the crazy one for trying to reason with an unreasonable man. Although she said it without fore-thought, it was the truth, consequences be damned.

A growl grew in her uncle's throat, reaching its highest pitch as he hurled his fresh glass of Port at the balcony floor and swiped the table full of bottles and ashtrays with his elbow. Aware of her bare feet near the shattered glass, Talia clenched her knees as far above the floor as the ropes allowed. The sky lit up with a streak of light.

"What are you doing, Talia?" Nuno breathed in her ear in an attempt to calm her, but she was aware of his intentions. She no longer allowed Nuno to dictate her actions.

"Your beloved grandmother made me who I am," Carlos said. "It was her witch doctor that first told me of my gifts when I was nine years old."

Talia was in no mood to listen to an old wives' tale about her uncle discovering his dark side while Jared rotted in the *terreiro* alone. But then it occurred to her that Vovó's witch doctor had been Pai Paolo, and he claimed she never brought in a little boy.

After all she had uncovered in the last few days, Talia had to question whether it was yet another in Vovó's string of lies. Talia couldn't blame Pai Pedro if he had kept his promise to hold

Vovó's secret, even after death. But her uncle had a history of embellishing the truth. Talia didn't know whom to believe.

The maid returned, handing her uncle a fresh glass of wine, which shook with the rumble of thunder. One thing was clear: the maid could only balance that line for so long. Talia could not determine whether the warm looks she gave her uncle were real. Could they be real? A nagging feeling convinced Talia that the maid's meek demeanor masked one fact—like Vovó, she knew a lot of things she should not know.

Talia gleaned all her knowledge about body language from her own personal therapist, her best friend. In their junior year, after Talia got her license, she and Caryn spent their sunny weekend afternoons at the park, dissecting picnickers' lives while stealing each other's potato chips. Caryn could always spot the lovers, even when it was obvious they were dating other people. It was more titillating than a soap opera—reassembling people's life stories based on one interaction. It was a real life lesson in sociology. Carlos and the maid seemed like the type of couple Caryn would call out as suspicious.

Besides being great fodder for writing, these outings taught Talia how to separate suitors who wanted a relationship from those just looking for a one-night-stand. It didn't always work, but the odds were more often in her favor—as they were the night she met Jared.

The maid was a bit harder to read than Jared, and her uncle harder still. As far as Talia could deduce, the sole means of getting Carlos to talk was to fire up his Mediterranean passion and watch him lose control. It wasn't her safest bet, as men like him are unpredictable and lethal, but the stakes were mounting by the second. Being tied to a chair and drugged while the man you love is being held captive in a dungeon tends to change one's priorities.

"Okay, I'll bite, what did my grandmother do to you at nine years old?" Talia humored her uncle while she brainstormed ways of getting back to the *terreiro*. Every great idea she came up with was impossible to execute. Her only option was to convince Carlos and Nuno to take her back to the *terreiro*, even if it meant she'd get there in shackles.

A procession of white marched through the moonlit grapevines, down a similar path as the one Talia charted the night before. A woman in a red headdress circled the sanctuary and lit all of its seven-day candles, including the two Talia extinguished the night before. A few stragglers carried paper bags, crock pots, and caged animals into the stone building. Their shadows danced in the windows. Something was starting.

"I was possessed, Natalia," Carlos said. "I was scared at first, but once I realized it was my *Orishá*, I opened my soul to him, and my power grew stronger. It was a life changing moment. Have you ever had a life changing moment, Natalia?"

"I've had a few since I've been here," Talia said.

The term *Orishá* had previously surfaced in her research of Macumba and it referred to the follower's spiritual possessor. The spirits are believed to enter the follower's body when conjured through pagan rituals, and through outbursts by the possessed, *Orishás* reveal truths about life, give advice, and even cure disease. There are too many to name them all, but there are a known few who many claim to exist for the sole purpose of performing evil deeds. Talia guessed Carlos's spirit was not one who spread world peace or cured cancer.

Her uncle eyed the gold watch covering his tattoo and waved his finger at Nuno, who began undoing the knots at Talia's ankles. Talia raised her bare feet to Nuno's face, threatening to kick him once she was set free.

"*Com boca fechada as moscas não têm entrada,*" Nuno recited a

Portuguese proverb her father recited in her chatty childhood days, warning to mind one's tongue.

Talia lowered her calves.

"We will be taking a walk," Carlos said. "I hear you know the route well."

Before Talia could lift herself onto her feet, Nuno reached from behind and tied a monogrammed handkerchief over her eyes. Though startled, she didn't attempt to flee. She knew their destination, and blindfolded or not, it was exactly where she wanted to be.

———

THE GROUND CRACKLED underneath Talia's bare feet, the sky echoed above. The dewy grass along the vineyards cooled her toes, unlike the gravel surrounding the *terreiro*, where tiptoeing intensified the sting. A fruity breeze picked up speed and sent a shudder up Talia's torso. The red dress Nuno clothed her in fluttered, but it was difficult to control with her roped arms.

Entra com o pé direito, her mother advised her before big life events. It literally translated to, *Enter with your right foot*, but as most Portuguese sayings, underlying was a religious play on words. Following the same principle as the ear burning, her right leg was led by God—her left by the devil—and by physically entering the room with her right foot, she was inviting him along for the ride. Talia could use the help, if it were true.

She squinted and wrinkled her cheeks to shift the handkerchief off her eyes. The guards weren't concerned about Talia's impaired vision, dragging her whenever she couldn't keep their pace. It became clear that a man capable of harming her and the people she loved would not think twice about murdering a couple of young girls in an alley. Carlos had the means and the connections to do so. Even his practice in black magic fit the witnesses' account. It was the same with her older cousin, Armando, the one who died with a red candle in his hand.

What Talia still couldn't piece together was the motive. Why would Carlos want to murder their cousins? How menacing can two tweens be? Talia and Armando were adults carrying their own vendetta, their own history of deception and sin. It was no surprise they'd be one of his targets. These little girls couldn't have wronged him at their young age. They hadn't even finished the sixth grade.

Talia tripped on what felt like the threshold, and unable to steady herself, toppled to the cold cement floor without the chance to watch her right step. She pictured herself mere feet away from where Jared laid earlier that day.

"Jared?" Talia called into the dark.

No one answered.

Before she could crawl away, a set of clammy forearms dragged Talia to her feet and steered her further into the building. Sighs haunted her from every angle. A dozen or so paces in, and two steps up, Talia felt her body release, and then bind again around a wide pole. The pole's rough edges splintered her fingers as she struggled once more to unknot herself. Nuno's familiar sandalwood scent overwhelmed her, and something heavy thumped onto her chest.

Nuno tugged at her tangled hair until she could see again. Though the room was dimmed in candlelight, Talia blinked to quench her unadjusted eyes. Blobs of white dotted her vision, and as the apparitions formed into human shapes, Talia noticed a hushed audience gawking at her from the pews. She scoured the packed room for any sign of Jared, but he was missing. Her shoulders dropped.

Stone sculptures of African and Christian deities such as

Saint George and Saint Anthony stood atop a red table runner. Unglazed clay bowls brimming with colored sand lined the floor, along with bags of beans, trays of baked goods, caged live animals, and other offerings. Beaded rosaries adorned the walls, side by side with framed paintings reminiscent of those etched into the stained glass of cathedrals, which depicted scenes of dark figures in white kneeling or dancing around a mother figure in an embroidered red gown and matching headdress.

Marking the center of the half ring of pews, a woman in white chalked the floor with a circle. Inside its circumference she sketched a crisscross of lines. At the end of each line she drew a symbol. Some represented pitchforks, others the moon and stars.

Another woman struck a long match against an already sooted area of the stone wall and lit a large bowl of potpourri situated to the left of the platform. It burst into a rainbow of flames to the spectators' oohs and aahs. The flame lapped against Talia's skin, loose threads of her dress catching fire and fizzling out. Talia looked to the audience for help as she leaned back against the pole to which she clung.

Inhaling a plume of almond and aloe, Talia coughed, her eyes watering from her parched throat. To the crowd, she was an animal in a zoo. The dancing women swung their hips ever closer, and Talia sensed a familiar setting. It was happening again. Her nightmare was becoming reality—she was about to be burned alive at the stake.

A faint drumbeat escalated from outside the building and a line of shirtless men in red harem pants marched in the doorway, tapping to the beat of an African hymn on the drums strapped to their shoulders. They filed along the sides, continuing the rhythm. The older women stirred their hips at the center of the symbol until women of all ages joined one by one, opening a pathway for two men carrying a man in grayed pants to the altar on which Talia was strapped.

"Jared!" Talia screamed and stomped her feet.

Jared had help from his two new friends. His eyelids fluttering and mouth agape, the two men, who Talia now recognized as the guards in different garb, tied Jared to the wooden pole on the opposite end of the altar.

Her teeth clenched. "Jared," she said. Jared didn't respond.

A few in the herd voiced concern over the beat of the drums, but her focus returned to Jared's groan. "Can you hear me, baby? Stay with me. What did they do to you?"

Jared bobbed his head and mumbled, but she was too far away to hear his words over the music. If Talia believed in God, that moment would have been the perfect opportunity to use it to her advantage—to pray to God to take her life instead of Jared's, to save him from this fate that she laid out for him. Talia tried to ask for forgiveness, knowing deep down it would never work. She couldn't fake it.

By the time Talia noticed, the dancing had halted to allow for Nuno's entrance. He made his way to the podium where she hung, gripping a live rabbit by its ankles with his fist. The gray bunny kicked its hind legs and contorted its body upwards to attack Nuno, but there was no hope.

Nuno walked across the altar to Talia. As he leaned in to breathe into her ear, the rabbit latched onto her dress. "This is all for you, *gatinha*."

His exhalation shook in Talia's eardrum, causing her to knock her skull backwards onto the pole at her most vulnerable spot, still sore from her accident in the wine cellar. This pole was softer, but splintered.

Nuno dangled the rabbit above his head as the dancers flocked, then struck it with his hand, cracking the rabbit's neck. It no longer wrestled. Nuno positioned its carcass near similar offerings and sat at the closest pew to Talia's end of the stage. This ritual did not faze Talia. It wasn't the first time she'd witnessed someone take the life of an animal. Her family called it farm-fresh, the circle of life.

Jared moaned.

"Jared," Talia called. "Please wake up, baby. I need your help."

Jared's head fell forward and he dribbled onto the side of his shirt, no longer aware of his surroundings. Held up by nothing but the rope that bound him, an occasional twitch reassured Talia he was still alive.

The eldest woman in the group, her headdress a foot tall with jewels tucked in its crevices, reappeared from the back room, which Talia presumed to be the kitchen. In her hand, protected by a monogrammed towel, the old woman balanced a mug of warm liquid and passed it on to Nuno, who greeted her.

Nuno blew into his cup, took a long sip of a liquid that painted his lips purple, and lifted it up to the sky for his applauding audience. The drums faded to a heartbeat. Talia watched as Jared regained consciousness, aware that Nuno was also approaching her. Assuming she'd be the next to take a sip, she screamed to Jared through tight lips.

"This will not hurt you, it will help you," Nuno said.

Talia mumbled incoherently, refusing to allow Nuno to medicate her once again. He forced the chalice to her lips, but he could not break the seal. He pinched her nose, but she shook him off. Talia tried to shoot Nuno the evil eye like her ancestors, squinting and wrinkling her brow so much, she suspected she looked as cartoonish as a character in a graphic novel. He stepped back, and Talia spat in his face. "Is this what you used on Jared?"

Fire burning in his eyes, Nuno wiped her spit from his chin and smashed the cup into her mouth, splitting her lip. Without her arms to protect her, it wasn't long before he succeeded in prying her mouth open and pouring the warm liquid down her throat. It reeked of malted wine, but tasted of sunflower seeds.

"Jared," Talia moaned, watching his silhouette stir.

She saw the mug passed to a half dozen elders before she began to feel its effects. This surprised her because she knew ingested drugs can take up to an hour to start working. She was positive it hadn't been that long, yet the room rotated around her.

Nuno held hands with his neighbors and danced in and out of Talia's distorted vision as the drumbeat lilted. It appeared to Talia as if Nuno held a better grip on reality at that moment than she did, even though they both drank the same poison. Her constraints grew tiresome and sweat gathered at the seams of her dress, even as the potpourri fire bowl quieted and the breeze opened a path to her neck.

"Talia?" Jared replied.

"Jared?" she slurred, spit pooling at the corners of her lips. "I'm so sorry."

"I'm sorry, too." Jared's voice melded with the music, warping with the steady thump. Talia didn't understand another word he said, but she appreciated his persistence. It was getting harder to keep her eyes open.

A hush swelled over the pews. The mass that once parted for Nuno opened wider in anticipation of who Talia assumed to be the night's guest of honor. Through distortions of colors and faces, Talia saw Carlos hiding underneath a crimson hat, gold chains, and a loose pantsuit as he sauntered in from the main entrance to everyone's bow.

A crash of thunder quaked the congregation. The shake loosened Talia's wrists, now raw from her constant wrenching, allowing them to fall to a more comfortable height behind her. Carlos moved towards her, shaking hands with his devotees along the way. He winked at Talia, who turned in time to find Nuno observing her from the pews.

Carlos took the stage with a grin that wrinkled his forehead. He shouted from the altar, "May the universe give evidence that in this *terreiro*, I, Domingos Raposo, praise the all-powerful *Orishás*. With these offerings and traditions, I forge a link with my ancestors so that Exu, who knows all, will chart our paths together."

The room erupted in applause, and then silenced again, echoing for a moment before stillness. Someone who resembled the maid snuck in unnoticed by the crowd. She looked like a different person in her religious garb, praising Carlos like one of his pawns. It was still unclear why Padilha, the maid, would risk her job, her life, to help Talia find Jared.

"Brothers and sisters, we are here tonight to welcome a new member," Carlos said. "She will help us with our service tonight, along with her friend."

Was Talia a new member or a sacrifice? She wouldn't put it past her uncle to strap her to a stake and roast her in front of his entire congregation.

An urgent sense of calm overwhelmed Talia, and though she fought against it, her shoulders slouched and eyelids grew heavy. The swirling around her relaxed as she felt the weight of her body transfer to her bindings. Jared shouted her name again, but she could not find the strength to reply, her tongue heavy and swollen. She hung there like a botched anesthesia patient, capable of hearing and feeling everything, but powerless to move or speak to protect herself. If there was a hell, that may have been it.

A muffled church bell echoed twelve times in the distance,

faint over the din of the drumbeat, which soon mimicked it.

"It is time," Talia saw Nuno mouth to Carlos. "It is almost nine past midnight."

Nine past midnight. Twelve-oh-nine. It wasn't an address—it was a time of day, just like Vovó told her in her dream. That meant it was happening soon, whatever they had planned. She had to do something.

Nuno pushed through the multitudes towards Jared, who was struggling to free himself. No one within the stone walls reacted to Jared's cries, slumped motionless on the altar. From the corner of her eye, she saw Jared's shadow dancing in the candlelight.

"Nuno, stop!" she shouted, not a syllable distinct. Talia's limbs were immobile, but her mind raced through the previous few days as if they were her last. Every word, every motion. She cursed herself for not remembering any detail that could save them, or more so, for allowing Nuno to deceive her. Talia threw a punch, but it never landed, it never even took flight.

Carlos settled into his dais as Nuno fussed with the bindings around Jared's wrists and murmured something in his ear. Whatever Nuno was saying, Talia could tell by the motion of his lips that it was repetitive, like a prayer.

Though her mind commanded her limbs to break free, they did not obey. She tried to speak telepathically, as if that were a valid option, but it didn't work. Jared couldn't hear her screaming thoughts. Collapsing as his ropes released, Jared's knees buckled before Nuno could catch him. He dragged Jared's body toward the throne, dropped him a few feet before Carlos, and then positioned Jared's limbs into a cross, opposite the chalked symbol. Jared's head pointed to the pews.

In a language jumbling Portuguese and African tribal, Carlos sang, his eyes rocking back into his head. Talia understood every other verse, as even the Portuguese lyrics traced an African dialect. The few words that slipped through were *Exu, tonight*, and *sacrifice*. Talia was also certain she heard her full birth name.

Exu in Macumba is the messenger between humans and their Gods, but he is also considered in some *terreiros* to be a close friend of the devil. Though Exu was always present, he was invoked for powerful spells resulting in the harm of unsuspecting, though not quite innocent, individuals.

Nuno crept from the circle balancing a white porcelain bowl full of a red chalky substance in his right hand. With the sweep of his left thumb, his lips chattering under his breath, he marked Talia's forehead with a cross in a ceremony reminiscent of the Catholic Ash Wednesday services her parents forced her to attend as a child.

While cringing, Talia wiggled her big toes again. Jared lay motionless as Carlos splattered him with the red fluid gathering at the tip of his brass dagger, staining Jared's white pajamas and pale skin. A fleck of burgundy caught the corner of Jared's eyelid and trickled down his cheek to his earlobe like a tear.

The harmony of Carlos's prayer combined with the congregation's *Amen* appeared to have hypnotized Jared into a deep trance. Carlos's body jerked as he hobbled to his niece, his limbs draped in the air by a set of invisible strings, his pupils dilated and hollow. Talia screamed but only a mumble escaped. Progress.

The thumping escalated from the barrels and the women resumed swaying to the rhythm, more attuned to their every step. Talia managed to jiggle one of her legs, but it wasn't enough to dissuade Carlos from continuing, his musk intensifying with every step.

"*Bom dia, Pomba Gira.* The birds fly in circles." Carlos's fermented breath shook her eardrum before he pecked her cheek, leaving behind enough slobber that Talia could sense a draft from the entrance. Circling his finger to the ceiling, Carlos surrendered backward into the maid's embrace, as if in a psycho-logical game of trust.

The maid's neck beads outnumbered those of her peers, and her headdress was dyed a thick crimson to match her belt. She was the only other woman in the room besides Talia in red apparel. The bold color was sure to make an appearance in a ritual such as this one, but Talia was uncertain of its significance in this case. Often a pigment used in the dark arts, red has been known to represent Maria Padilha, the entity of the *Pomba Gira*, who always wore a hip-hugging scarlet dress and matching head-band in the many existing portraits for which she was its artist's muse. It was a dress much like the one in which Talia had been clothed.

Twisting her neck a little more, Talia found a better view of Jared, who lay unconscious on the floor, tied to the pole, clasping a red candle. Her stomach dropped. Armando was found with a red candle in his hand. It was also not an uncommon color for a candle used in occult rituals. She knew it was most likely not coincidental.

Talia's fingertips tingled to life, now capable of bending her index fingers and thumbs to unravel a knot. A flame raged in her chest. Able to kink her neck downward, she realized that Vovó's amulet had been searing her sternum. Desperate to quench her blistering skin, Talia slumped her body forward with every ounce of energy, causing the collar of her dress to sink. Talia sighed with relief. The sensation in her body now restored, she focused on appearing paralyzed while loosening her bonds.

"Tonight a new chapter begins!" Nuno shouted from Carlos's throne to a thunderous crowd, turning his back to Talia.

If Talia was coming down from her forced tea high, why wasn't Jared moving yet?

Nuno caught her eye and, as much as she feigned a cold

vacancy, Talia knew he could see the life returned to them. Her heart sped against her ribs. A smirk staining his face, Nuno slinked behind Talia and caressed her exposed shoulder, raising the hair on her arms.

"Be a good girl and Jared will be spared," he whispered, squeezing her backside as he unchained her. Nuno dragged Talia by the wrists to the center of the room, eager to receive the adulation in her gaze he so unmistakably returned.

Exhausted and with limited mobility, Talia couldn't give Nuno what he wanted, even to manipulate him out of that nightmare. His fervor heightened with this realization, and he jutted his foot in front of her, laughing as she tripped forward, her arms unavailable to break her fall. Nuno tore at her elbow to elevate her, nearly dislocating her shoulder, his fingernails burrowing into her skin.

The sea of dancers parted once more to reveal the chalked symbol on the sandy floor, now smudged from the festivities. Talia combed the room for the maid, but was unable to find her. Carlos perched with the weathered *Book of Saint Cyprian* Talia found in his office bookcase, the bookmark still intact, and continued to chant.

"I don't understand." Talia said, her voice crude. "What were you and Carlos planning to do to me?"

"Oh, *gatinha*, you are so blind. Can you not see? You have the power he needs to survive. Your uncle is dying and only your energy can save him."

"My energy? You mean my life?"

"If it must be. Your uncle takes what he needs. What becomes of you is unimportant to him. But now I know you have a different destiny, Talia," Nuno said. "You belong with me."

Talia fought the urge to spit at him. "I'm in control of my

destiny, Nuno, not you." It came out a bit garbled, but she made her point.

Nuno chuckled as he forced a kiss on her lips. Carlos, who was now under a deep trance, recited an African prayer without moving his lips, yet the prayer drowned Talia's thoughts.

She was overcome by a heightened awareness in all living beings around her, down to the grapes maturing on the vines outside, the scent of the rainwater that collected on its fruit, and the thoughts of every living being in her fifty-foot circumference.

No longer able to feel the surface under her feet, Talia resisted the swarm of voices flooding her mind, suspended in the space between life and death, unable to decipher the difference. She plugged her fingers in her ears to block the chaos that was unraveling her, but the voices weren't coming from outside. Talia could hear them speak, praying for more money, more love, more everything, but their mouths remained motionless.

"STOP!" Talia screamed. Her shriek reached into all four corners of the room, bouncing off the exposed wooden beams. Talia collapsed into Nuno's arms, her brain fragmenting with an overdose of knowledge. The prayers persisted, but Talia could hear Jared's muffled voice above the rest, hollering her name. It sounded Greek or Russian, not familiar like her own.

Nuno threw Talia to the floor in order to defend himself against a now-awakened and enraged Jared. Some heroes in the congregation charged Jared, but Talia raised her hand without thinking and they halted in place, as if hit by an invisible wall.

Talia examined her palm. Did she just do that?

Jared threw the first punch. Stumbling around in what resembled one of his high school wrestling matches, Jared kicked the bloody dagger out of Nuno's grip, landing it by the altar stairs near Talia. Immobile from the migraine, she couldn't muster the strength in her upper arms to drag herself towards the blade. Her head slumped.

Her legs were looser than the rest of her limbs, so Talia scooted until the knife's handle sat near her toes. Not at all ambidextrous, grasping the handle with her feet looked much easier in her head. Nuno, well aware of Talia's plan, kicked the knife away from her grasp when he briefly escaped Jared's hold. The tussle between the men escalated, crashing into the shrine and knocking over a lit candle. Bowls collided and figurines split, creating a pool of broken ceramic pieces on the floor.

Nuno slid into the shards, the blood from his gashes already soaking through his white shirt. Talia shrugged away the ounce of care she still held for Nuno with a cheer for Jared, disappointed that it lingered. Arms stronger, Talia crawled toward the knife, which had been kicked to the other side of the altar, jutting out of a couple of sacrificed animal carcasses.

Mounting above the other voices swirling in her head was that of the maid, reciting the counter spell she wrote for her on a napkin the night before. She wasn't sure if it was real or lunacy, but Talia sang along anyway, quieting the madness long enough to muster the strength to reach for the dagger. But it was too late. Nuno broke free from Jared's grip and grabbed the dagger from Talia's fingers, striking Jared in the shoulder in an outburst of pure instinct.

"Jared, no!" Talia scrambled to reach Jared to nurse his wounds.

"Stay where you are, Talia. I got this." Jared raised his hand.

Talia could tell he was bluffing, trying not crouch in anguish, but he was right. They were a larger threat on opposite ends of the room, splitting their enemies' attention. Talia faked a faint and fell to her knees, prompting Nuno to come to her rescue as she'd hoped.

Jared scowled, and waited until Nuno was fixed on curing Talia's ailment before striking him from behind with a painted statuette of Saint Sebastian. Nuno extended his hand in Talia's direction as Jared plunged forward. Talia jerked back at the last moment. Talia and Jared locked eyes, now a few feet apart, but before Talia could interpret Jared's look of horror, she felt a blade against her throat.

"Where are you going, *menina*?" Carlos asked with a hoarse voice, twisting Talia's arm behind her back. "Did you forget about me?"

"Talia, please, don't fight him. Just do as you're told," Jared pleaded. "His eyes…"

Talia struggled to get into a more comfortable position, her back warped by her twisted arm, but the blade sliced into the top layer of her skin and stung like a paper cut on a knuckle.

"Talia, please!" Jared shouted, his hands hovering above his head.

No one else dared to help Carlos or Nuno. The congregation now huddled at the corners of the room with singed hair and ragged tops, waiting for the right time to leave without creating more danger. Talia empathized with Carlos's clan—they didn't realize the consequences of their actions. They had been lied to just like her.

"Why do you resist? This is your destiny," Carlos said.

"My destiny does not involve a human sacrifice, I promise you that," Talia said. "You don't want Jared, you want me. So let him go."

"No, Talia, it's not your choice," Jared said.

"It *is* my choice, Jared. I got you into this, I'm getting you out. This was always my fight, not yours."

"Just because you do not see the truth does not mean it does not exist." Carlos lost his hat during the ritual. The few hairs on his dome now stood on end with static, a sheen of sweat beading on his forehead.

Was he suggesting that she was the one out of touch with reality?

"You have felt the power of the *Pomba Gira*." Carlos pressed harder on her neck. "How can you turn your back on her?"

"I don't know what you want from me," Talia said. "I haven't felt anything."

"The amulet burned your flesh, you are the one." Carlos cleared his throat. "You felt its powers like no one else can."

Her inflamed chest. That explained the damage done to her pelvis by the amulet when she fell in the wine cellar. It wasn't just smashed into her. It was searing her skin, literally branding her.

"I told you she was the one," Nuno said. Jared followed close behind as they moved towards Talia. "This is why I brought her here, why we need her."

Jared looked ready to pounce, shuffling his feet, but he held his shoulders high in solidarity, winking to assure her his winces were harmless. So much damage had been done already, the altar in shambles, the children crying with their parents under the fractured pews.

"You possess a power, Natalia. It can change the world," Carlos said. "We all need you."

"Then why are you hurting me and these people?" Talia strained to keep her words to a minimum, as every movement cut deeper. "What am I sacrificing for? I want to know before I die."

Carlos hesitated, but Nuno didn't hold back. "You could save his life, Talia. You could save your uncle's life."

Carlos was dying from emphysema, like his father. They believed Talia possessed the power to save him, but that was impossible. "He expects me to sacrifice my life for his?"

"He would save other lives with your sacrifice." Nuno took

her hand, and with Carlos still holding the knife at her throat she had no choice but to allow it. "Is that not why you are a journalist, so you can help people?"

"You said you loved me, now you want me to die?"

"I do love you, Talia." Nuno raised his head. "This is about more than love."

Before Talia could respond, a blaze exploded from the shrine and the flock of sixty-plus screaming, coughing believers stampeded, knocking Talia to the ground, and Carlos unconscious. Behind them, the animals thrashed in their cages, chickens clucking, rabbits squealing, some managed to escape, some scraped Talia with their claws in haste. To avoid a trampling was difficult. After a few more knocks and bruises, Talia resurfaced, just in time to find Jared riding the wave towards her.

"I'm sorry." Talia wrapped her arms around his neck. "I love you so much."

"Don't be sorry," Jared said. "It's not your fault. I should have listened to you."

Jared cupped her face, leaning in for a kiss. His lips were as salty and soft as she had remembered from the shores of Cascais earlier that week. The crowd knocked them around the room, the hands of the clock dragging. Nothing else mattered.

Talia felt the front of her dress dampen, as if a water balloon had burst between them. Jared's lips drooped, his hands clutched at his stomach. Talia looked down to see her blouse had been torn, and a blade pierced through Jared's linen shirt. She didn't understand what was happening, staring at her bloody hands as if they were a figment of her imagination.

Jared collapsed atop the chalked symbol, one limb at a time, his red hands clasping at his shirt.

TWENTY-ONE

"THIS CAN'T BE HAPPENING. Jared. Jared! Stay with me, baby, stay with me," Talia cried. "I love you. I can't lose you now. I–I just got you back."

"Love you, too," Jared groaned, tilting his head back, his eyelids twitching. Talia rocked with him, sliding her fingers through his greased mane to keep his head steady. "I'm sorry. That girl … nothing happened."

"Don't talk. You need your energy."

"No. I have to tell you. This may be my last chance."

"Don't say that."

"I wanted something to happen, but I couldn't do it. I'm sorry." Jared's eyes rolled back and his head dropped into Talia's lap. His chest collapsed.

"No, no. I'm the one who's sorry. Please wake up. Don't leave me."

Nuno hovered above them, the ceiling of smoke sinking lower and lower above his head.

"What have you done? You monster!" Talia shouted.

Jared's blood beaded along the grout, gathering at the center of the mysterious symbol upon which he lay. Talia pressed herself against his wound, blotting the flow of blood in vain. His lips were already cold.

"Someone's blood must be shed tonight," Nuno said. "*Vez*, I love you, Talia. I spared your life."

"You're delusional," Talia said. "And a murderer, just like my uncle."

Nuno no longer hid behind false concern and European courtesy, his shattered mask unveiling the psychopath underneath. "There are a lot of things you still need to learn, Talia. This sacrifice will bring us closer together and to our Orishas. We will rule this *terreiro*, together!"

"What about Carlos?" Talia asked. "I thought he was your mentor?"

"No amount of spells can cure your uncle. His reign must be passed down," Nuno said. "There can only be one *pai-do-santo*."

"I'm guessing Carlos doesn't know this." Talia pointed at her uncle's unconscious body, now partially covered in ashes and rubble.

"It is not luck. Your uncle will know my plans soon enough, and he will accept them as truth." Nuno stretched out his hand. "Come with me."

Talia wrapped herself around Jared's body. "If I go, he goes."

"Jared's dead," Nuno said. "And if you do not come with me, you will be too."

Talia hated that Nuno finally told the truth, but not as much as she hated the truth he told. Jared's face was devoid of color, his veins emptied onto the pavement that cradled him. Talia kissed him on the forehead, wiped her nose with the back of her blood-soaked hands, and whispered, "I love you."

Though her bruised body still convulsed with anger and

agony, she accepted the risk to follow Nuno to what could be her doom. Staying put meant being consumed by fire, the smell of her own seared flesh still fresh from her nightmare.

"If you only understood how important you are, Talia." Nuno squeezed her knuckles as he dragged her to what was left of the altar. "Not just to your uncle, but to me as well. I found you by his orders, but I brought you here to be with me. With your powers, we could change everything."

She could either rule a cult with a lunatic or die. Great options.

"I can't rule with you, Nuno," Talia said. "But if you let me go, I won't get in your way."

Nuno growled. "You will change your mind or you will not leave here alive."

She would rather die. Jared's lifeless body sat out in the wreckage left by the mass exodus, the fire still smoldering in the corners. Talia stared at the smudged chalk symbol, the flattened drum parts strewn across the floor. One of the flags that hung from the rafters now dangled by a single frayed rope. The one layered on Carlos's legs was embroidered with a symbol of a pitchfork, which Talia found befitting. Only the devil could do this to his own flesh and blood.

The fire that consumed most of the offerings still smoldered near Talia's area of the altar, and she weaved as best as she could through the embers with care, keeping with Nuno's longer stride while protecting her face with her free hand.

"*Aqui.*" Nuno pointed at another symbol, this one carved into the stone floor where the table once stood. "Now kneel down."

"Not a chance," Talia said, a sink in her gut.

"Kneel down and pray." Nuno yanked Talia down by her sore wrist.

She recognized the mark on the floor. A *Vévé*, as it was called in the Macumba religion, consisted of the Ichthys, most commonly known as the Jesus fish, tilted on its tail with a cross made of stars above the left fin and a half moon below its mouth to the right. The stone tile it was engraved into was worn a few shades darker than the ones surrounding it. It looked as though it had always been there, as if Carlos or whoever owned this property before him, built this *terreiro* around that symbol and hid it in plain sight.

Nuno weighed Talia down with his hand on her shoulder, slamming her bended knee on a shard of clay. Talia gasped. The piece of pottery embedded itself into her kneecap, but she was forced to tilt her head down, to find some peace in the crackle of the waning fire that drowned Nuno's chanting.

Her throbbing knee numbed after several focused breaths. Nuno's vocals grew shriller and Talia realized she had unwillingly joined in his melody. No longer able to decipher between reality and dream, Talia found herself face-to-face with a smiling olive-skinned woman in a scarlet corset. Her half-pinned, raven locks hovered in a breeze as her strawberry lips mouthed the chant a second off-tempo. Talia could not blink, her dry pupils pasted onto the majesty before her.

"Foi uma rosa que eu plantei para a minha Rainha Maria Padilha," she heard her own voice chant from somewhere outside of her body. *It was a rose I planted for my Queen Maria Padilha.*

At every repetition the scarlet lady floated nearer, her smile warping. Her arms widened for Talia, who embraced the woman, full-hearted, eyes welling.

Talia's body tingled with a strange sensation that triggered her to levitate a few feet off the ground. First her heels lifted, then her toes, until her entire body floated in the air, as if the earth's gravity had lost its pull.

She towered above Nuno, who continued to chant through

his full eyes, his knees in a prayer position just below her. Talia experienced an overwhelming confidence she had never felt. She was invincible. She was omnipotent. Confident she could put an end to Nuno's plan in an instant with one flick of her fingertips, her desire for revenge tapered into empathy.

Nuno sobbed into his stained palms, and when he glared into her eyes, simpering, she realized they were not tears of sorrow but rather of joy.

"I have been praying for you, *minha rainha!*" Nuno exclaimed in the way she imagined her parents would if their God had decided to visit, heaving their clasped white knuckles into the air in a plea for salvation.

Talia's hand slapped Nuno's cheek, a satisfied grin in his doe-eyes, stinging the raised areas of her palm. Most of her senses were deep in sleep, but the smack tingled in her fingertips. It was cathartic.

"You are not worthy of my presence," Talia heard herself say, her voice lighter and in a thick Portuguese accent she only dreamed of attaining on her own. "You have spilled the blood of the innocent. You shall not be forgiven."

"I did it for you," Nuno pleaded, his knees bleeding from the glass shards on which he knelt. "They were for you."

"You have failed me, Nuno," Talia spoke as Queen Maria Padilha, the woman she believed had taken control of her body. A flick of Talia's finger unhooked a wooden board and tore off the leg of a chair, resurrecting the blaze on the other side of the room. Talia could not stop herself, because she was not herself.

"I will make it up to you, I promise, *Rainha.*" Nuno sunk deeper into his knees, his tone gentler than when he'd sweet talked Talia into his bed.

"There is nothing that can be done." And like that, the queen disappeared.

Talia stumbled, not in control of her limbs when they hit the ground. The ring of fire descended with her. The scarlet lady reappeared, blew Talia a kiss, and then dissipated into the smoke gathering at the peak of the torn ceiling. Talia cursed herself for no longer being able recall the breadth of knowledge she possessed moments before, when the world sat at her fingertips. All that remained were glimpses of Nuno's desperate pleas.

Talia's pupils itched but her arm lay dormant at her side as she sprawled the altar ledge, the dying fire tickling the air above her head. She heard it crackle. Nuno scooped Talia up and laid her upon the stone slab, and then prayed above her.

She tried to make sense of her out-of-body encounter with the woman who Nuno kept referring to as *Rainha Padilha*. She dressed like the queen when compared to the many renderings of her found on the internet. Her experience could have also been induced. It wouldn't have been the first time Nuno had poisoned her. But this time felt different.

"Stop," a voice called from the gallows.

Nuno paused and rolled his bloodshot eyes. "This is no longer your *terreiro, velhoto*," he said without turning.

"What are you doing?" Carlos asked. "She is the *Pomba Gira*, Nuno. She cannot be sacrificed."

"You did not see what I saw," Nuno said.

"I have seen enough." Carlos trudged through the rubble, a burning flag looming above him, threatening to fall.

"She will not let her in, *Tio*," Nuno said. "This is the only way."

"Give her time. She will see what is best for her," Carlos said, a groan announcing his every step. Blood leaked out of his left pant leg, but Talia could not see the wound.

"It is too late." Nuno raised the dagger above his head, the sharp end pointed at Talia's chest. "My Orisha says it must be done."

"No," Carlos shouted as Nuno lowered the blade towards Talia's thumping chest. The dagger's sharpened edges reflected the mounds of orange flames encompassing it. The flames or the dagger, one would be her death.

In an impulse that may have been divine intervention, Talia rolled herself onto the floor by striking her heel against the slab, the edge of Nuno's dagger nicking her neck on the way down. With only moments to react, she pitched a flaming bowl in Nuno's direction, the adrenaline pumping through her shoulder. Talia cooled her charred hands on the floor, crouching to listen for a response.

Nuno's pant leg caught on fire and he struggled to squelch it with spilt animal blood and holy water.

"I trusted you, Nuno," Carlos said. "You said you would bring her to me unharmed."

Nuno turned, his burnt pant leg hanging at his knee. "There was a time I worshipped you. I have killed for you."

Talia wormed between the altar's stone legs for protection and a better view. Though she was interested in the conversation, there wasn't much time before the smoldering rafters collapsed and the building crumbled, crushing everyone inside. Talia needed to find a way out.

"I never asked you to kill for me, Nuno. All I ever wanted from you was to be loyal," Carlos said. "I thought we agreed that she could not be sacrificed. You say you *love* her."

"I no longer worship you or the *Pomba Gira*," Nuno said. "Talia has failed us all."

"How can you say that after all we have suffered?" Carlos gasped for air, the smoke exacerbating his shallow breathing.

"This is what we wanted, what we've been praying for all these years. Now we can speak to our *Rainha* whenever we wish."

"I have spoken to her." Nuno gazed into the fire. "She will never return for me. I cannot be forgiven."

"This cannot be true. What have you done, *rapaz*?" Carlos's fingertips quivered against his forehead. "She will forgive you."

"It is unforgivable. She told me herself," Nuno said. "They were innocent."

Talia's ears perked. Nuno blocked the lone exit on her side of the building, and she didn't have the faith to run through the rubble and flames to her freedom. It was too risky, even if Carlos decided to help. It was still up in the air whether Carlos valued her life enough to protect her, or if Nuno had become too much of a son to lose.

"Talia's friends were far from innocent." Carlos assumed, like Talia, that Nuno was confessing to hurting Caryn and Jared. "We did what we could to keep them alive. That was not their fate."

"Enough with the interrogation, *velhoto*," Nuno said. "You do not know what you speak. They may have been young girls, but they were a threat to our lives."

Carlos stepped back, his mouth agape, almost tripping on the rubble, cheeks crimsoned. "It was you who murdered those little girls."

Talia fell onto her backside in shock. Throughout her search for the man who had been murdering her family, the murderer was there with her, laughing with her, sleeping with her. A shiver crawled up her spine. He convinced her he was a lackey, doing as he was told and nothing more—he wasn't paid to think. But it was all a lie, every piece of it. She covered her mouth to stifle her grunts, holding back a dry heave. Nuno was the biggest mistake of her life.

"I needed your family blood," Nuno said, his face gaunt.

"Innocent blood. They would not cooperate with me. I did what I had to do. You always said I was family, whether or not we shared blood."

For the first time since she discovered Nuno's rich friend was her uncle Carlos, her flesh and blood, she sympathized with him. Her heart raced as he approached Nuno. She wanted to help, to scream at him to be careful. Now that she knew Carlos was not the murderer, his reputation notwithstanding, Talia felt a glint of guilt for suspecting him on circumstantial evidence alone.

Yet she could not forget that Carlos wasn't innocent either. His plan for Talia and her friends was the catalyst for this nightmare, giving Nuno the opportunity to execute his plot—even inspiring him to craft it. Carlos had trained Nuno to be his protector, his yes man, his disciple. He gave him the ammo and sent him to war, expecting no casualties. It was naïve and reckless, marks of an amateur like herself.

Carlos was a powerful man, with dozens of followers, and the means to control the law to ensure his safety and freedom, despite his shady dealings. Nuno was likely not the first who coveted Carlos's position, but he was the only one with open access to Carlos's life. As her father warned Talia as a teen, your best friends can become your worst enemies. They know all your secrets.

"Do you know what you have done in my name?" Carlos asked, steadying himself on the leg of an overturned table. "Imagine if I had sacrificed you when I found you on the streets. You have grown into a brave man with my guidance. I cannot allow this, Nuno. This could ruin us all."

"It was to save *you*, but I no longer find you worthy of saving," Nuno said, ice in his eyes. "I do not need your approval. You have been dying for years. You must choose a successor. Will you die without passing down your power to your worthy children?"

"You are not worthy, Nuno. You lied to me. I sent you to find the amulet, not to murder my family. They will find you, and when they do, you will take us all to hell with you."

"You do not care about your family," Nuno said. "You have been denouncing them for years. I realized during my journey that you were not worthy of my adoration. You took advantage of me, trained me to be your assassin, and now you are disappointed to hear that I have done precisely what you have taught me to do? These children would one day destroy us, I saw it in a vision. My Orisha spoke to me. She told me twins with great powers from your family would one day curse you. I needed their blood to save you."

In most pagan religions, an Orisha is a fairy godmother or godfather of sorts, appearing when invoked through rituals and offerings, possessing the body of its summoner. Young or inexperienced members of the congregations were often barred from these rituals, the weight on their fragile souls too heavy. It would be years before her twin cousins would gain the power to overturn Carlos, but as it turns out, Nuno was capable on his own.

"An assassin kills who he is paid to kill, not for his own vengeance," Carlos said. "Your thoughtless actions could send us all to hell. I am sorry, but you can never be my successor. I will not allow it. You are careless. Your reign would be the end of us all."

"You no longer have a choice," Nuno blew his tangled curls from his face. "Tonight I claim my place on the throne. You do not have the strength to stop me."

This was Talia's cue, as the throne sat mere feet away. She spotted an escape route through an archway to the back room on the opposite side of the platform, the altar no longer aflame. If she could stay low and to the right, she could make it there without being seen, and possibly avoid being burnt to a crisp.

But she couldn't leave now. She sacrificed everything for this moment. Even if the outcome was different than what she imagined, she needed to know her friends' deaths wouldn't be in vain, that something of worth came of their sacrifice. Talia wished she could record this conversation for proof. No one would ever believe her, if she ever made it out of there alive.

"You are not innocent yourself, *velhoto*," Nuno said. "I know what you have done."

"This is not the time to discuss the past," Carlos said.

"I think it is the perfect time to discuss your cousin. Talia—where are you? You should thank your uncle for giving you your first story. Isn't that right, *Tio*? You killed your cousin Armando on the streets of New Falls, in cold blood. What was your silly reason again?"

"That is enough, Nuno."

"It was jealous rage, right, *Tio*? You killed him for sleeping with your precious girlfriend. What you did not know was that she slept with everyone you knew. Including me. And he was not even your first kill. Tell us whose blood you shed first. These are your last breaths, you should repent. Tell us why you were banished from your family."

"I have had *enough*, Nuno," Carlos said.

"You murdered your first girlfriend, right, Tio? An innocent little girl. You were both young, but you were powerful even then. Oh, what I would have done with that kind of power."

"I did not mean to kill her. She… she got in the way. I tried to warn her… she would not listen." Carlos dropped his head, and then raised it with gnashed teeth. "That is past now. I have done what I have needed to survive."

"I have also done what *you* have needed to survive. You are turning your back on me for saving your life, just like your parents turned their back on you for your choices." Nuno stepped closer, careful not to take his gaze off his mentor.

Talia eyed the exit, no longer blocked, and panicked. She was stuck in a burning building with two serial killers, one her ex-lover and one who shared her bloodline. She felt claustrophobic, as if the walls were caving in on her. And in fact, they were.

"I am glad you cared for me so deeply, but you have not saved me yet," Carlos wheezed. "I am still dying, and your loyalty does not erase the errors you have made. I cannot convince the *Pomba Gira* to forgive you for this sin. There is nothing I can do. You cannot lead this *terreiro* without her approval. Our *Rainha* has spoken. Hopefully your sins will not ruin us all, *se Deus quiser*."

"If you cannot, then I will." Nuno raced to the altar.

Startled by Nuno's sudden torrent of energy, Talia stole a fragment of stone for defense and slunk toward the archway, but Nuno ambushed her at the edge of the table.

"Where are you going, *gatinha*?" Nuno asked, evoking in Talia a nauseating dejavú that crept up her neck. Nuno forced a kiss onto Talia's pressed lips and shouted when Talia didn't concede. Nuno's grip on her elbows constricted her while he planted another one.

Repeating the maid's protection chant under her breath without thought, Talia maintained her calm while evading Nuno's advances. She stepped on his toes, kicked his shins, kneed his thighs, but Nuno didn't react. He was possessed. Not in the way Talia had faced earlier. This was a psychological breakdown.

"You are my *Pomba Gira*," Nuno said, a twisted vacancy in his eyes.

"Of course." Talia tucked the shard behind her back. "Anything for you. You're all I have left." She played a tough game, but it was her only way out. If Nuno felt he still had a chance with her, Talia might survive long enough to walk off that godforsaken property.

Nuno, softened by Talia's gesture, embraced her with vigor, and Talia tolerated him, pretending to return the sentiment. "Always this or always that or always another thing or never another thing nor another," Nuno babbled, reciting a line from Pessoa's *Tabácaria*, a complaint about the uncertainty and pain of the human condition.

"Stay away from him, Natalia," Carlos said.

"We don't need your help." Talia scowled at her uncle. The tension in Nuno's fingers loosened and the blood tingled back into her veins. Talia clutched the shard harder behind Nuno's back, even as it sliced into the creases of her palm, retracing her fortune. Finally at an angle that could cause some damage, Talia lifted her fist of shard, drawing blood from her palms at its jagged edges.

Just then, Carlos shouted something in an African dialect, and what felt like a bolt of lightning wedged between Nuno and Talia, ripping them apart from their embrace. Talia tripped backwards to the floor, landing on her elbow in order to protect the sharp stone still embedded into her hand, the ache masked by a surge of adrenaline. Her sooty dress caught on a sharp edge on the way down, shredding the skirt's edges. She tore off the petticoat underneath her dress with a relieved grunt. She was free.

The earth rattled, the chalked tiles Jared laid upon cracked first, outlining the symbol in a web of veins. Talia judged the archway, but Nuno waited in her path. Trapped again.

"You cannot stop this," Nuno said.

"You killed to save me so you can watch me die?" Carlos asked as he hiked through the rubble, his balance wavering through the tectonic shifts.

"Everything has changed." Nuno lowered his head.

"Are you going to let this girl destroy everything we have worked so hard for?" Carlos's balance was now firm, as if his feet were glued to his hovering stage.

"You mean what *I* have worked so hard for," Nuno said. "You have done nothing but sit and watch, hiding behind your money and your sickness. I am the one that makes the sacrifices."

"I took care of you. I raised you like a son. That was a sacrifice." Carlos snuck closer. "I gave you everything I did not have."

"You … you had everything … and you threw it away. Your family loved you." Nuno moved to the center of the room, where Jared's body rested unscathed under a steel table. "You abandoned them. The way you have abandoned me."

"They abandoned me when they kidnapped me from my home," Carlos said. "I did what I had to do to return. You were not there to see how easily they let go, how quickly they disowned me. If I had not returned, I would not have been there to save you."

"I never knew my father. My mother was a whore. I was a mistake from one of her many lovers, and she reminded me of it every chance she could. I moved to Portugal to escape her."

"My family forgot me as well, Nuno. My niece didn't even know I existed. They were happy to be rid of me."

"I went to America to find out more about you, my mentor, the closest I had to a father. I expected to find … I do not know. The way you speak of them, I expected mush worse."

"I did not send you there to spy on my family," Carlos said. "I sent you there to take the jewelry box before someone tossed it away without realizing its powers. The amulet could not end up in the hands of a novice."

"How else was I to find the amulet without your mother?" Nuno asked.

"What does it matter now? My mother is dead."

"When I mentioned your name to her, she broke down in front of me," Nuno said. "She confessed her guilt, her anger, and how she could no longer live with the burden."

"*Maluco*. She was already dead when I sent you there." Carlos laughed.

"Who told you she was dead?"

Carlos paused.

"I knew you would send me to search for the amulet when your mother passed, so I rushed the process," Nuno said. "I told you she was dead so you could send me to America, as I had dreamed since the first story you told me about her in the tunnels of Lisboa. She was a powerful *Pomba Gira*, a legend. I had to meet her. But she suspected my intentions, as I should have known. She refused give me the amulet. She said she would die before she would give it to me. So I granted her that wish."

TWENTY-TWO

"NO!" Talia's scream echoed into every corner of the smoky room and ruined any chance she had at a clean escape.

With nothing to lose, Talia lunged at Nuno with the shard and struck him in the heart when he twisted to catch her. Talia knew the shard wasn't long enough to fatally wound and when she reached for another makeshift weapon from the debris, Nuno struck her down to the floor and straddled her. The shard was still lodged in his chest, blood trickling from its edges and vanishing into Talia's dress.

"Talia." Nuno blocked her persistent thrashing. "Please let me explain. I did not feel then what I feel now. I did not know you then."

"You killed my grandmother," Talia shouted.

He disgusted her—his sweaty palms, his beady eyes, his bloody lip. His usual hypnotic scent nauseated her, consuming her with a rage she could no longer control.

"Your uncle lied to me my whole life," he whispered, calming Talia down like a pet, but it only made her angrier.

In the corner of her eye, Talia saw a glimmer of light. Underneath one of the burnt flags a few feet away, peeking through one of its tears, was Nuno's dagger, scratched and dented, but just as sharp. She transferred her weight to the side as she continued to struggle, towing Nuno toward the knife without his knowledge.

Two steps forward, one step back, like the tango. Talia learned the rhythm of Nuno's movements, when he leaned, pivoted, relaxed his grip. When the dagger neared, Talia twisted her leg sideways, prompting Nuno to widen his legs and over-power her with his arms, which left the back of his knee exposed.

Seizing the moment, Talia swung her leg and knocked Nuno's knee into a buckle, crashing them both onto the floor. Though Nuno had dampened her fall, the loose stones managed to bruise her shoulders and legs, yet spared her skull. Nuno didn't have the same luck. His face was bruised and cut, the back of his head leaking as the energy drained from his limbs.

She released herself from his arms and scrambled toward the flag, the dagger hiding underneath. She fumbled to get a good grasp, then pivoted with its blade pointing outward, ready for battle. Nuno was still on the floor, waking from his slumber.

"You killed my grandmother, you bastard." Talia's vision blurred with tears and hate, the knife quivering in front of her. "I loved her."

"Your grandmother wanted to save her son, as any good mother would." Nuno lifted himself to a seated position. "I gave her the chance to save the son she abandoned, Talia. She wanted this."

"Her death was for nothing. If she died to save him then why is he still sick? Why haven't you saved him like you promised?" Talia held the dagger in the air, her body stiff.

"It did not work." Carlos limped in her direction. "We held a service a few weeks ago."

"A sacrifice?" Talia asked.

"Of course, Talia." Nuno tried to manipulate her with his wide eyes. "Your uncle is not as innocent as he claims."

"Joaquim asked to be sacrificed," Carlos said. "To save me. We were like family."

Talia lifted herself up on her sore elbow and then shifted her weight to the other. Nuno regained his grip on her wrists and legs, but Talia wrangled herself free.

"Someone had to die. Just not you, Talia. Not the *Pomba Gira*. We planned to prepare your friend Caryn to donate blood, as you say, but our scoundrel guards did not allow her to live long enough," Carlos said. "Jared was much harder to prepare. He was not cooperative."

Talia battled the urge to vomit. She didn't dare search for similarities between herself and Carlos, but they crept into her thoughts anyway. Her friends' deaths weren't planned, but she had been careless with their safety, abandoning them while tracking a mass murderer around a foreign country. They sacrificed their lives for her. How was that any different than what Carlos had done? She was just as guilty of murder.

Nuno rushed toward Carlos, passing Talia on the way. Without blinking, Talia sliced the dagger into Nuno's abdomen as he passed. A warm flood oozed over her hand and wrist. Talia could not let go of its handle, her fury hurling him to the floor. Even as the blood pooled from the side of his torso, he did not cease, crawling across the rocky surface in Talia's direction.

"Stay where you are." Talia threatened him with the dagger still soaked in his blood. "I *will* kill you, Nuno."

A flash brightened the room into daylight for a split second.

Nuno didn't speak, his pain seemingly too much, though not enough to deter him from his crawl. As he drew closer, Talia prepared to pounce. Without warning, Nuno wrapped his elbow around Talia's ankle and yanked her down to his level.

The crashing thunder muffled Talia's screams, and the dagger slid into a crack when her arm hit the ground. This time she swore she heard a bone crack. Nuno released her ankle in a momentary slump, enabling Talia to reach for a headless statuette and strike it across his right temple. His head whipped to the side as he plummeted face first onto the altar.

"You killed everyone I love." Talia's cheeks flushed. The rage controlled her, consumed her, and a sensation she felt for the first time earlier that night resurfaced.

Talia spun her head to look, and the amulet twinkled from the altar. It called to her, and with the force of an electric magnet, the amulet flew toward her. Shaking, sliding, scratching, until it was at her feet.

Time slowed. The rain decelerated down the rafters, looping over and over again in slow motion. She swiped her hand across the dirt, lifted the amulet into the air on her fingertips, and pinned it to the waist of her tattered dress. It no longer burned.

"Not everyone." Carlos emerged from the rubble. "Thank you for saving my life, Natalia."

"Stop," Talia lifted her hand, halting Carlos's movements. "Don't tempt me to change my mind, old man. I no longer have the patience."

"I did not murder those girls or your friends." Carlos dusted the soot off his clothes and started walking toward Talia. "You have no reason to kill me."

"You may as well have," she said. "You put all our lives in danger with your psychotic plans. You killed our cousin

Armando. And you premeditated at least one person's death tonight."

"Better you than him." Carlos looked over at Nuno's bloody body on the altar as he limped past it.

"Let's can the mysterious responses, Uncle Carlos. I've had enough bull for one lifetime. Step back." With a flick of her wrist, Carlos tripped backwards, landing on a pile of wet two by fours, still steaming.

Her mouth fell open as she stared at her palms. She didn't know where this new power came from. She certainly wasn't controlling it, though it would be useful if she could.

"I still need you, Natalia." Carlos groaned, the urgency increasing in his twisted pupils. "She—you can help me."

"If you're talking about your *queen*, she's never coming back. This is me now, and you're both going to pay for what you've done. Only one of us is leaving this hell hole tonight."

Nuno regained his consciousness slowly, but not his strength, and just a look from Talia slammed him back into the ground. Her necklace slapped heat against her chest. The amulet. That was the source of her newfound powers.

"*Por favor*, Natalia," Carlos said. "We are blood. Do not let me die. He is the one who wronged you, not I."

"Is that what you told yourself while your precious protégé was brainwashing me to get in my pants? Apparently, that's how you treat family around here. If you want to know, I have no preference either way. You live or you die, whichever one keeps me safe. I'm thinking the latter."

"I did not know Nuno's intentions." Carlos raised his palms in the air. "I cannot be blamed for his shameful actions."

"I guess we'll have to agree to disagree then." Talia stood taller than ever.

"You will not kill me, we are family." Carlos pressed forward.

"Do not underestimate me, Carlos. You don't know what I'm capable of," Talia said. "If I can do it to Nuno, what makes you think I won't do it to you?"

"I do not think you will, Natalia," Carlos said. "You are not a murderer."

"Call me a survivor if you prefer," she said, fire burning in her fingertips. "I want justice. I want you to pay for all the harm you've done, all the people you've sacrificed, all the lives you've ruined. Including mine. My friends will not die in vain."

"I will make it up to you, Natalia. *Eu prometo*." Carlos struggled to move forward. A sudden downpour crashed onto the roof, every drop adding to its white noise, a damp gust raged through the windows.

"And what am I? You would not have known or cared for her had it not been for me," Nuno croaked, awakened from his slumber. Talia could feel his energy and fed from it, as if storing it for later use.

The two men chanted, each a different hymn, competing for the highest decibel. Talia strained to bury the confusion by reciting the maid's prayer in her head, but it wasn't working.

The two storms clashed, creating an earthquake below them. The largest crack in the stone floor tore open a sink hole that devoured everything within five feet of its opening. Jared's legs dangled off the edge, threatening to pull the rest of his corpse with them.

By sheer will, Talia pressed the shard deeper into Nuno's chest. Nuno winced and fell backward into a pile of debris. When he didn't crawl out, Talia tripped toward the abyss, her hair slicked to her blustered cheeks. The blow deterred Nuno for a moment before he regained momentum.

Clutching his shoulders as the fracture in the floor widened,

Talia groaned as she hauled Jared's body to the far wall and settled him into a safe area dampened by spilt holy water. The dying inferno reflected against something in Jared's right hand. She lifted his fingers and smiled. Her *Figa* necklace. Jared was still taking care of her, even after all the terrible things she had done.

Talia wrapped the silver chain around her wrists and scrambled to fasten the clasp with her tattered fingernails. Its weight pressed against her pulse, the jade stone knocking against her bones with the cool of an icicle. Her breath grew deeper.

The last of the rafters plunged to the ground, exposing the center half of the building to the deluge outside. It just missed Talia, who deterred it with a glance and raced to the nearest exit. The clouds multiplied the claw of lightning that slashed through the sky, echoing the deafening thunder that soon trailed. The smoldering fire fizzled in the sprinkles sneaking into the holes in the roof.

The side door had been bolted shut with a rusted iron lock, no key in sight. Talia jostled a ragged corner of the broken floor tile and ran toward the lock with all she had left, but it didn't budge. Adrenaline pumping the discomfort from her perforated hand, Talia cracked the tile against the lock with the swiftness of a hammer, chipping rusty sparks into the air. After a few good cracks, it snapped open.

Talia surveyed the area one more time, just in case, and spotted a young boy, maybe eight years old, stuck between a rafter and one of the few remaining stone walls. Her stomach sank. She needed to leave at that moment in order to save herself, but there he was, helpless and alone. His parents were probably worried sick. And though Talia knew she was likely giving up the only opportunity she may get to escape, she ran to the boy to pull him out.

Talia hushed the boy's cries as she tugged harder at his pant leg, but he wouldn't budge. Remembering her newfound powers, Talia pulled the rafter as hard as she could, flinging herself a few feet back into a black puddle. The rafter shook and Talia, in a panic, screamed out a chant in Portuguese. Her energy waned. The rafter shook again, but this time it splintered, allowing just enough room for the boy to break free and run toward the front door. She tried to tell him there was no way out, but the boy managed to squeeze through a tiny opening in the rubble to safety.

The chanting stopped with a clash. Talia ran back to the door, hoping she could still escape. She twisted the rusted lock to remove it from its latch. But as she wrenched at it, she felt something thrust against her back, smashing her head first into the door. It slammed it shut. She crumpled to the floor, rain and blood dribbling into her eye.

"Not so fast," Nuno yelled.

Talia watched a hazy Nuno limp with bloody statue in hand. Carlos was missing.

"How did you—" Talia squinted. "Where's Carlos?"

"Never mind your uncle, Talia," Nuno said. "It is you and me now."

"No, Nuno, this can't happen." The split roof now dripped on Talia's forehead, the odor of wet burnt wood intensifying.

"It is fate that we have found each other, Talia," Nuno said. "I know you will realize this one day."

"This isn't right." She slid her torso in the opposite direction with bent knees. The slicked floors eased the process. "I'm not the one."

His shadow preceded him, and Talia could no longer avoid it. The rain flooded into the puddles that filled the cracks in the stone floor, the depths not easy to measure. There was nowhere to run. With a grunt that shook the building, Talia lobbed Nuno ten feet onto the stone steps of the altar with a thrust of her arms. He had tricked her so many times, Talia couldn't believe he was truly dead this time. His arm twitched. Before she realized her thoughts, a cement block dislocated itself from the wall and hovered above Nuno's head, awaiting Talia's signal.

<hr>

TALIA WAS NOT A MURDERER. She was a survivor and this was self-defense. Her lip trembled, her heart pounded, her eyes widened. The cement block teetered above Nuno, threatening to fall. And then suddenly, a loud crash echoed through the room and roused Talia into sobriety.

"Don't do it, Talia," the maid said with a sneaky American accent, her voice firmer and more confident than before. Her brown curls wrapped into a low bun, and her eyes hid behind black-rimmed glasses balancing at the slope of her small nose. She still wore her red dress. Hers fared better than Talia's, whose dress was now shredded like a grass miniskirt. "This is not who you are."

The maid raised her right hand up in the air. Talia felt her try to pry the cement block away from her grip, but Talia wouldn't let go.

"Listen to Mira, Talia," a man with a familiar French accent called from the front entrance. His footsteps accelerated.

Talia saw the man pointing a gun at Nuno's chest. "You. How would you know what I'm capable of?"

A man who resembled Pierre, dressed in a dark uniform and gold badge, gripped Nuno's collar. "*Calma*, Talia, I am here to help you."

Talia hesitated, and the cement block hesitated with her. Their first encounter came to mind—his limp hand, his greasy smile, his tattered loafers. He looked less slimy in uniform. "You kidnapped my friend."

"I expected that greeting." Pierre lowered his eyes. "I tried to help your friend, but when I told her my plan, she begged to leave. I thought I convinced her, but then she left for Porto while I was sleeping. I could not stop her."

"A move Caryn perfected," Talia said. "You could have kept a better eye on her, being a cop and all. Maybe if you weren't sleeping with her."

"I did not do anything with Caryn, although she was persistent. We are officers of the National Republican Guard, similar to what you call in America the CIA," Pierre said. "I have been tracking your uncle for years. Nuno may have been guilty of the harm done to your family, but your uncle hurt many others in his past."

The block shook and dropped lower with Talia's waning force.

"Jared escaped my men and headed to Porto," Pierre continued, his face stern. "Once he left, Caryn found a way to escape."

It sure sounded like Caryn. If Pierre spoke the truth, Caryn would've been safe had Jared not been compelled to be the hero. She couldn't fault him for it—she would have done the same for him. Talia exhaled and shifted her gaze. The cement block jerked to the right and landed on a rafter wrapped in a flag.

Pierre put his gun back in its holster, disarmed the dagger from Nuno's hand, and tucked it into his belt, pinning Nuno to the ground with a boot to his neck. "Where did your uncle go?" he asked, not taking his eyes off his prisoner.

"I don't know. He disappeared. I thought Nuno killed him," Talia said.

The storm calmer and the building now in shambles, she found a clear view of the river, a stubby shadow tracing its bed. "There he is." Talia ran to the cliff's edge.

"Talia, wait," the maid, or as Pierre called her, Mira shouted after her.

Every minute mattered. It was her duty to catch him, to finally bring him to justice. "Stop right there!" Talia shouted at the shadow.

It stopped, to her disbelief, and so she stopped too. Though he was far off she could still recognize Carlos, as if their eyes met, even at that distance. The maid caught up to her, inspiring Carlos's shadow to dive off the cliff into the river. Talia screamed after him, but it was too late. When she arrived at the edge, nothing bobbed with the river's current outside of a few leaves and branches.

Mira wrapped her arm around Talia's neck, whispered, "I'm sorry," and walked Talia back to the dilapidated stone shack from which she had finally freed herself. Talia welcomed the warmth of a friendly embrace.

"So you're not a maid, you're a witch. And an undercover agent?"

"It's complicated." Mira paused. "I really want to believe you had nothing to do with your uncle's death."

"He's not dead if there's no body," Talia joked and then stopped. "Wait, are you serious? How could you even think that after everything that just happened?"

"Because he left you everything in his will."

"He what?"

"Your uncle left you properties all over Europe," Mira said, "including this entire vineyard estate. That's a pretty solid motive for murder."

"I didn't know he did that, or why he even would." Talia

resumed walking at a faster pace. "I want nothing to do with that hell house. Burn it down for all I care, vines and all. Just get me out of here first."

As they approached the front of the *terreiro*, the signs now trampled and broken, Pierre rushed out the door.

"I am guessing you did not find Carlos?" Pierre's face was flush. The phone in his belt buzzed in a methodical, almost peaceful rhythm.

Mira shook her head and frowned.

The *terreiro* looked surreal in the budding daylight, auburn and cool. Nuno lay on his back at Pierre's feet, unconscious or dead, the latter preferable.

"I think he jumped off the cliff," Mira said.

"*Merda*. What happened to Jared?" Pierre grumbled.

"He's dead," Talia interrupted, the lump in her throat choking the syllables. She tiptoed toward Nuno's body, anxious to see for herself if he was really gone.

The pool of red spread around his torso indicated that he had bled out from the wound near his kidney. The shard of stone remained lodged in his chest. Nuno didn't die easily. He was a survivor. Unfortunately for him, so was Talia.

"He is unconscious from the blood loss," Mira said. She consoled Talia as if she were mourning him. "He may be dead already, I have not checked in a bit. The ambulance is on its way, but I'm afraid it may not make it in time."

Talia kicked Nuno's shin, expecting an involuntary reaction. When he didn't respond, she crouched in closer, extending her hand to take his pulse. Just then, Nuno sprung back to life, twisting her wrist until she kneeled in closer, her squeal spurring him to twist deeper. He whispered a chant in Talia's ear too faint to comprehend, then pulled her in closer, "You are my *Pomba Gira*." When his grip loosened, Talia screamed.

"Step away from Nuno, Talia," Mira commanded, the gleaming dagger now a natural extension of her arm. She must have gotten it from Pierre.

Talia obeyed her orders and stepped back, Nuno's grip unyielding. He lifted his other arm and the dagger sliced into his eye. Talia shrieked as he dropped his hand.

"I'm sorry, Talia. It was the only way to be sure." The maid's distorted voice quieted, but her lips persisted. The room rotated with a ring in Talia's ear. Talia tripped on a lifted rock and tumbled backward into a heap of wood and stone, knocking her head against a rafter. A jolt of pain raced from the back of her head to her temples like a live wire.

"Talia? Talia?" a medley of voices repeated.

Talia awakened with a deep shiver from her toes to her neck, the weight in the air constrained her breathing. She hoped it was just a nightmare, but when she looked around at the sooty walls and blood-splattered stones, Talia knew it was all painfully real. Jared and Caryn were still dead, and she was ultimately to blame.

"Nuno can no longer harm you, Talia," Mira whispered as she pet Talia's sore head.

But Talia wasn't scared. No matter how he'd destroyed her life, she couldn't help but feel a strange loss from Nuno's death. She should have felt relieved or redeemed, but her heart grieved for him instead. She hated herself for it.

A reflection in the wreckage caught Talia's eye. Vóvó's amulet basked in a ray of moonlight near the rim of the crater that had engulfed Jared's body. The amulet's gold chain dangled off a loose rock. Talia reached for it, despite its distance, using the last of her energy to rescue it. She grunted. The amulet jolted up from the rubble and then crashed onto the crater's edge.

Talia closed her eyes for one last attempt and the stone floor shifted. She held her breath and squinted, but it didn't work. The chain slithered into the crater, dragging the amulet with it into the darkness.

O FIM

ACKNOWLEDGMENTS

It is a bit surreal expressing my gratitude to the many amazing people who have helped me on this journey. First, I want to give love and thanks to my husband and number one fan, Aaron Dixon, whose patience through sleepless nights and endless rewrites never faltered. Thank you to my parents, who always nurtured my creative side, and taught me how to love and appreciate both my heritage and my country.

Much appreciation to my extraordinary editor, John Cotter, who helped me mold this novel into a publishable piece with patience and, especially, humor. Thank you to my proofreader and link to the publishing world, Michael O'Donnell. Without your sound advice this novel would not have made it here.

A special, teary shout out to my best friend and fearless cheerleader, Kristin McFetridge. Thank you for believing in me and for being my unyielding soundboard. I have no idea what I'd do without you.

Many more thanks to my close friends Kristina Dadekian and

Melinda Pepler, who took the time to read unpolished manuscripts and give thoughtful critiques on short notice.

To my many friends and family members who listened to me rattle on about my writing career over the years, and even read some of my short stories, thank you for taking the time and acting genuinely interested, even when you may not have been. Those small gestures inspired me to continue following my dreams.

Finally, I would like to thank you, the reader, for taking a chance on my first novel. I hope you enjoyed it. Obrigada!

ABOUT THE AUTHOR

Suzanne Ferreira is a former journalist, raised bicultural by a Portuguese immigrant family in New England. After publishing her first poem at age twelve, she earned a degree in journalism at Emerson College. Suzanne continued as a reporter in the Boston area before moving to Los Angeles for a career in web design. She now lives in Burbank with her husband and twin sons.

For more books and updates:
www.suzanneferreira.com

facebook.com/SFerreiraDixon

twitter.com/SFerreiraDixon

goodreads.com/SFerreiraDixon

pinterest.com/SFerreiraDixon

instagram.com/SoozFerreira